The Ghost
of
Jimmy Savile

The Ghost of Jimmy Savile

by

E.G.Taylor

First published as *The Whores of Coxcomb Hall* in 2010. This
edition published in 2013 by what tradition books
Contents both editions © what tradition books

British Library Cataloguing in Publication Data available

ISBN 978-0-9565093-0-7

Printed by Lightning Source

Also from what tradition books:

The Ghost of Neil Diamond by David Milnes
To Have Nothing by David Milnes

All hail *The Ghost of Neil Diamond*:

Acknowledgements

Allusions to the reportage of R.M.Macoll
in the second part of Chapter Eleven are
made openly and with respect.

E. G. Taylor & Ms. A. M. M. Taylor

Edward George Taylor was born in Boston,
Lincs. on 12th March 1908 and died on 3rd
December 1969 in Caistor Sands, Gt.
Yarmouth. He was an itinerant piano tutor
and tuner by profession, covering the East
Midlands and much of East Anglia. *The
Ghost of Jimmy Savile* is his only known
work.

The assistance of his sister and sole
executor, Alice Margaret Munro Taylor
(1910-2007), in the granting of all
permissions, including the right to change
or update references to actual places or
persons, is acknowledged with gratitude.

The Ghost of Jimmy Savile

Egg Taylor

what tradition books

whattradition.co.uk

Chapter One

Parsons' Bones

There took place in the dark and freezing Games Room one Tuesday evening a fearful drawing of lots. A tight group was gathered around the broken billiards table. Around this inner core a second group patrolled in stops and starts, keeping a watchful eye, each praying he'd be called back into contention. Then a third and utterly desolate group lay dashed against the walls and windowsills, taking what comfort they could from lukewarm radiators. These were the most sinister. Their eyes were heavy and their expressions swollen with appetite. They knew their fate. They would not go. Under the silent flickering of the black and white television, where Jack Warner mouthed his epilogue to *Dixon of Dock Green*, these wallflowers, with their heads roughly shorn and their skin lumpy with acne, with their downy beards that grew in patches where they could not shave, these lost souls looked quite as ugly and sinister as they felt, and capable of anything, any crime.

The billiards table was full-size and there was ample room for eleven bodies standing round. Another of Rowell's hand-me-downs from the Royal Air Force, it was a ruined and useless thing. The baize was torn and ragged and the slate bed had been cracked long ago in some berserk act of anger or bravado.

No less than a hundred seniors had entered for selection. Only ten would go.

Only ten.

The decision was made on the roll of Parsons' ancient, yellowed, bone poker dice, which were spilled by Parsons himself from an antique leather cup. Savouring his role at the head of the billiards table, the sententious Parsons had announced to the hundred before they began - even though everyone had heard the story countless times - that his dice and cup were the last effects of a long dead relative, a seafarer who'd actually drowned at sea, an old sea dog who'd lost every possession in the world save this plain leather cup - held aloft - and these lonely bones now cast before them on the green sea bed, as it were -

"He's well out of it!" came an effete cry from the back. "Jack Tar!"

"We know all this, Parsons," said another.

"May his spirit be with us!" intoned those closest to the table.

Each winner was selected from a sub-group of ten hopefuls. He who took the highest score over three throws went through, the other nine were discarded. But there were many draws, settled on the roll of a single die. The tension was fierce when two players drew again, and yet again, as happened several times. These contestants insisted the crowd step back to give Parsons more room, and then, as all surged forward to see the fourth result, more time was lost in re-establishing order. But results were emerging. Six of the ten had already been selected. From the middle group there were calls for a revision of the rules, as some of these six had failed to score as well as those who'd already been rejected. Jack Tar's honour was invoked, in the name of fair play. But Parsons wouldn't entertain pleas of that kind, and in this atmosphere it seemed as if the six who'd been chosen would gladly have murdered the protesters rather than give up their places.

All this was the outcome of what Parsons had taken to be a chance encounter with Clara White – the witch of the woods, the bitch of the woods - late Monday afternoon.

Like all seniors, Parsons smoked, but he liked to smoke alone and to combine his smoking with other solitary pursuits. To guarantee his isolation he walked half a mile or so away from the Quad, another quarter of a mile beyond Woodlands, the tied cottage of Dr. & Mrs. White. There were certain trees, old friends, Parsons had marked out in a shady clearing. He would lean against one of these and enjoy the ritual of opening his packet of ten Player's No. 6 and lighting up. He always smoked two cigarettes. For the first he stood looking up through the bare branches at the still, grey skies, while he savoured the momentary high of the nicotine, and the pleasure of caressing himself through his trousers. When this first cigarette was finished and its butt extinguished in the damp humus of the woodland floor, he would turn and set one arm against the tree, lean his head on his forearm, undo his trousers and take out his erect cock. After fondling himself for a few moments he masturbated quickly onto the tree trunk, his excitement driven hard, chased down by fear of discovery. The orgasm over, he wiped any mess away from his trousers and underwear with some toilet paper, discarded the paper on the fallen leaves, then moved to a clean tree, another friend, where he smoked his second cigarette. Since the onset of puberty this had been Parsons' chief pleasure in life.

He was a pleasant looking, full bodied youth, who would have been handsome but for his ears, which were small, cupped and protrusive, shaped like a seal's ears. They were always red and veiny, as if someone had just boxed or flicked them, as bullies had done without ceasing, approaching him from behind at any time of day or night all through his junior years. He could not grow his hair to protect himself and improve his appearance because all boys were shorn in the darkness of the barber's van that visited every fortnight, without fail. Despite his seal's ears two things set Parsons apart as personable and self-confident. Firstly, he was one of the few blessed with a clear skin. The institutional diet of brisket, tapioca and suet didn't seem to trouble his system at all. He thrived on it, and never had so much as a blackhead on his cheek, neck or back. Secondly, he was one of the very, very few who'd had a sexual relationship with someone not of his own sex. It was rumoured that he had been walking out with a dark lady on Hemsby Lows, the common ground behind Hemsby's council estate. The looks and age of the lady were not known, but there were various stories about her being a single mother or a divorcee. Some said she was more than fifty.

Perhaps it was this woman he thought of on his walks through the woods, and who filled his fantasy to bursting when he masturbated against the tree. If it was, and she had any emotional attachment to the young Parsons, so much the worse for her, because she was about to be displaced in his affections.

Clara White had noted Parsons' habits and the hours he kept. Well before his arrival she had come to the clearing where he liked to stop. She knew she was at the right place from the toilet tissue lying about, in various states of sodden decay. The tree she had chosen to hide behind was no more than twenty-five paces from his favourite place. She wanted as little distance separating them as possible. She had trodden the leafy steps she would take two or three times already to remove any treacherous twigs.

Thus she had accounted for her prey's senses of sight and hearing, but foolishly she had forgotten about his sense of smell. She wore as always her patchouli oil, with which she had heavily laced the evening air on these practice steps to and from her hideaway.

When Parsons arrived in his clearing he sniffed the air in alarm and stood very still. He frowned and glanced about. But he had smelled this scent - though nothing like as strong – on more than one occasion over the last few weeks, and it had not signified anything then, no human presence. As far as he knew it could be the scent of some strange shrub given up to the evening air. After a minute or so he relaxed, leant back against his favourite tree, and took out his cigarettes as usual. Once he had lit up his Player's No. 6 the smell of patchouli oil was forgotten and he drifted off into his usual luxurious fantasies.

Clara watched and bided her time until Parsons finished his first cigarette, put it out, turned to the tree and undid his trousers. On her feet she wore rope sandals. She trod in silence the damp and leafy floor to where he stood braced against the tree. The patchouli oil went undetected until she was upon him, and even as he turned she reached round and took his firm warm cock in her hand.

"Let me help you," she said, in her softest whisper, as if nothing would give her more pleasure. And her tone was in part sincere, because she did find the act pleasing in a way she never found doing such things for her husband pleasing. Here there was no overlay of reward, reconciliation, obligation. Here was the simple pleasure of feeling the young man's strength in her hands and seeing him submit to the wondrous relief she was offering him. Clara imagined she was fulfilling his most sublime and long-held fantasy. She reached round and cupped his balls and he came in a matter of seconds. While he stood slumped against the tree she leant against him, pressing her small breasts against his back, and whispered: "Tomorrow you can bring a friend . . . Only one. Any friend - except Ossaf - of course."

Without explanation for either the offer or the exception, she turned and disappeared into the woods, leaving Parsons to understand of the episode, the miracle, what he could, and to enjoy his second Player's No. 6 in peace.

Woodlands was a dark cottage and its small windows were inset, close set, and darker still, so that it always looked blind, stupid and deserted. Parsons had grown complacent, believing that once he was off the beaten path (well worn by Dr. White's anxious steps, head down, three or four times a day) the trees were so dense it was unlikely Dr. or Mrs. White could see him from those pitted windows, even if he or she had wanted to.

From the safety of her kitchen, staring out over a pile of dirty dishes, Clara White had spied on Parsons. She had wanted to see him. She had looked out for him.

It was all very well winkling five pounds a week from Dick Baker, Crafts Master, but he, it seemed, could take or leave her services these days - on two occasions recently he had not even showed up. And little Jimmy Newlings, History Master, though a more secure source of revenue, had his problems too. She had begun to find his short, hard body repugnant in the extreme, and his desperate gasps as he became excited, and the spots of saliva that dried in the corners of his mouth, were sounds and sights which lingered afterwards in her mind, triggering post-coital depression. No. One way or another Newlings was not going to last. She had noticed a whiff of strong beer or liquor on his breath several times in recent weeks. He was slipping away. The discipline had gone. The iron in his soul, the resilience and willpower that the little man was renowned for, had turned out to be pewter, fit only to make tankards out of. But for her part at least, the 'relationship' - Newlings had started to use this word: "*I want to talk about our relationship*" - had been a success. She had been seeing him for more than six months and had put away some seven hundred pounds of Newlings' salary and savings.

But Clara was inclined to think that she must go on accumulating much more, much, much more, in order to win her freedom from serfdom and gain a measure of control over her life, and arrangements with the likes of Newlings and Baker were not going to secure the capital she needed in the long term. *Capital* - that was the word. Her ambition, which seemed even to her a touch fantastical, this idea of the sheer quantity of money she must get hold of, had been inspired by her reading from

The Age of Leisure. Capital seemed to sit there as an immovable ballast at the bottom of Jane Austen's novels; capital remained the underlying preoccupation in Trollope's books, and in Eliot's *Middlemarch*, and Thackeray's *Vanity Fair* - and most particularly, of course, in the character of Rebecca Sharp. Clara kept remembering, for her courage and comfort and inspiration, Becky Sharp's working maxim: All men are fools.

Newlings, Baker and her husband all confirmed that idea, and gave her confidence in the potential of her circumstances. At Coxcomb Hall, a quarter of a mile up the woodland path, there was a source of wealth Bob Rowell - that lazy and perverted swindler! - had not even begun to tap. Just a quarter of a mile up the woodland path were scores of young men at the peak of their sexual potency, and in their education, if that is what it had to be called, that ungovernable force was ignored, dismissed, treated as a nuisance, an embarrassment. A mere quarter of a mile up the woodland path there was the equivalent of maybe a whole gallon, a half-bucketful of semen thrown out every week, slopped out, poured down the drain, or left to dry on cold, soiled sheets. And the supply was inexhaustible. All that was required was a plan bold enough and ingenious enough to tap it at source, to cream it off for a mutual profit.

There were certain blessings to be counted here. After all, it was not as if she was having to sell her services at closing time on freezing backstreets to reeling drunks, nor to the likes of Jimmy Newlings several times over, week in and week out. Instead her clientele was a stream of pure youth, of frustrated, naïve, unquestioning, and deeply appreciative young men. She would not even have to sell herself entirely - not unless the price was right, and the mate agreeable.

These boys were by and large the sons of the English lower middle or middle-classes. This was no Charterhouse or Harrow. The parents of these boys would not have a great deal of money, but they would have enough, collectively, to make Clara White a sum of capital within, perhaps, a year at most. And here she also remembered from her reading what it is that divides English people more effectively even than education or class, love or marriage - all obstacles with which one can come to terms, reach some compromise, in one way or another – no, the division that mattered above all, where there could be no compromise, the hardest, fastest, and most bare-fisted fact of life, was the uncrossable divide between those who started out possessing a few thousand pounds, and those who started out borrowing a few thousand pounds.

She had quizzed Baker and Newlings about the parents of these boys. Many of them were not even in the country. They were service people abroad in places like Aden, Cyprus, Kenya, Papua New Guinea; confused soldiers wrestling with the mess of vestigial empire. Other boys were the children of naïve foreigners who hoped to get their offspring an advantage in life from an English boarding school education, who believed Rowell's assurances that after Coxcomb Hall their sons would – as a matter of course - attend Oxford or Cambridge university, whichever they preferred. These people were at an even more remote distance, in every sense, from the realities of life at the Hall, and their social pretensions made them all the more gullible and exploitable. And there was another, much smaller group she had identified: those who had already been cast out from other systems, streetwise neo-criminal elements who had been placed here prior to a proper tempering in borstal or prison. These she would have to watch out for, no doubt, but they could not spoil her plans if she were circumspect.

The arithmetic was dazzling. To start with there would be ten boys, each week, each of whom would pay five pounds. What Clara had in mind was a group variation on what she'd done with Parsons. It would all be over in quarter of an hour. She was confident she could ensure that. The boys would be so excited on arrival, having thought of little else all week, that she would be able to stroke them to orgasm within a few seconds. If some had cunningly masturbated already in order to enjoy her attention longer, she could make timing part of the conditions: a boy who took more than his allotted time would be left to finish the job himself, while she moved on to the next.

There was a snag, of course. She was dealing with something instinctive here, and according to Baker and Newlings and her own husband, these young men had reverted to behaviour that could properly be called bestial. The stories she had heard from her husband about the sadistic Ossaf, for example, were really quite appalling. Newlings referred to the boys as 'beasts' or 'brutes' at every opportunity: they were 'beasts, young beasts, nothing more nor less'. And he did not use the word 'beast' with any humorous hyperbole. What was to stop a boy, then, whom she had brought to the verge of climax, turning on her, trying to hold her hand on him, trying to pull her to him, trying to kiss her, perhaps? No doubt at first they would be too nervous to question her authority, but once one of them had sensed that when he took hold of her he dominated her, what could not happen? There would be ten of them against her. What could they not do? What could they not plan in advance?

Their own self-interest was at stake: one false

move on their part and the sessions would be over - but Clara knew the folly of that line of thought. No, the solution, of course, lay in avoiding any confrontation, it lay in strategy and diplomacy and in forging an alliance. There was a *mutual* benefit here. There should not be division and distrust. To forge such an alliance she first had to find a leader, and this was why she had focused on Parsons. From her enquiries she knew that Parsons, though friendless as any other boy, was one of the oldest and strongest and not to be crossed lightly.

Hallett was so handsome. Parsons wanted to bring along someone whom Mrs. White might find appealing, and Hallett was the very best Coxcomb Hall could offer, except perhaps for his younger brother Christopher, but Christopher's heavenly features were as yet untested by the uglification of puberty. Anthony Hallett, with his cowlick of blonde hair, his pale clear skin and retroussé nose, had an air of superiority and purity that made him sought after by all the boys, junior and senior alike, and by Rowell himself and all other homosexuals on the staff. He'd had to fight off the latter suitors ever since he was a junior. Though not shy, Hallett was by nature a rather private soul, and not the arrogant sensualist reflected in the swooning eyes of others. He was artistic and sensitive and, like Parsons, enjoyed his own company. But his elusiveness only added to his reputation, made him all the more desired. Hallett did not relish this attention. He was no more vain than any young man of his age.

He liked the usual solitary pursuits - music, reading, even poetry – but his favourite pastime was to spend the afternoon alone in the Art Loft, hunched over an art book, copying the nudes of old masters, or, very occasionally, nudes of himself from photographs he had taken with his own expensive automatic camera. Hallett did nothing with all his nudes, never flaunted himself or his paintings in any way, and was not at all flirtatious or promiscuous, but by virtue of his sheer desirability he was known as Whore Hallett. The name had stuck for so long few knew his real name was Anthony.

Clara was dressed all in black as usual, but the outfit was deceptive. She wore a double-breasted raincoat, though the evening was as fine and mild as it had been the previous day, and, most strange, she wore a veil. She needed the veil to give her confidence. She did not want to address these young men unobscured. Yesterday she had approached Parsons from behind: one could dispense with so many words that way. But today there would have to be many more words and they would have to be spoken eyeball to eyeball.

When Parsons and Hallett arrived, she watched them for some time from her hideaway, while she gauged their mood and gathered courage.

Parsons took out his cigarettes and he and Hallett smoked nervously together. Parsons had told Hallett what had happened but did not want to say anything speculative about this second meeting. He did not want to raise Hallett's hopes too much in case Mrs. White - the witch of the woods, the bitch of the woods - didn't turn up, and he would look a fool, or a liar, and his motives - alone with Whore Hallett deep in the woods? - *Really*? - might be misconstrued.

As they put out their first cigarettes the petite, veiled form of Clara White emerged from the shadows and walked towards them head down, like a nun. Parsons and Hallett felt self-conscious and ill at ease as she came closer.

Only when Clara raised her head to speak to them did she appreciate how tall and strong these young men were. She felt a fleeting panic. She was vulnerable here in the middle of the woods. What folly this was. And at her request there were two of them now. But she smiled, pulled her wits together and carried on. After all, there was not much else she could do.

"We have to talk about terms."

She looked first into Parsons' eyes, and then into Hallett's, afraid of the sinister intentions she might find. Parsons' eyes were grey and very slightly protuberant: there was a frankness and steadiness there. In Hallett's blue eyes she saw a wiliness, but it seemed more humorous than cunning, and she liked him immediately. She was pleased and relieved. There was humour too in the curl of his mouth. She understood in this moment that her idea of these boys had been conceived from the stories she'd heard of Newlings' and Baker's sufferings, and her husband's sufferings, at their hands. But these were just the stories of a few whining and inadequate middle-aged men, who no doubt blamed these 'young beasts' for all their own professional and personal failings. Clara's fears fell away. She began to relax and felt ready to assume command.

But Hallett spoke next. He said, with a flick of his blond hair and a winning smile:

"Of course."

He seemed much quicker than the ponderous Parsons, and Clara addressed her next remark to him.

"I need to make money," she said. She glanced back at Parsons, who shifted his weight under her gaze. "I'm happy to give you the help I gave you yesterday . . . as often as you like. But for a fee."

"How much?" Hallett asked, assuming what was to Clara a disheartening gravity of tone. She looked back at him. He swallowed under her gaze, and her hopes dipped with his Adam's apple. Perhaps what she had in mind really would be too much, be out of the question.

"Five pounds," she said, without wavering. "Each."

Hallett took a sharp intake of breath and a frown creased his brow. But Clara was not to be put off. She had to see her proposal through. There was no choice now.

"You may not have that kind of money with you," she said, looking up into Hallett's eyes, which now swam with unspoken, probing questions, "but I'm sure you can get it if you try. Try very hard." She finished with a smile to Hallett, and was rewarded by Hallett offering his own long and subtle smile.

Clara did not want to talk for much longer – the fewer words between them the better. When she spoke again she accompanied her words with actions. It was time to appeal to instinct.

"I'm prepared to see the two of you, and up to eight of your friends . . ." she said, and as she spoke she undid the top buttons of her coat. Keeping her head down, she let the flap of her coat fall wide to reveal her pale, pert, thirty-one-year-old breast, slightly dipped, her nipple erect in the evening air. Without looking up she refastened her coat, then, smiling first at Hallett, then at Parsons, she completed what she was saying, "On Friday, here, at five o'clock." The boys' eyes were tight and their mouths pursed. "Each boy must wear long trousers and a belt," Clara added. She had been right to be so bold, and to come here prepared to be so bold. "I shall show you why on Friday. Why we need the belt, that is," she added, smiling again at Hallett. "And I must have the money in advance, at the very start, or I shall just go away again."

Hallett said: "You'll have the money."

Clara took great heart at his attempt to assume some adult authority and decisiveness, when it was obvious from his eyes that he could hardly contain his excitement.

"Oh," Clara added, as if she'd nearly forgotten, "and Ossaf cannot come."

"Of course not," Hallett agreed. They seemed to have assumed his exception.

Clara nodded, smiled farewell to each of them, then turned and left without another word.

Chapter Two

Counsel of Perfection

One dry autumn night, outside the Victorian wing where Rowell, O'Donnell, Jackson and Newlings had their apartments, some distance from their rotting sash windows - those tall, sad casements, battered by the coastal winds and rains - there stood a dark-skinned, bulky figure, with a pair of binoculars trained on the second floor of the building. He was focusing in particular on the lonely windows of Jimmy Newlings' sitting room. He'd been standing there, binoculars raised, perfectly still, for some time, and his polished toecaps had sunk in the dewy lawn.

From his vantage point, standing there in the dark, in the centre of Rowell's immaculate horseshoe of rose beds, the trespasser had spied upon a pivotal meeting of minds.

The back of Dr. White's learned head was discernible through the barrels of the binoculars in some detail. Above the wispy dogtooth of his Harris Tweed stretched a pale celery stalk of muscle, either side of which were hairy hollows of flesh. The hair from these hollows, in wiry curls, lifted a straggling grey mullet, long and neglected. It was the residual of what once had been, in younger days, a smooth and oily DA, or duck's arse. From time to time Dr. White's head moved energetically on its stalk, reflecting the gravity and earnestness of his part in the conversation. Sometimes his head pitched down and forward, as he strained to make a point, and his mullet was lifted clear on its wiry grey hairs. At other moments, in response to something Newlings had said, his head retracted and shook with weary denial, as if the very depths of despond had been plumbed in this conference, and the mullet broke up on the collar of his greasy Harris Tweed.

Dr. White and Jimmy Newlings had been talking for more than an hour and a half. They had exchanged more words on this occasion than they had exchanged over the entire decade they had spent working together at Coxcomb Hall. It was an extraordinarily intense and personal meeting of minds.

But the spying trespasser, who had been where he stood for nearly twenty minutes, had had enough. He returned his binoculars to their case and took his leave. He noticed the tell-tale footprints he left behind in Rowell's lawn, but they did not concern him.

This was Ossaf, Head Boy, going about his endless, unfathomable and insidious business.

The meeting between Jimmy Newlings and Dr. White had begun in the staff room at the end of the day. As

White finished sifting through some circulars in his pigeon hole, Newlings had approached him from the refreshment area with an unopened bottle of what he claimed to be twelve-year-old, single malt whisky. Dr. White hesitated. The bottle had, to the eye of Dr. White, a lurid look and a bogus label - too many thistles, cudgels and what have you. (In fact, it was ironically reminiscent of the Coxcomb crest, with its phoney dragon, tridents and crossed halberds. Had Newlings sunk to home-brew?)

"Er . . . One for the woods, Whitey? What d'you say?"

Something in Newlings' thin-lipped smile and watery gaze was pitiful this autumnal afternoon. White had noticed, as had others, that Newlings often smelled of the bottle these days. Ah, it was noted, with satisfaction, the crapulous habits were creeping up on him at last. Dr. White's seat at chapel was next to Newlings', and for the last few weeks he'd had to put up with the noisome stench of sour booze on Newlings' breath - always at evensong, sometimes at matins too. For nearly ten years Principal and Choirmaster Bob Rowell had flattered Jimmy Newlings that he could have been a professional baritone, but for want of good training and a bit of luck. So Newlings never failed to belt out verse after verse of whatever godforsaken hymn or collect they'd been given without inhibition, as if this were the only outlet of feeling in his life, which for so many years it actually had been.

But here was Newlings with the bottle in his hand by the dusty pigeon holes, with his straggling eyebrows pointing upwards in a plaintive way, and to Dr. White it seemed churlish in the extreme not to give in to this appeal, from one man to another, to share a glass of the good malt, and with that sharing of a glass or two share also, no doubt, woes of a fairly predictable and tedious kind for a master living alone at the Hall. Woes that he himself had exchanged, about a year ago, for the woes of marriage to an attractive and much younger woman.

Failure has its gradations, and all who had worked at Coxcomb Hall for more than a few months knew the gradation of Newlings' failure. The pupils of Newlings' history classes subjected him to tortures classical, medieval and modern. He had somehow become inured to it, had learned to get through the day, endure the week, shoulder the terms and years as his private burden, and such fortitude had made him an immovable part of the institution, staggering out each morning from his quarters under Rowell's apartments (which leant him no protection at all) and returning thereto in the evenings to mark the worthless rubbish of his pupils, to tear out from their exercise books the shameful pictures of himself scrawled in blue biro in obscene acts and pleasures, of Jimmy Newlings gobbling his own faeces or his own cock and balls, of Jimmy Newlings bent with both hands up his arse, sucking his own cock, with the words '*Your COCK!*' scrawled large, and with a pulsating arrow pointing and so on and so forth. Newlings would sit at his desk each evening, under the lamplight, tearing out these pages, lest O'Donnell or some other master or monster should see them, putting the books to rights, rendering them thinner and thinner before returning them to their owners for more drawings and messages – *'Your KNOB!' "Your GOB!" 'Your ARSE!'* - the next heavy day.

The great solace of Newlings' life, until recently the only solace of his life, had been to make a daily calculation of his savings, and to study daily the progress of his investments. Newlings' savings were the source of endless rumours at Coxcomb – inflamed, exaggerated rumours that he had done nothing to inspire and which, he was sure, all began with Baker's jealousy and spite. But perhaps it didn't help that he took the 'pink 'un', the *Financial Times*, the one pretension and luxury he had never denied himself. The paper connected him with a world about which he knew very little, but the delivery of the fresh, pressed pink pages to his apartment every day made him a part of that world nonetheless. The journalists and commentators addressed him as part of their readership, treated him with due respect, and commented upon the stocks he too had watched, and agreed with him, more often than not, about what would go up or down or stay the same. The pink 'un had a symbolic value in his life quite as important as its usefulness, lending meaning and direction to this course he'd charted into the doldrums of middle age.

Newlings' life was a life well known, well mythologized, almost obituarised already. To others it was a warning, a marker buoy held in view when they too began to feel the undertow of dissipation and self-contempt, and the years slipping by beneath them. But now, evidently, Newlings' life had changed, something had given up, some cable of perdurable toughness had become so tense and chafed that it had snapped, casting adrift the buoy upon the open seas. Newlings had taken to the bottle. And Dr. White, old Whitey, still with some bourgeois pretensions of what it was to do the decent thing, had acceded to his colleague's invitation to share a few glasses of the amber liquid this foul Wednesday afternoon. They were not even halfway through the week: on Saturday came more duties to keep the beasts occupied with sports and CCF, and a multitude of energy-sapping and time-wasting pursuits, and on Sunday there the week's marking still to be done.

But the extraordinary thing about this Wednesday

meeting was that the main subject of their conversation did not derive from any outpouring from Newlings at all. Quite the reverse. It was Dr. White who was holding forth. Dr. White was not accustomed to drink. His wife kept him away from it. Early in their marriage she had discovered that a few glasses of wine or a finger or two of whisky all too often led to a dropping of inhibitions from the good doctor, led to lascivious petting and, on rejection, the beginnings of bad temper. So Clara had banned drink from the house. It was an unnecessary and burdensome evil and expense, she said. Their budget was modest and if she could do without it, he could too. (Clara was as good as her word. She never drank. For her own diversion she smoked hashish, wheedled from the aging trendy and mock-reprobate Dick Baker, sometimes as payment in kind.)

After just a couple of glasses of whisky White's manner had become unguarded. He looked about Newlings' neat bachelor nest, with its sprinkling of heirlooms and antiques, such as the rather fine rosewood table he sat at now, with misplaced envy. It all seemed very warm and cosy and rather satisfactory to him this evening, this bachelor existence. Newlings had some nice things. Some very nice things. This oval rosewood table, French polished, Newlings said, was particularly nice. Of course he knew, as everyone did, that Newlings hoarded his money and invested shrewdly, and the thought of that financial security appealed very deeply to White as well. He had begun to worry about why he and Clara, with no mortgage or rates to pay, somehow never managed to have any money left at the end of the month, despite his cutting back on old indulgences.

"No, married life's not all it's cracked up to be, Newlings," he had reflected after a couple of glasses, with a rueful wince, and he shifted in his chair on saying this, as if the admission had caused some painful wind.

Newlings looked down, he had to, and found himself staring at the good doctor's hands, so large and furry, curled inwards on his rosewood table. What a study of hopelessness there was in those hands, for any half-competent artist! He reached across and topped up his guest's glass. He tipped in some water too, just a drop, from a miniature crystal jug.

"Oh come on, Whitey," Jimmy Newlings teased. "You have so much now! You, of any of us, surely can't complain. You have Woodlands, a lovely wife, holidays away from here, if not abroad, I shouldn't wonder . . ."

White stared into the gentle brown grain of the rosewood, and looked at the light playing in the crystal jug. He was not used to drink at all, he reflected. He had already taken on board more than he could handle. Up to the gunnels, in fact.

"But I'm not happy, Newlings," he said, with one of those grave, sincere shakes of the head. "I am not a happy man."

Newlings laughed. "But which of us is, Doctor? We all have our crosses to bear, I'm sure. I'm sure we all do."

Newlings was not adept at the conversational finesse required here, having lived such an isolated life for so long, and his wooden flattery, his feigned naivety about Dr. White's marital circumstances, was clumsily done. There was about him this afternoon a bonhomie and sympathy of spirit which was actually very uncharacteristic, but White was already too drunk and self-obsessed to notice, or if he did notice, to care.

Newlings could hardly contain his curiosity. This was not what he had anticipated at all. Dr. White, 'the good doctor', to borrow Baker's impertinence, had broken down into confessional mode after just three or four fingers! He was drinking on an empty stomach, of course, and was plainly out of practice. Newlings felt cock-a-hoop about bringing the good doctor to his rooms and getting him so loose-tongued, but this very success only excited a new need in him, a need to extract more, much more from the good doctor, to probe and pick at the pain like a dentist, deeper and deeper still. So far he was safe. White clearly imagined he had been the soul of courtesy in agreeing to have a drink in the first place, and was now under the drunk's delusion that he'd been hearing his companion out, rather than blathering on himself.

Newlings had arranged this meeting because he had not been able to endure the uncertainty of his relationship with the good doctor's wife any longer. He was torn between two very different ideas about Clara White. The first was that she was nothing but a merciless whore, bent on draining him of every penny he had for no other reason but her selfish gain. Sometimes he thought he saw signs of this in her dark eyes - a coldness, an indifference to him as he climbed on top of her and she took his cock and put it inside her. She always shut her eyes as he began to climax, but he kept his open, not wanting to miss a moment of her nakedness, of her small, perfectly edible breasts below him. On a couple of occasions he had seen her open her eyes as he came and look up into his face, in particular at his mouth, and there had been something like distaste in her eyes, something like disgust, he sometimes worried.

Or was it, rather, that her face, at the moment of climax, showed a distaste for what she was doing, for the strain and duplicity of her life?

Still waters run deep, and Newlings' other idea about Clara was that her coolness and shameless greed were just a front to cover deeper feelings. It could not be, Newlings considered, that she felt nothing at all: sexual desire was always flowing one way or another, it did not simply ebb away. If she felt no desire for White, then she felt it for someone else, or she repressed her feelings for someone else, but she did not feel nothing. Desirelessness was an illusion, the repressed foolery of monks and mystics. This much insight into human nature Newlings had gained from his own existence of frustration, paedophilia, and masturbation. He could also see that Clara White must know that her marriage to the good doctor had been a mistake. It was a sham. White had been too old, and was anyway too ill-favoured, to be an object of love and constancy. That part of White's life had passed him by. And old Whitey, to be perfectly fair, should have accepted that, in Newlings' view, gracefully, instead of chasing after the unattainable and causing everyone such inevitable unhappiness. But the fact was that White had not accepted it. He had thought he could bring this lovely young woman back to Woodlands and live contentedly in his rural idyll. And now Clara had turned to other men. Baker was a loose cannon, a cowboy, a buffoon - there was no future there. But with him, with Jimmy Newlings, it could be a different story. He was still young enough to fulfil her and to challenge her in what he called 'physical love', and he was prepared to give her his undivided devotion. Above all he could offer her a degree of financial security White and Baker could only dream about, couldn't even muster between them. It was the possibilities of their relationship that caused her strain. She appeared cold and calculating, hard and mercenary, simply because it was the easiest game to play under the circumstances. She had to stifle the side of her nature that yearned for comfort, devotion and security – all that he could so readily offer her.

Generally this idea of Clara White gained substance only after two or three fairly large glasses of whisky, with just the one cube of ice for all three, but tonight, hearing Dr. White's confession of his marital unhappiness, Newlings' lover, White's wife, was virtually there, present in the room with them, with hardly any alcohol to heat Newlings' fantasy, with hardly any clothes on at all. Clara White had become an ectoplasmic figure in his living room, small and dark and perfectly formed, brought into being by the sheer power of White's disillusionment and Newlings' lust. Newlings was not drunk by any means. He had faked a drink or two, even poured one down the sink in his kitchenette, because he was so concerned to hold on to every word of the good doctor's confession.

"Couples have their rough patches," old Whitey began again, turning his glass on the polished table in maudlin meditation. "I know that. Of course. But Clara has never, even from the start . . . "

But the enormity of what he was about to say out loud dragged White back from the brink. An inner panic shut him up, literally shut his mouth, made him gulp.

Newlings was at a loss as to how to make his guest open wide again, so that he could probe and pick deeper and deeper still, and somehow hook the nerve that would make White cry out in agony and complete that line of thought. He sensed that the things he really wanted to hear were at the very front of the good doctor's mind, but not quite in the right order for utterance. He feared that more whisky would prove counter-productive, would turn back or dissolve the befuddled queue of words, and White would become less likely to express anything really satisfying and important.

31

"She is a lovely woman, your wife," Newlings prompted, setting his foot patiently across his knee.

White looked up sharply. His soggy eyes focused on his host.

"I mean, you are very lucky," Newlings repeated quickly, stupidly.

"No I'm not, Jimmy. I'm not lucky at all." White shook his head. The maudlin earnestness returned. "I've got no luck at all. No luck at all, Newlings."

Newlings slapped the calf of his leg. "But you are! You are *so* lucky! Lovely house. Lovely wife . . ."

Dr. White braced himself in his seat. His jaw clenched, his nostrils flared. His face was suffused with blood. What came next was ejected from him, like some bile his system had to get rid of despite his efforts to contain it. It burst out. It burst through him -

"I think Dick Baker is fucking my wife!"

White's milky eyeballs trembled in pools of feeling. Newlings was fearful. He had never expected a breakdown of this kind, something so without self-respect. White's whole head was trembling now in tiny, involuntary shakes. Here it came again -

"I think Dick Baker is fucking my wife!"

Newlings frowned back in utter disbelief. "Oh come on, Doctor! You are *drunk*!"

But Newlings was inadequate to the situation he had created and he well knew it. This scene was all of his making, and he had lost control of it. He'd half filled the good doctor with whisky and the man had become emotionally incontinent. He looked horrible, quite bloated with feeling. His eyes bulged. His cheeks were flushed and puffy, almost like - like O'Donnell's, for goodness' sake.

The way White appeared to Newlings was not at all an exaggeration of how he felt. The whisky had seeped into the very warp and weft of his defences, and all the fears and miseries he kept so tightly bound up twenty-four hours a day, both at home and at work, had pressed through their softened confines. The ill feeling and unhappiness was like some sweat or lymph opening up the pores of his skin and leaking out into the open, and creating an awful stink. Doctor White was on the verge of complete incontinence, of breaking into tears.

"Mine is a loveless marriage, Newlings . . ." he confessed at last.

Newlings felt such a deep satisfaction and relief on hearing this he had no idea what to do or say. After a decent pause, he murmured: "Oh, come along now . . ."

He had to take a break. He stood and went out to his kitchenette on the pretext of refilling the crystal jug with water.

In his kitchenette he put the jug on the drainer and leant over the sink.

What kind of crisis had he precipitated here? Wasn't this just the kind of thing English etiquette had trained people to avoid at all costs? How on earth would he and White face each other in the staff room tomorrow morning? The workplace must be free of personal sentiment - a golden, a glistering rule. What could they say or do now when they passed each other in the Quad? To show how we truly felt about all that went on around us, about ourselves, about each other, was madness - we would walk around with tears streaming down our faces all day long. It just wasn't on. Feelings had to be kept in check in order to get everything done, get organised, get through the day. Yet here he was breaking up the very defences poor old Whitey needed in order to cope, to survive. Newlings felt ashamed of himself. Thoroughly ashamed. Not only of what he'd done tonight, obviously, but of what he'd been doing these last seven months or so. Of how he, too, had been making love to the good doctor's wife. Ah, but there was the difference, Newlings noted, and he bit his thin lower lip and closed his eyes, considering this difference. For Baker it was simply a biological thing. It really was what the good doctor had said it was. But for him, for Newlings, it was something else again. White's confession had allowed him to see past his usual preoccupations - his jealousy of Baker; his anxiety about being found out - to his real feelings for Clara. And despite her ruses and strategies, Newlings began to see that he was in part responsible for the corrosion of Clara's feelings for her husband. His relationship with her had drained the marriage of its brief vitality, displaced whatever she felt for the good doctor, and trapped these people in a loveless union. Oh, what a mess.

"I had better go."

Dr. White was standing at the doorway of the kitchenette. The fever of sentiment had subsided. He seemed quite self-possessed once more.

Newlings looked at him, still with his thin lip bitten, buttoned.

"Forget what I said just now, Newlings. I was drunk. It was nonsense."

Newlings nodded. "Of course, old man."

"Good night."

"Good night."

Chapter Three

Dr. & Mrs. White

Lovers. Lovers, lovers, lovers - he saw them everywhere. He saw smiling twosomes, contented threesomes, chattering foursomes. No sooner had he woken up in the morning, or in the middle of the night, than the fear of cuckoldry drew tight over his eyes like a blindfold of fishnet stockings. This is why he sat in moody silence in the staff room, on his own, watching, scowling. This explained his snappishness, his wild and violent behaviour towards any good-looking boy who upset him, in or outside his laboratories.

The four hundred yards of dry, leafy path that led

from the Quad to Woodlands, very beautiful in October and April, were walked blindfold by Dr. White at a fierce and jerky pace, nearly a jog, several times a day, as he went home to share a cup of tea at eleven, or a salad at one, or afternoon tea at three, with his attractive young wife. She was always there waiting for him, with a cold cup of tea or a wet, droopy salad, and some new lie or pretence.

Clara cultivated a sense of mystery about herself, a sense of the occult, by dressing in widow's weeds and by dabbing her body and her clothes with cheap but exotic scents, such as her Indian patchouli oil. As soon as she'd arrived at the Hall as Whitey's lovely young bride, she was named 'the witch of the woods' or 'the bitch of the woods'. 'Have you seen the witch of the woods? Have you seen the bitch of the woods?' But it was as if that was what she'd expected, or even wanted. It was as if, from the start, she was one step ahead of the game.

With her affairs Clara played her part in maintaining the status quo at Coxcomb. She helped to keep safe the isolation of the community against the tide of worldly influence, the social upheaval of the mid-sixties, that washed in such flotsam as the enlightened pornographer, Ray Hooley, or the strange offbeat musician, Egg Taylor. The sexual needs which might have driven men like Jimmy Newlings to seek relief in Gt. Yarmouth, the nearest town large enough to support prostitution, were more than satisfied in Woodlands, deep within the grounds of the Hall itself. Bob Rowell approved of and encouraged these affairs. He even urged headmaster O'Donnell to visit Clara White. And O'Donnell did visit. After carefully checking Dr. White's timetable, and the timetables of Baker and Newlings, he rolled all the way down the path to Woodlands on his bony shanks. But on arrival he was rebuffed. Clara didn't even let him inside the house. Rowell had a word with Clara on O'Donnell's behalf, and explained to her that the more staff became accustomed to the Hall as their own hermetic world, their own England, their scepter'd isle entire unto itself, the better for everyone concerned. His words had no effect on Clara.

In some ways Clara appeared to have a perfectly traditional, not to say Victorian view of life and marriage. The forging of a sound alliance, a keen sense of economy and good husbandry, guided her judgement in most matters. But this attitude was very new. Before her marriage to Dr. White she had spent a thriftless and shiftless youth, sharing various untidy flats and slovenly households, and moving from one lowly secretarial position to another until she finished up, at the age of thirty, living on her own in a boarding house, earning her living as a receptionist at Gt. Yarmouth's Eastern Electricity showrooms. One miserable December morning, in an early snowfall, walking towards the bright orange logo of the showrooms in Mare Street, Clara Evans, as she was then, had had a moment of epiphany. She stopped there, on the pavement, in the snow, and looked ahead at the overbearing orange logo, and she'd understood in this moment that unless she acted decisively, her life would become so oppressed by the drudgery of her working days it would not be worth living. Worse still, she knew that she would, in fact, just carry on, carry on and live it out, wear it out, like some old coat she hated but couldn't afford to replace, until she was seventy or eighty years old, and then die somewhere not far from where she'd started out, a burden to the state in some home or hospice. In this moment the future was entirely clear and true to her.

Though she carried on to the showrooms that December morning, in her mind she had reached a turning point. She was thirty and she was still single. She knew herself to be reasonably attractive. She thought her hips too broad and her breasts too small, but she knew from the way men looked at her and quickly looked away that these were minor blemishes, if blemishes at all. But all of the men in all of her offices had always seemed so lumpy and middle-aged, so lecherous and treacherous, and they dressed all year round in Marks & Spencers beige or brown. They talked of nothing but football, cars and television. Hopeless prospects.

Clara Evans had needed to change her life. But how? *How?*

In the end she could think of nothing more imaginative than the irksome business of evening classes, the slow climb up the ladder of second-rate qualifications that might one day lead to a third-rate career. It was at these evening classes, at the Technical Institute, that she met the beaky, quite elderly, and very unappealing Dr. White. He was teaching CSE mathematics and science in the evenings to supplement Bob Rowell's paltry salary, and to get him away from what he thought of sometimes as the madness of his life at the Hall.

But Clara Evans found that maths and science, taught by Dr. White, made as little sense to her second time round as they had at school. Her days were filled with the tedium of filling in Electricity Board forms and her evenings, in her chilly, lonely digs, were now filled with turning pages of grey, incomprehensible diagrams under a lowly Woolworths table lamp. A terminal disillusionment set in and a defeated soul became manipulative and vindictive. From Dr. White's uncertain manner with the women in his class - with all the women in his class - it was obvious that he was a deeply frustrated man, and, very probably, a very inexperienced man. Whenever he introduced a new theorem or equation, he took every opportunity to rush to the women's desks to explain things to them personally, but then held back from them, all confidence lost, no sooner than he'd started. And the younger and more attractive the woman the more flustered he became. Such agitation, such buzzing lust, made his teaching infuriatingly ineffective to the young fathers and young farmers waiting with sharpened pencils, logarithms and protractors in hand, ready to move on in life.

The idea settled in Clara's mind that if she could seduce this beaky, hairy-eared, aging schoolmaster into supporting her indefinitely, this would be, in the short term at least, prize enough to compensate for his age and his shameful unattractiveness, and in the long term it might lead to other possibilities, opportunities, any of which had to be better than things as they stood.

Married life had worked out very much as she'd wanted and expected. She loved the isolation from worldly cares of Dr. White's cottage in the woods. She loved the freedom to get up when she liked and to eat and drink as she pleased. Above all, and this was her greatest pleasure, she loved to sit and read whatever she chose. Alongside her maths and science classes, she had started and abandoned a course in English Literature. The teacher was a passionate young graduate who had inspired her to buy the set classic - *Emma,* by Jane Austen – before she quit.

In Woodlands, this introduction blossomed into inspiration.

Without the stultifying effect of work on her leisure hours she found herself, after some effort, able to cope with the antique, circumlocutory language, and then to enjoy it. After *Emma* came *Mansfield Park*, and then *Sense & Sensibility*, *Pride & Prejudice* and even *Northanger Abbey*. In Woodlands, Clara White discovered the wonderful ease of living in fictional worlds. Rising when she chose and travelling to Hartfield or Mansfield Park or Norland Park every day, clip-clopping through landscapes not dissimilar to those she now inhabited at Woodlands, was a great deal different to walking up the dark streets of Gt. Yarmouth at 7.30 sharp towards the orange logo of the Eastern Electricity showrooms.

Clara White had found her vocation. She was to be a lady of leisure.

But after a while her monologues about literary characters and great authors filled her husband with a smouldering anger. At first he tried to read a book or two himself to keep up, but he quickly gave up these attempts. He was not a reader and she was already too far ahead. Now she'd been through the Edwardians. Now she was reading poetry. Now she'd started Hemingway . . . Her husband's attempts to share in her new passion, his tentative contributions to discussion, such as he could manage, made no difference, never stemmed her flow, never interested her. All of a sudden, he was too ignorant.

Dr. White had imagined that he had married a woman who was so many years his junior she was almost a child, an innocent. He had relished the idea of bringing her to Woodlands where he could ravish that innocence. Where he could, at last, explore all the possibilities of sex, about which he'd fantasised so heatedly through a long and lonely bachelorhood. But this was not all he had hoped for. He had hoped – and he had told her, passionately, of this hope - that they would have a child, before it was altogether too late for him. Clara had assured him that this was what she wanted too, oh yes, that she felt the same need, the very same need, and the same urgency.

But these books of hers - these wretched books! - as he saw it, had changed all that, had somehow taken her innocence away and taken her away too. He had to work all day and mark all evening - what chance did he stand of keeping up with her reading, of being able to talk back to her about this book or that book? Inside he ranted and railed against his young wife. Instead of enjoying the fruits of marriage in his rural idyll he found himself living with a lazy and slatternly bookworm. Cursed with the bourgeois repression of his own upbringing, Dr. White's anger and sexual frustration grew worse, grew into a weighty sickness, a source of depression that became more acute the more he tried to deny it to himself.

This weakness of his, this repressive tendency, had been obvious to Clara from the outset. His outmoded, patronizing, gentlemanly posturing when he'd courted her had never fooled her for a moment. She had seen it for what it was. An aping of high English manners, inhibition and constipation of thought and feeling. Once married and settled in Woodlands she was quick to turn this weakness against him. An unwanted advance – and they were all unwanted - was rebuked with silence and cold withdrawal. His slightest impatience or irritation hurt her feelings for days and he found himself shunned for his barbarous incivility. And her withdrawal, by and large, meant withdrawal into another book, another imagined world.

She caught him watching her as she neared the end of a novel, waiting for the vacant period when she might give him some attention, by and by. If he had offended in any way she arranged to have another book to hand, but out of sight. When she finished the current read she sighed, closed the book, and looked for a long, reflective moment at its covers, and seemed about to say something, but then did not.

At these signs Dr. White made himself more comfortable on the sofa, and tidied a space next to him for his young wife.

"Now, my dear . . . "

But she would be on her feet even as he spoke. She would stretch her lovely young body in front of the fire, and then, feigning a frown of pleased surprise, she would take up her next volume, thicker than the last, from where she'd hidden it round the side of the mantelpiece, or from under the Daily Mail. She sat down again and curled her legs up beneath her in what had once been Dr. White's very own fireside chair, a club chair, but which had now become her 'reading chair'. She ignored his fretful sighs. To her he was not there. She was immersed again between the sheets of another book.

Within a few minutes Dr. White left the room to do some chore in the kitchen, or to iron his clothes for work the next day.

By this pattern of provocation and withdrawal Clara secured much solitude from her husband and smothered any criticism firstly of her reading, and then, as time passed, of her housework too. Little by little she stopped doing things. She got out of the habit of ironing regularly, of washing up after supper, of sweeping and cleaning the ancient lino of the mouldy kitchen. She left things until, in the end, her husband began to take them up. He was orderly and could not bear living amid shabbiness, dirt and waste. Of course she had to be careful not to let things go too far. When she sensed that he was on the verge of breaking down under the strain of his day job at the Hall, and his night shift of housework at Woodlands, when he was on the verge of mental collapse, and of losing, at last, his precious temper, she had strategies to relieve him and to dissipate ill-feeling. She would have a sudden burst of energy herself and clean the kitchen or the living room from top to bottom. And she would cook a good meal for him. And she would tidy away all the bills into their respective files. She would accept no praise or recognition for these sudden spurts of industry. Tacitly she implied that she was perfectly happy to do the housework, the effort meant nothing to her - *but she would not do it at his command!* Neither was she his guilt-slave, and the more he tried to treat her as such the less she would do.

These pretences schooled her husband to further patience and silence, and, most importantly, into doing more and more of the things he wanted done himself. He assumed the burden of the routine chores - shopping, which he loathed, which he felt to be a public disgrace; cooking, washing up, putting out the washing, taking in the washing, ironing - and as he worked harder so his young wife, from the corner of her eye, as it were, monitored his behaviour and timed the deployment of her other stratagem, when it was time to reward rather than punish.

The harder he worked and the more he took on, the more likely it became that she would come to him, quite out of the blue, to give him some sexual treat or favour. He stood washing up at the sink, after cooking and clearing away the Sunday lunch, and she came through from the living room, where she had been sitting reading in front of the fire, and slipped her hand between his legs. He stopped still where he was as she undid his trousers, stroked his furry belly and felt him through his underpants. When he tried to turn to embrace her she held him to the sink with her forearm across his back.

"Carry on washing up," she whispered into his hairy ear.

Obediently he took up another pan and dipped it into the suds. She stooped, pulled down his pants and drew his cock back between his legs to give herself room. He moved to assist. Then she began gently to squeeze and stroke him - to milk him, as it were - as he stood there at the sink.

"Carry on washing up," she whispered, very low, when he stopped again, his hands flat on the bottom of the greasy sink, his rolled sleeves getting wet, his face twisted in ecstasy, and in agony also, in the agony of all his repressed ill-feeling welling up against him. And until he resumed his chore she would only hold him, but as he began to scrub and rinse more vigorously so she would begin to rub and milk him vigorously, until he could bear it no more and he climaxed and his trunk slumped over the sink. With his orgasm, which she prolonged to the full, all his pent up fury was released, all the private rants and rages were expunged and once again he was cleaned out and ready to go to work on Monday morning, and begin another hellish week in the servitude of Rowell and O'Donnell, in the company of the dullards of the Hall, to earn the soldier's pay that would keep his wife in the style to which she had become accustomed.

But in fact Clara was not as dependent upon him as he might have supposed, and was becoming less so as the months passed. His tied house, Woodlands, had become for her not only a comfortable retreat from the world, but an ideally lucrative situation. From the first week they were married she had put much of the housekeeping money into her own deposit account; she'd added to this with the revenue from Baker and Newlings, which she banked each Friday morning. Not only were there these sums, which had enjoyed a steady growth over the last year, there was also, in prospect now, a vein of income which was potentially far, far greater than that she currently mined at the Hall, or that her husband mined, for that matter.

She had no competition. Matron was the only other female in the confines. Despite her more privileged access to the boys, Matron wasn't even in contention. A very tall, virgin spinster in her mid-sixties, she attempted to be the shipshape-and-Bristol-fashion stereotype, the pristine battleship, she believed everyone expected her to be. Her double-breasted tunic was firmly pressed, and her long, flowing grey hair was pinned back in a bun so extended and so severe it lent her head a weathervane for seeking out mischief. For such pains she was ignored: no one cared in which direction, down which corridor, she headed. No one, not even Rowell himself (he had long forgotten), even knew her real name. She was simply, solely, only, 'Matron'. Beneath her forlorn attempts at starched white efficiency, Matron was just another lost and unhappy soul whom Rowell had trapped in his employ for personal gain rather than professional purpose. Matron was an alcoholic. The battleship could be discovered run aground and rudderless any time of day or night. This meant that more often than not Rowell himself was obliged to minister to first aid cases, and from there it was but a short step for him to instruct boys generally on other matronly matters, such as personal hygiene. For some of the more sporty boys, this might mean a long hot shower and a rubdown in the warm, red luxury of Rowell's apartments, and perhaps even a massage with various oils and creams to ease the strains of rugby or cross-country. For the very small ones a soothing balm on the buttocks might be needed for the wounds left by O'Donnell. O'Donnell's excesses were at their worst when provoked not by his passion, where there was a discernible patterning to the wounds, a gentle, climactic patterning either side of a central stripe – tending to these wounds had its rewards for Rowell too, which he never failed to mention to O'Donnell. No, O'Donnell's excesses were at their worst, at their most reckless, bruised, bloody, and quite unerotic, when provoked by Dick Baker.

Chapter Four

Crafts Master

In a round of belt tightening in 1962 Rowell promoted the bluff and easy-going, unqualified Dick Baker, to Crafts Master. The sports jacketed, sports car driving Baker, originally employed as an itinerant teacher of art and ceramics in 1959, found himself, by 1965, and past the age of forty, in charge of gluing canoes together, fixing clay ovens, and instructing in basic car mechanics. It was a miscellany that could be added to as the demand arose, giving Rowell the flexibility he needed to maximise slender profits.

Baker's hail-fellow-well-met manner was beguiling. Affably he agreed to do whatever Rowell required, and then affably did nothing about it. He had discerned long ago that Coxcomb Hall was in such a parlous state Rowell couldn't enforce the terms of his contracts, and the more thinly he deployed his masters the more indispensable they became. Even as Baker assumed more and more roles, he did less and less actual work. He was one of the few who lived off site, which left Rowell and O'Donnell little control. All too often Baker didn't even show up, leaving his classes to the direction of the long suffering technician, Pez Rankin - Pez or Peasant Rankin because of his broad Norfolk accent, broad shoulders, and broad beard - or to the blustering O'Donnell, something which infuriated the headmaster and ex-quartermaster, 'the old man', as Baker called O'Donnell, to apoplexy. For O'Donnell hated above all to be dragged from the warm fug of his study into a classroom or workshop brimful with tension and fear. But Baker did not care. To him the old man was just another old man: he saw only too many of them on the streets of Gorleston where he lived. Gorleston, at this time, was becoming Gt. Yarmouth's premier retirement suburb.

Some days Baker might arrive at work and then spend every lesson tinkering with his sick and aging Austin Healey Sprite in the car mechanics pit, while his classes drank tea, played cards and fetched him spanners and rags. The only work he set on such a day was the cleaning and polishing of his car when he'd finished.

In fact, Baker's attendance and duties at the Hall were more dictated by Dr. White's timetable than his own. While 'the good Doctor' (another of Baker's epithets) was pinned down, straightjacketed, as it were, in his labs, by a bunch of jeering seniors in white coats, Dick Baker gave himself up to half an hour of sexual abandon back at Woodlands with Clara White. The affair didn't mean much in itself. Its significance lay in the endless frictions it provoked between the mock-worldly Baker and the passionate but inadequate Jimmy Newlings.

'Little Jimmy roll-your-own.'

Though they both paid, there was an essential difference. Baker knew that Clara White enjoyed intercourse with him quite as much as he did with her, perhaps more most of the time, and so when she tried to increase her charge, even though the increase was to come with a licence for him to do something to her that she had always refused, he said quite flatly, frankly, No, he would not pay a penny more. In fact he laughed in her face. Clara recoiled, smiled, and for a moment negotiations faltered. They met a firmness in each other's eyes at this moment, but also a humorousness, as if each had found the other out, as if a truth had been laid bare. After a tussle, a little roughing up, Baker continued to pay, but, he told himself, there was more a self-interested generosity in his paying now. He knew Clara was salting his money away, and though it was an obvious risk on his part, he felt inclined to invest in her prospects. The truth was that Dick Baker, however ludicrous it seemed to him at times – he too! - had allowed himself to fantasize of a life of blissful monogamy with Clara White. Past forty, Baker was acutely aware that time was running out for him. He was reminded of this depressing fact day in and day out by living in Gorleston. He hated Gorleston. He loathed Gorleston. The last young family in his street had just sold out to an arthritic couple from Essex, up for their last gasps of sea air. He had no neighbour either side of the street, and it was such a long street, and he lived right in the middle of it, less than seventy years old.

Baker had sufficient wit and cunning never to utter a word of his innermost feelings to Clara White – the witch of the woods, the bitch of the woods – and as things turned out he did well to keep his own counsel.

But between Newlings and Clara the relationship

was quite different. Though he imagined otherwise, to Clara, Newlings was actually much the same kind of creature as the man she had married, except that physically he was even less appealing. His skin was dry and flaky, prone to eczema, and he smelled, at any time of day, of a bitter combination of his own anxious sweat and the school's tallow soap. In middle age his mouth had incurled to a lipless slot, a hard dry hole for ejecting dates, battles and rebukes. When sexually excited clots of spit dried at the corners of his mouth-slot, and this was something that disgusted Clara White, this all-too-predictable frothing over and drying up. She imagined, quite rightly, that it was the same when he ranted and railed at the boys in his desperate lessons - she could remember faces and mouths just like Newlings' before the blackboards of her own classrooms, half her lifetime away. From their very first week of intercourse her charges to Newlings had never stopped increasing. Newlings cursed himself for his spinelessness in acceding to her demands, but when he considered the alternative, a return to his masturbatory ways, fantasising about the younger boys, taking up Rowell's offers to come upstairs and help with first aid instruction with the seven- and eight-year-olds, when he remembered all that his life had been at Coxcomb Hall, and all that his youth had been, the years and years that had already passed by in such depravity and isolation, all the time he had torn up and wasted before the arrival of Mrs. White, when he remembered all of that, he could not contemplate his existence without her. He *had* to see her once a week at least. It was a compulsion. The spirit of self-denial, that until her arrival had enabled him to put aside considerable savings, even on Rowell's pitiful salary, that spirit, which he'd always mistaken for strength of character, had been broken. He dreaded the holidays when

Dr. White would take his wife away to Cornwall or the Lake District in his single berth caravan, towed behind his tiny Fiat motor car, while he would have to pack up and take a train in the opposite direction, to somewhere increasingly modest these days, all because of the crippling expense of Clara's services.

All this might have been tolerable to Newlings while he still could afford it, if not for the attitude of his rival, Dick Baker, the unqualified Crafts Master who didn't know his place. Dick's attitude was pushing Newlings to the very brink.

"Why on earth do you pay her so much, old boy?" he whispered to Newlings as they collected their coffee and biscuits at morning break. "It's costing you a bloody fortune. You must have money to burn. Pay her ten. Not a penny more."

Ten!

"I pay five," Baker said, and his eyelids lowered smugly. He snapped a chocolate bourbon between his teeth. "Not a penny more. Or she can forget it. I told her so. Not interested." He looked about, crunching his biscuit. "Do better under the pier, says I."

Newlings stared down into his milky coffee, then reached for his own bourbon with a trembling hand.

Baker watched Newlings' hand: such thin and wasted fingers reaching for sweetness - no wonder Clara put a premium on a hand like that coming near her young flesh.

"She tells me you pay twenty-five a throw. *A pony!* Why, Jimmy Newlings! Hold on to those savings, old boy! Is it love or something?"

No, Newlings said to himself, it certainly is not that, and he lifted his chin, stretching for a little dignity here. The humiliation of knowing that she had told Baker, and that they must have laughed about this together, laughed at his desperation, at how she was bleeding him dry like a blackmailer - he could see it all, he could see them lying in Dr. White's bed together, with Dr. White's counterpane, the yellow candlewick, tucked under their chins, chatting and laughing under the yellow candlewick - the humiliation was mixed with a sense of wild panic, because Baker had mentioned his savings. Newlings was careful, he had always been so careful, never to talk about his savings, yet everyone knew about his savings. Everyone knew! And talked, and whispered, and cast knowing nods and sullen, swollen looks in his direction. And now Baker and Clara openly discussed his savings in Dr. White's bed. They chuckled and made plans. They were *after* his savings. The woods were truly burning now.

On the subject of money Baker and Newlings were as chalk and cheese. Baker was always broke and living beyond his means, shoring up his debts with more loans, while Newlings personified the principle of cautious husbandry. He had never been in the red in his life, had never crossed that line, and was now a long, long way from that square in the game. It was very galling to him to know that Baker found some stupid delight in seeing him throw his money away like this, paying five times as much for the goods Baker got for a mere five pounds, the price of a whore under Yarmouth pier.

Newlings looked out the window, down at the Quad. There was that malnourished looking boy again, Scott, one of the outcasts, scratching around the edge of the tuck box shed.

"What is that boy doing?"

Baker wrapped the skin from his milky coffee on a chocolate finger, sucked off the skin and ate the biscuit. He looked out the window and spoke with his mouth full.

"Burying something, by the looks of things . . . His treasure, Newlings. Pocket money, Newlings. Saving it all up for a rainy day, Newlings. Looking after the future like a sensible little chappie, like a sensible little *roll-your-own*."

Newlings' mouth curled in tighter in a grim smile of anger and hurt, acknowledging the score, and Baker, satisfied at last that he had cut the bloodless Newlings, strolled off to chat with deputy Tim Jackson, the young pretender, who'd that moment drifted in to the smoky fug of the staff room.

Newlings sipped and watched.

It put some salve on his dry wounds to note that of these two younger masters, and there were none younger than Tim Jackson, Jackson was by far the more attractive man. He made Baker look paunchy and middle-aged. Baker's curly fair hair, brushed high from his forehead and too well groomed, was beginning to recede, while Jackson's rich dark hair was cut trimly, a firm and springy force kept under control, like his athletic figure. His Roman nose made him the hawkish side of handsome, and he looked particularly sharp and hawkish now, frowning and looking down at the floor, as he always did when Baker approached. It had puzzled Newlings how Rowell had managed to recruit such a promising and accomplished fellow as Tim Jackson. Because Jackson was no fool. He wouldn't be charmed by Baker, who seemed to be putting some effort into getting on his right side these days. In his responses to Baker's bluff remarks, jokes and appeals, Jackson only looked suspicious, unamused, reserved.

Newlings turned back to the Quad window. The boy Scott was making some kind of private gestures over the hole he'd dug, as if crossing himself in prayer or casting a spell – had he fallen to a belief in God or magic?

Now he was scuffing dirt and gravel over his hole with his bare hands, like an animal covering its excrement. What was he up to, for goodness' sake? It looked quite hopeless. Newlings had seen this performance several times at different points around the school. As an outcast, an untouchable, Scott was left to his own devices, forbidden from taking part in lessons, denied even the basics of pen and paper so as to keep him at a distance from the masters; and for their part the masters would not give him a second thought in their struggle to maintain supremacy over the bigger brutes. It was quite possible that Scott had made no progress at all, even after four or five years. He might be going backwards, becoming illiterate and innumerate, deaf and dumb.

Of course the disapproving Christian Tim Jackson was trying to take this kind of thing in hand, he was identifying the outcasts, caring for the weak and persecuted. He had a long list of 'reforms' to implement. He had fenced off the Dell, the private rubbish pit - and the private retreat, the only playground, for the likes of Scott. He had expressed concerns about what went on in the darkness of the tuck box shed and the Games Room, and he was trying to take on the tyrannical corruption of the prefects. At this recollection Newlings frowned too. The prefect body was so strong it was like a praetorian guard, set around the dark and dreaded figure of Ossaf - seldom seen these days, thank the Lord. It would be interesting, Newlings thought, jutting out his jaw, taking stock, to see how the young pretender fared, how he endured, when up against a monster like Ossaf.

Then his thoughts turned to Clara White again and the blood rushed to his head. He took the last custard cream and glanced about for a chair.

Chapter Five

Reform

Sweets, cake, fruit and sundry comforts were stored in the bleak and forbidding tuck box shed. Five hundred boxes lined the shelves. Most were tough as teak, with weighty padlocks, but some - on lower shelves, in easy reach - were pale and new and quite defenceless. By order, the shed doubled as storage for shoe polish kit and the air was thick with Cherry Blossom wax. The wax was a great leveller. Every item in the boxes was scented with it, and the duckboard floor was black and treacherous from the buffing of a thousand toecaps.

This was an emotive place. Within the boxes were those things that had been packed by mothers, and here and there, by fathers too. Special things parents had wrapped with their own hands. Gifts they had tried to disguise from covetous eyes and fingers. These items, deep down in the boxes, despite the Cherry Blossom, still had the scent of home, of brave farewells and concealed regrets. To see these things snatched away and eaten, or stolen and discarded, kicked about by bored and greedy thugs, or to discover some piece of food that months before had been secreted in a corner with a kind or humorous remark, to find it rotten in that corner - this sort of thing was emotional for boys not yet even eight years of age. Under lock and key the boxes held tokens of the world from which they had been wrested. This windowless shed, grim and utilitarian, was a place both of solace and despair, where things of the old life could be held and treasured or mocked and trampled underfoot.

O'Donnell, Rowell, and even Jackson, were of one mind about this place. It was off limits. Row upon row, box upon box, filled to the brim with sentiment, constituted a powder keg. The overlaying seal of wax could not cover the smaller boys' yearnings for hearth and home. It was disturbing just to open the flapping door and peer into the dimness of the tuck box shed, and to see along the upper shelves pale knees and calves, bedraggled socks, dangling there as if from lifeless young bodies - a mass childhood suicide. O'Donnell, Rowell and Jackson felt it best to leave this place as uncontested territory. On their patrols they glanced in, then let the door flap shut in the winds that swirled the gravel Quad.

As an ex-quartermaster, and indeed as headmaster, O'Donnell had an obligation to be more attentive, but he was one for whom the atrophy of feeling that accompanies old age had set in prematurely. His fight against lifelong weaknesses - stripping, flogging, drinking - had hollowed both principles and health. He had become a gentleman without presence, a potbellied figure in crumpled suits on bony shanks. Each morning he walked the length of the Quad with his painful, rolling gait, his flushed face lowered, his shoulders hunched against the cold, and he seemed to drag the bad weather in with him, the cast-iron skies and endless coastal storms. Unless summoned by Rowell he kept to his inner sanctum all day under a fug of Gold Leaf and whisky fumes.

Coxcomb's owner and paymaster, Bob Rowell, self-styled Principal as distinct from headmaster, a bogus and confusing distinction, was unlikely to be spotted much about the grounds either. For Rowell, an incorrigible posturer, the stance of absentee landlord, of English country squire, was his preferred attitude during term time. His own apartments were well removed, high up in the Victorian wing, overlooking the playing fields and the misty woods and streams beyond. His vigilance amounted to nothing more than boy-gazing from the casements of his third storey windows.

Which left reform largely to Jackson, the new man, full of Christian decency and worthy intent. Tall and handsome and with exquisite manners, Tim Jackson was truly a likable young fellow, and very capable as well, but he too had a weakness. He was impetuous.

Coxcomb had its fads, its cults, things the old-timers just passed by but which Jackson could not leave be.

In the autumn of 1965 Doctor Who was still in his infancy. The long-haired William Hartnell had not yet given way to Patrick Troughton, nor Troughton to Jon Pertwee, and Christopher Eccleston was but a babe in arms. On Wednesday nights the mysterious programme drew a large gathering in the Games Room. Chairs were borrowed from every corner and the lights were put out. The younger boys, seven to ten years old, lay in the laps of the prefects and were stroked and fondled there under the flickering black and white screen, while the Tardis panted back and forth and the Daleks rolled by. Jackson stared in through the steamy windows and was appalled at what he saw, at the undone buttons and loosened zips, at the stroking hands and the groping hands, and the prefects' eyes fixed on Hartnell's long-haired and wooden performance. As he watched, the ancient, humourless face of Dr. Who loomed in close-up, scowling down on the degenerate scene.

The boys assumed, turning to the window, that Jackson's interest was prurient. Because he was new, and because he lived in the same remote apartments as Rowell, and because neither was attached, it was taken they enjoyed a homosexual relationship. Nothing could have been further from the truth: Jackson had rejected Rowell's advances, his favours, the use of his sagging Jaguar at weekends, the loan of his Holland & Holland shotguns, his expensive sea-fishing tackle, and so on. Jackson was earnest about his Christian reforms. But it was neither in the tuck box shed nor the Games Room that he first made his presence felt.

The Dell, a natural pit in the woods beyond the Quad, served as both cesspit overflow and general dump for garden and kitchen refuse. Apart from its smell, which hung over the Quad on windless summer days, there was nothing much harmful about the Dell. Mother Nature had provided a most useful and economical convenience, according to Rowell. But on his patrols Jackson had noticed something else and he took a different line. The Dell had become a haunt for small boys looking for adventure, boys searching for hideaways and dens, for mystery and magic, and such pursuits represented a weakness, a regressive tendency, in his view. Furthermore the Dell was dangerous. Besides the risk of breaking an ankle on the builders' rubble or broken furniture, or picking up a disease from the sewage mulch, there was the chemical and biological waste. Jackson had seen acids from the science laboratories hiss and steam in the grass cuttings. He'd seen slashed rats, slashed bulls' eyes, bits of dissected frog, chicken, locust and other animal matter.

Jackson protested first to O'Donnell, who said and did nothing, who did not even speak or move from his chair, who just shook his head once in disbelief at the young reformer. So Jackson took his complaint to Rowell himself. He persuaded the Principal that stakes and barbed wire, and some signs - in Latin - were needed to protect the boys from the dangers of the Dell, and from their own misguided and unhealthy tendencies. Hoping to charm, Rowell agreed. The reform was implemented in full and with immediate effect.

One day Jackson would look back upon this petty business as a triumph.

Bob Rowell had served in the Royal Air Force during the second World War and when he heard that the de Havilland Vampire was being taken out of service, broken up, or used for aerial target practice, he talked old friends at R.A.F. Coltishall into letting him have a carcass for his CCF. There was sufficient room on the Hall playing fields for a final touch down and after some haggling over costs his plan was executed.

The plane had stood in the corner of the playing fields, its engine removed, lopsided on its flat tyres, since 1960. In the coastal rains boys sheltered under its motherly wings, and when that space was all taken one or two smaller boys might climb into the engine cowling between the fuselage struts. It was not comfortable in there: the coiled walls of the cowling were covered in severed pipes and cable runs, sharp lugs and brackets. But the pleasure of listening to the driving rain clatter on the aluminium shell, and of watching the world go by through the engine's exhaust, was lure enough to a bored and wet seven- or eight-year-old.

Once inside the engine cowling a boy was trapped: there were some naïve and playful juniors who wanted to be trapped, or who had a subliminal desire to be trapped by some of the prettier, older boys, and in this there lay harmless homosexual amusement. But for others getting trapped in the womb of the Vampire was a mistake never to be repeated or forgotten, and it was the suffering of these that Jackson tried to relieve with his second reform.

Rowell wouldn't listen this time. The Vampire, lopsided and dangerous, pleasure palace for sadistic homosexual bullying, remained a looming grey eminence pointing across the rugby fields. Rowell would not hear of its removal or destruction. It was a feature of Coxcomb, he said, staring absently over the playing fields at the grey aeroplane, and the misty woods and streams beyond. It was a unique asset, he said. They were very lucky to have such a relic. Very lucky indeed.

In the same way that the appearance of the tuck box shed had an emotional resonance for the boys where an adult might see something only dull and utilitarian, so the Vampire had a significance for Bob Rowell quite beyond its usefulness to the CCF. It was an attachment the impetuous Jackson had not even tried to understand.

Bob Rowell had spent most of his years in the Royal Air Force discovering and nurturing male vocal talent. There was no more beautiful sound than the unaccompanied male voice, he'd always maintained. At

Coltishall he'd built up a choir of such professional standing they were invited to sing carols every Christmas, in their flying jackets and fancy scarves, on the BBC's *Look East* programme, the region's nightly news magazine.

While at Coltishall Rowell had made a discovery that stayed with him, haunted him, for the rest of his life. A handsome young flight lieutenant, one of the lucky few who'd buzzed about in Hurricanes and Spitfires during the war, arrived in '56 with four years to run before he finished his commission. This young man's name was John Cussack. He had a full and clear tenor voice such as Rowell had never heard outside a concert hall. It was Rowell who discovered, nurtured and trained the voice of Johnny Cussack, destined to become a star of the stage, radio and television. It was Rowell who coaxed, then coerced, the rather frivolous and dandified flight lieutenant into taking his talent seriously. Cussack became his protégé, and when early British show-business luminaries such as Cliff Adams and George Mitchell started their radio and tv favourites - *Sing Something Simple* and *The Black and White Minstrel Show* - Rowell had the connections to see to it that his man became a lead singer in every troupe. And from there a named star. Outside the Victoria Palace in London, the theatrical home of *The Black and White Minstrel Show* (where they didn't sing a note: the Palace was too big for live performance) Johnny Cussack's name was up in lights, along with the rather quacky but popular Welsh baritone, Dai Thomas, and bass Clive Winthrop.

It was Johnny Cussack, willingly and good-humouredly performing one last stunt for command, and doing a favour for his old mentor, who touched the Vampire down on the Coxcomb playing fields. The Christian reformer Jackson had no idea what he was up against when he sought to have the aeroplane given away to a local air museum. Rowell wouldn't listen to this petition for a moment. Jackson couldn't understand the significance of Rowell's wince, when he informed Rowell the Vampire was used day in and day out for sadistic bullying, and should be cut up with oxyacetylene torches and removed.

Jackson had to make do with keeping a private vigil. The plane was central to the lives of the top brass in the CCF, a vicious and crack elite. They had access to the cockpit and more than once Jackson found an eight- or nine-year-old up there with no clothes on, shivering and crying behind the joystick, too ashamed to escape. One rainy Sunday afternoon Jackson found a pair of twins naked in the Vampire, one in the cockpit and the other curled up in the engine cowling, which was slowly filling with water. Shocked by the ineffectiveness of his own vigilance he went again to Rowell - but Rowell would not give an inch.

"Boys will be boys, Jackson."

"What if their parents knew of this?"

"O'Donnell deals with that, you know."

It was a duty for the boys to write home each week but this was done under O'Donnell's supervision, in the dining hall, after Chapel on Sundays. It was the one time of the week when O'Donnell was genuinely alert to the world.

Rowell was sitting in his antique captain's chair in his Principal's study. He leant back, his reading glasses dangling from his fingers, surprised at Jackson's persistence and tenacity. Before Jackson's interruption he had been immersed in J.R.R.Tolkien's, *The Lord of the Rings*, a book he never tired of rereading. He wanted to sink again into the gnomish imagination of the lauded

Oxford don, into the *Inklings*, and the misty woods and streams just beyond the rugby pitches, a few hundred yards from his rotting third floor casements. The points Jackson had raised were of no interest to him at all. He dismissed Jackson. "You must have a class waiting, Mr. Jackson."

With this snub all Jackson's reforms ran into the sand.

Chapter Six

The Strumpet's Plague

No one knew what he was talking about, and Jackson understood that. He could keep these seniors more or less in line, but he could get them to do no serious work. The text in front of them was Othello, no less, and they were already at Act 1V, having understood virtually nothing. The last few lessons had been the worst. A further shortening of attention span, an unwillingness to engage with anything, even on the crudest level. Something was preoccupying them, disturbing them: Jackson thought of animals, a herd of beasts, made restive by some collective instinct, a herd about to migrate, following signs no one yet understood - seasonal winds, celestial maps. Or a herd bitten into stampede by mosquito swarms, a plague of tics.

He frowned. His handsome forehead was habitually creased in frowns these days. Puzzled frowns. Disapproving frowns. Louring scowls. He had read somewhere that it took twenty thousand frowns to make a wrinkle. So be it. Perhaps the job, the reforms, were too much for him after all. Perhaps the place was getting the better of him.

But what was eating them? What was making them itch so? Crabs? Lice? Crotch rot? Jock itch? What was going on between them, and between their spotty, mouldy thighs? Hallett and Parsons. These two had taken to sitting together to one side of the form. They seemed the most severely bitten. And yet he would have said these two were the very least susceptible, suggestible. The others stole glances in their direction from time to time, then passed notes and sotto voce remarks. It was not difficult to work out what was in those glances, notes, remarks. Something covetous. Something imploring, desperate. Each boy seemed to be saying, when he glanced across at Parsons or at Hallett:

Remember me! At your peril! Do not leave me behind!

Jackson had been forced to presume it was sexual, some kind of collective crush, a mass hysteria - Whore Hallett, as usual, being the irresistible attraction. When that failed to make any sense it crossed his mind, for one vain moment, that if not Hallett, perhaps the main attraction was, in fact, himself. But they were *all* involved! (Or virtually all: the untouchable, Leery, was forgotten about and kept in the dark as always. He sat alone at the back of the classroom drawing sketches and cartoons of

Spiderman, Hulk, Donald Duck . . .)

By coincidence, the dreadful sessions of uninhibited pawing and stroking that went on in the Games Room on Wednesday evenings, during Dr. Who, seemed to have abated. Without any further action on his part. Perhaps just the awareness that someone was prepared to step inside and act, as he had done, storming the sacred preserve of the Games Room, putting on the lights, switching off the television, and telling them to dress themselves properly and sit in an orderly fashion before he'd switch it on again and let the Tardis return - perhaps that was all that had been necessary. But he thought not. He suspected he'd merely driven the lust underground, and not by any authority in his threats either, but simply by his invasion of their privacy. Quite possibly he had only succeeded in putting more juniors into seniors' beds after lights-out, having denied them their mutual comfort in the twilight of the Games Room. Following his intervention the most disturbing thing had been the behaviour of the juniors. The next Wednesday he had witnessed new problems: boys of seven, eight and nine years old running wild around the room, at a loss for what to do with themselves, desperately seeking attention from their erstwhile molesters. There was regression: chasing, hitting, biting, baby talk. The younger boys had been thrown back upon each other and were vying for each other's petting. They behaved like excitable infants after a party where there had been some terrible upset, the magic had failed, the rabbit had been pulled dead from the top hat.

What connection could there be, though, between the sudden abatement of overt homosexual behaviour among the seniors, and their behaviour towards the ponderous but admirable Parsons, and the wily, attractive Hallett? Were these two having a liaison? Hence the covetousness? Had Whore Hallett chosen, at last? The cup-eared, seal-eared Parsons?

Whatever was going on Jackson knew it to be corrupt and ungodly. It might even be dangerous, to themselves and to others. Insurrection. A mass breakout, perhaps. A plan to slaughter all of those in charge, then run riot and desert. Arson. Looting. (But what could they loot?) Mayhem. Sometimes it seemed to Jackson that, given the circumstances, anything was possible here. Coxcomb reminded him of a mutinous ship from centuries past: intolerable conditions leading to frenzies of destruction and lunacy.

There was another piece to the puzzle, though, concerning Jackson personally. Something else had happened.

Was there a connection between these changes he had noted, and had discussed with others in the staff room, and with a blithely indifferent Bob Rowell, and the serious theft (£40: his monthly allowance) that Jackson had recently suffered? He was sure it was these seniors who had stolen from him, not the juniors or another member of staff, or poor Rankin, Pez Rankin, the caretaker, whom Baker had immediately accused. (He'd pointed a finger at Rankin with a knowing nod - there's your culprit, there's your thief. Baker was full of the most malicious and ridiculous slander!) Looking up now from his battered copy of Othello, Act 1V Scene 1 - Jackson considered that, yes, very likely the theft had been planned and executed by those who sat before him now. He was sure it was these. This very class. This bunch. This bloody lot!

To confront them with an accusation was pointless, so he was biding his time, looking for clues, trying to build up some picture of the crime itself and the identity of those behind it. He needed to be patient, to watch, to listen, but how much time did he have before some other, bolder and more dangerous exploit was executed?

"Parsons? Iago, if you please. From, '*tis the strumpet's plague* . . ."

All eyes seized the excuse to look to the cup-eared Parsons, who began to read without expression from the text he shared with Whore Hallett, his ears burning fiercely.

"Wait a moment! What have you there?"

Jackson approached their desk. "Give that to me!" he commanded. "Open your hand."

Parsons dutifully opened his hand to reveal nothing more than a smooth, shaped piece of wood, something like a wedge or peg or an enormous tooth.

"What is that?"

"A piece of wood, sir."

Jackson nodded. "Put it away. Continue."

Parsons put the wood into his blazer pocket. Whore Hallett held a finger on the text until Parsons was ready to resume.

" . . . . . . *'tis the strumpet's plague*
To beguile many, and be beguiled by one."

There was a ripple of amusement on Parsons' reading of these lines. Jackson noted that. He looked across the class. What did it mean? And the piece of wood, smoothed, shaped? They all knew what it was, what it was for, but of course he could not ask. They would lie and turn it into a joke, make a fool of him. The best he could do was pretend he had no interest in it. It was important, though. He knew it was. He was on the very edge of finding something out. He could feel it.

"He, when he hears of her, cannot refrain
From the excess of laughter - "

At this there was a sudden outburst of quite raucous laughter from half the class or more, and a good deal of smiling, tittering and smirking from the rest.

Ah.

At last Jackson had his clue.

Chapter Seven

The Untouchables

The Mauritian Christofalos was not yet strong enough to take on seniors who dominated territories such as the Quad or the Games Room, but he was a powerful figure in the community nonetheless. His fiercest boast was the wrenching off of Coke bottle tops with his bare teeth. The glint and snap and hiss of this act, in the dimness of the tuck box shed, was terrifying to the new boys forced to stand and watch. To them he was Count Christofalos, and the Count's appetites knew no restraint. One by one he heaved their boxes up into his corner and sat gorging himself, like an ape up a tree, scoffing and farting until there was nothing left, only wrappers and rinds scattered on the waxy duckboards below.

But he ate alone.

The Count could not share his feasts with anyone even if he wanted to. Suspicion and anxiety laid waste the ground where camaraderie, even among rapists, thugs and thieves, might take root. A sense of companionship only existed in the smiles of those new to the system - smiles soon perverted into seductive affection. But even against this background of each figure living within himself and for himself alone, the Count had receded further, isolated by the grossness of his appearance, his adult corpulence, his apish hairiness.

Yet he was content.

He looked around his domain, the dark and grubby tuck box shed, inhaled deeply its waxy smell, and considered himself lucky in comparison with others of similar or even loftier status. At least he was indoors. Leery, who stalked the beech trees in the Quad, seemed almost pitiful to Christofalos. But then again Leery's isolation was of a different order and had a deeper significance.

Leery had been born a syndactyl baby. The scars from the removal of the membrane between his fingers were bold as glove seams. Years ago, as a new boy of just seven years of age, he had been fool enough to explain what had happened to some nosy and treacherous new friend. From that moment he had been shunned by all around him. *Webby, Webman, Spiderman, Batman*, and worst of all, because of his ferocious temper when taunted - *Hulk*. The baiting went on until, in his rage and his agony, Leery abandoned his peers and grew vicious enough to silence the generations coming up behind.

The community needed its untouchables, such as Leery, in order to instil in those new to the system, by example, the behaviour expected by the homosexual elite.

Among those like Leery no bonding arose because they were so few in number and disparate in age: in any year just one was selected to join the caste, and once selected there could be no way back. He was lost for the duration. He might return from the summer holiday under the fond illusion that those who had shunned him the year before would have forgiven and forgotten, just as he was prepared to forgive and forget. But forgiveness was impossible. The selfish fear that a boy might himself be reduced to the status of untouchable by mere association guaranteed no breaking of ranks. And for his part the untouchable hid his suffering and showed no feeling because only by such stoicism, and a resolve to seek deeper and deeper isolation from his fellows, was there relief from persecution. So Jackson, the Christian protector of the weak, was silently cursed and hated by many of the most vulnerable, because he had taken from them the Dell, the rubbish pit which had become their accepted retreat, and left them nowhere to live out in privacy their years of misery and deprivation.

A physical blemish of some kind, or a speech defect, was always the primary cause of rejection, rather than issues of race or creed. Count Christofalos had never been troubled by anyone because of the colour of his skin or his bold insistence, to any who would listen, that he was a devout Muslim. Even when he painted a prayer arrow on the roof of the tuck box shed, pointing towards the Hook of Holland, no one jeered or sneered. No one cared. But just because of his gross size he had come closer than he knew to being the isolate of his year, and to having a very different destiny to that he enjoyed in the tuck box shed.

Then again, Scott's case broke the rules in a different way. He'd been elected untouchable virtually on arrival. A tiny, helpless child with a cauliflower ear, Colin Scott, from the very first day, cried for his mother at the slightest provocation. After just a few weeks this waif had become the spirit of the Dell, and four years later still spent most of his life in the rubbish tip, despite Jackson's barbed wire and Latinate signposts:

Cave!
Keep Out!

Scott was far from defeated, though. In fact, his plan, formed in his first year, was not just to fight back, but actually to annihilate this place where he had been incarcerated. Day in and day out he applied his childish cunning to this end. In all weathers, somewhere around the buildings, he could be found scraping away dust and soil under ledges, overhangs, in shady corners. To dig he used a treasured shiny dessertspoon that he had stolen from the dining hall. He dug in broad daylight, ignoring and ignored by passers-by. When he had made a hole big enough to accommodate it, Scott took from his blazer pocket an acorn. Lovingly he planted the acorn, together with a smidgen of compost he had brought from his den in the Dell. He buried the seed, muttering some spell or incantation or private prayer, and brushed the place over with his bare hands to hide what he had done. Scott had learned, years before he came to Coxcomb, on a nature walk in kindergarten, that plants grew swiftly in the dark, but he had not understood that they did so because they yearned for light, and that without light they withered and died. He only thought that the oak was a slow growing tree and immensely strong. He daydreamed of sedition all day, and at night, in the long, cold, bare dormitory, when all masturbation had ceased, and when he too, at last, fell asleep, young Scott dreamt of unstoppable trunks of oak, rising and swelling to break through brick and pipe and floorboard and destroy Coxcomb Hall forever.

Besides these institutionalised inmates, the home-grown ones as it were, there were the ingrates, older boys, in increasing numbers, who had arrived as fully fledged misfits, or even proven criminals. The former generally came from overseas, and the latter from over-stretched social services departments in inner-city boroughs. One day a pair of rich Turks arrived who could not speak, read or write a word of English. Spoiled and troublesome at home, they had been sent to receive the corrective discipline of an English boarding school education. The first phrase they were taught by their seniors and mentors, to be used as an all-purpose salutation, was: *Hello, old boy! You fucking shithead!* When smiling Christian Tim Jackson came across the Quad to introduce himself, his hand outstretched in haughty welcome, that is how they returned his handshake: *Hello, old boy! You fucking shithead!*

But inner-city imports like the pornographer Ray Hooley, from Newington Green in north London, were a case apart. It was Hooley's boast that he had been conceived during the making of a blue film. With his sideburns and long blonde hair and his lived-in eyes, his diverse sexual history, he seemed to his peers already adult. He had adult habits. He drank spirits and chain-smoked, and even had a preferred brand of cigarettes - Player's No. 6. And while he smoked and talked and played cards, a Player's No. 6 hanging from his lips, and bragged in his dreary monotone about his connections in the pornography trade, about paedophile films he had made, about the thousands of pounds his father turned over as a north London 'fence', he gained a kudos none could match.

Foreign elements like Hooley were important.

They opened the door to a new kind of commercialized corruption that in the end undermined Coxcomb's innocent ways.

Tim had them in the palm of his hand.

"I will arise and go now, and go to Innisfree . . ."

He had given some account of the music of Yeats' language. This had been his theme with these juniors from the start - assonance, consonance, alliteration, euphony - and now he was moving on to show some of the richer and more accessible examples from the heritage. He tested them regularly and kept them on their toes, and they were learning and responding well.

> *"And a small cabin build there, of clay and*
> *wattles made:*
> *Nine bean rows will I have there, a hive for*
> *the honey bee,*
> *And live alone in the bee-loud glade."*

The lines resonated, he liked to think, in the young and unformed minds before him, and for one fellow at least, at the back of the class, he was absolutely right. The untouchable Scott hung on his every word. Besides his cauliflower ear, which was not particularly noticeable, Scott had no obvious defect of body or speech that had made his election a matter of course. In his case it had been a subtler thing. It had been a question of manner. Scott was ingratiating, and his cartoon weediness complemented this quality. His face was large and pale and he wore adult, grey-rimmed glasses that gave an impression of top-heaviness, of a dull thing grown too heavy for its stalk. His voice was quick and nervous and under pressure broke down into gibbering. He was not a stutterer but his fellows turned on him the machine-gun mockery with which they strafed all stutterers, and this had driven him into permanent and sullen withdrawal.

Scott's unforgivable mistake had been to offer a fellow newcomer, on his very first day at Coxcomb, this rehearsed introduction, delivered in his mother's upper middle-class tones:

"Please pardon my curiosity, but would you mind telling me from whence you hail? My name is Colin Scott."

His mother had taught him the line, which she thought quite innocent and humorous, and how to deliver it. It was her anxious belief that her son, on account of his natural shyness and his unsightly ear, would need to take more care than others in making friends, and should treat his fellows with all due respect. At the same time he could not afford to back away from saying something first. She imagined the new boys would pair off quickly into protective partnerships, and that her son might be excluded if he did not make the first move. But Colin Scott, who'd been moving from one new boy to another like a lost puppy, came out with her introductory line to the wrong sort of fellow, to a fat farmer's son, a peasant, and Scott was snubbed for his trouble. This boy used the occasion to make himself popular by inviting others to laugh at "little toffy Scott", and he mimicked and mocked Scott's mother's line. By quick permutation Colin Scott became "little Scotty-dog", "Spotty-dog", "Doggy-spot", "Dog-end" or "Doggy-pot", and further punishment swiftly followed. Scott's head of dormitory began a nightly ritual where Scott was instructed to stand still at the end of his bed while others took it in turns to punch him in the belly as hard as they liked. The sport lasted until he finally won the election as outcast for his year. Then came immediate relief, because once elevated to that status his body, his clothes, and all his property became untouchable, contaminated. Even the soap he used was discarded, or thrown around in some wild sport: *'Scottysoap! Doggysoap! Pottysoap!'* Those who slept either side of his bed would not pass their own beds at the same time as him. Scott had to wait respectfully in his pyjamas for his neighbours to pass before he moved to his bedside and slipped between the safety of his sheets. Nor would it do to use the same side of the bed twice in a row, to show some preference for the side with the less vicious neighbour. That was taken as more ingratiating weakness and punished accordingly.

Punishments for someone you could not touch were necessarily inventive.

When sheets were changed Scott's bed could be tampered with. Scott had a phobia for cockroaches. He had never seen anything like a cockroach before, not at home, in any nook or cranny, not in his suburban garden, nor on any holiday abroad in sunnier climes. Nothing in his experience, in his seven years of life, had prepared him for the sight of an insect so large and quick and ugly, and with such terrifying antennae. Apart from the Victorian wing, which was regularly fumigated, Coxcomb was infested with cockroaches.

His first thought was that the loose threads in his pyjamas were itching him. Then sniggers from a bed across the way threw him into a panic. With a shriek he pulled back his bedding and ran for the light. There were a dozen or more cockroaches scattering in every direction, rushing for cover over his clean white sheets. Several more insects had fallen to the floor and were coming towards his bare feet, as if to give chase. Scott ran screaming down the corridor to the toilets.

A minute passed before he heard the spring door whine and slippered feet pad across the linoleum towards his cubicle. For one watery moment he thought his tormentors might have come to apologise and make amends. Unfailing human weakness. He did not move, hardly breathed. He was standing on the lidless toilet bowl, his arms braced against the sides of the cubicle.

Four cockroaches, still alive, had been impaled on the ends of undone coat hangers. In turn, anti-clockwise, the first three insects appeared under the cubicle panels. Terrified, Scott watched them coming up towards him, past the zone of his shortsightedness. Their undersides had burst where the coat hanger had come through the thorax, pushing out the creamy fondant of their innards. Their legs and antennae still struggled against the air, and against the metal pin of the coat hanger, in silent agony. Scott could not breathe. He arched his back against the freezing flush pipe and looked ahead bravely - only to see, straight ahead, a fourth insect, suspended from above the cubicle wall, being guided blindly but with intuitive accuracy, towards his face, his mouth. A breath escaped at last: a scream for mercy. It was a scream at a pitch no one had ever managed to extract from him before. But this reward was not enough. The more he screamed the more vigorously the dying insects were thrust this way and that towards him, touching him blindly, their fondant pasting his skin, their insect bodies breaking up against his human body.

'Score!'

When contact was made the cry went up.

Every term, for four years, the game had been replayed. He never knew when they would start. Novelty and surprise were everything.

But this term Tim Jackson put an end to the fun. He burst into the toilets, took Scott's tormentors by their necks and pushed them to the sinks. The cockroaches were dashed from the hangers, stamped on, and the hangers thrown violently under the urinals. Without a word Jackson shoved the boys over the sinks and beat them with a slipper discarded in the struggle, beat them again and again. When he'd finished he pointed at the door with the crumpled slipper and said not a word. The slipper, of tartan design, trembled with emotion in his hand.

The door of the toilet cubicle was still locked.

Inside, Scott got down. He slipped the latch, opened the door. On seeing the tall, breathless, dishevelled Jackson, with curls of black hair fallen across his pale and handsome face, on seeing his rescuer, protector and avenger, Scott shuffled back, sank into the lidless toilet bowl, and burst into tears.

In Jackson's classes Scott expressed his gratitude by working with exceptional industry, and by learning quickly what he was directed to learn. But he did not answer every question or volunteer for every chore. He was an insightful boy and knew that he should not risk embarrassing Jackson in any way. He also understood that he had to show an independent spirit and a willingness to deal with things as they were. This was the way to show his gratitude. By not becoming a burden. By surviving.

But Scott was also a dreamer. *The Lake Isle of Innisfree,* with its wistful talk of a solitary life in a rural idyll, of evenings full of the linnets' wings, and a longing for peace in the deep heart's core - these images caused his concentration to falter a moment, and nudge him gently into his own fantasy. For Scott too had his idyll. He too had a place where he enjoyed total solitude, but his haven was not so much bee-loud as flyblown.

The retreat Scott had made for himself in the Dell showed an unexpected side to his character: a keen practical intelligence. He had noted when Rankin dumped the grass cuttings. It took a whole week to fill his trailer. One Friday afternoon, after much careful observation and planning, Scott crouched at the side of the Dell, beyond the wire, out of sight, and from here he employed Rankin, in a sense, to construct his own Innisfree cabin.

Scott had dragged a broken form across to a position about two thirds down the slope of the Dell. With some bits and pieces of smashed chair and desk he had wedged the form in place and made it secure. Across the top of the seat he'd rested large hardboard offcuts to extend what would become the roof surface, and from these a section of rotten tennis net was draped that would form the lattice-work for the outer wall. Everything was held in place with the heaviest sods, rocks and lumps of wood he could lift up there. He'd trialled the structure in advance and had stored his materials close by in separate, innocent heaps to enable a swift assembly. On that Friday afternoon Scott finished re-erecting his structure just a few minutes before Rankin emptied his trailer down the slope of the Dell.

His plan was an outright success. The grass cuttings from the trailer tumbled down the slope to stop on the hardboard roof, covering it and forming a fresh, green, sweet smelling ledge. In his boy's imagination Scott had created a troglodytic Alpine home, something his mother had once pointed out to him on a skiing holiday. The achievement gave him more satisfaction than anything he had done before in his short life. He had created his own hideaway and he was the only one in the world who knew of its existence. Rankin, reversing the tractor to the edge of the Dell, could not see down the slope, and if he had come to look afterwards he would have seen nothing but an undulation on the way down to the rubble and rubbish at the bottom.

A few finishing touches were necessary to seal the thing and make it invisible and Scott attended to these as soon as the tractor had gone. The entrance was a stout cupboard frame with its door still attached. He covered this and the tennis net with branches, leaves and grass cuttings, hiding the structure completely. He only had to wait until the next Friday's load to have enough cuttings to smooth out the undulation. The original roof was then hardly visible. After three weeks Scott had a subterranean den that was so well hidden he had to set markers at either side of the Dell to give him a line on its position.

One problem about his refuge was that it had no natural light. Scott had to write home for a torch. He knew the kind of thing he wanted. A black, rubber-cased instrument, what his father called a 'flashlight'. He said he wanted it for November 5th, a harmless lie because bonfire night was never celebrated at the Hall and all fireworks were strictly banned. But in another secret sense, his pretext was the absolute truth. For the place he had created was not simply a cell where he could hide away from humankind and his own nature, as in Yeats' pitiful adolescent fantasy. In fact, Scott seldom used his den as a retreat, because it was so uncomfortable and boring in there, with just a torch light growing dimmer, pointing up at the mottled hardboard roof. The real purpose of this place was less innocent, less defeatist. Scott's den was a munitions silo. The materials he stored here would one day be used to burn down his prison. First there were the strategically buried acorns, the ongoing 'acorn-plan', and then there was this, the 'inferno-plan'. Scott thought of little else all day (except in Jackson's lessons) and dreamt all night of his plans to annihilate, to raze to the ground, this institution that was the source of such endless, grinding and profitless misery, and to do so for the common good.

Though they had done him great harm, Scott did not only blame the boys who tormented him, or those who had acquiesced to his rejection from the community at large. Of course there were individuals he hated but he also recognised, young as he was, that the Hall itself, or rather those who had created it, moulded it, or allowed it to become the way it was (Rowell and O'Donnell in particular) were the real tormentors, worthy of a special fate.

Around the grounds he was forever picking up pieces of scrap paper, dry twigs, nuts, kindling and wood shavings, empty aerosols, empty glue tubes, and so on. These things, week by week, he hid away in orderly piles deep in his den. The secret knowledge of this place gave him an inner warmth already, in advance of the conflagration itself. It gave him a sense of power which grew incrementally, like savings in a bank, with each new deposit. Some finds or funds were more precious than others. A half full can of spray paint in the bicycle sheds, discarded by a senior who had been doing up his bike, filled him with intense excitement. The absolute secrecy of his plan added to the thrill. He smiled up innocently when Newlings congratulated him for his civic-mindedness when he picked up a sheaf of biology notes in the quad.

"That fellow will be very grateful for the return of those notes, Scott. Well done! Well done indeed, sir! Jolly good show!"

It will be, Scott said to himself, smiling up at Newlings. It will be a jolly good show, sir.

Chapter Eight

Jimmy Tarbuck

It was a private conference arranged by Bob Rowell for a special announcement. Rowell's neck was flushed, his collar tight, his bald pate pink. He was trying to contain, even to pass over, a very powerful excitement.

"Guess who's coming to Great Yarmouth Pier, Tim?" After putting the question, there came a succession of tiny nods from Rowell, tremors of anticipated delight.

"To the Pier, Tim."

He allowed a further interval, but then couldn't wait for an answer -

"James Tarbuck! Jimmy Tarbuck!" He cleared a clot of feeling from his throat. "He is going to play the

84

Pier, Jackson!"

Jackson did not even know who Jimmy Tarbuck was. Some popular entertainer, presumably, some tv star. He sensed that his ignorance would be unexpected and disappointing. Out of touch, then. Tsk tsk tsk. But Jackson could not have cared less. He sat impassively across the desk from Rowell and said nothing. Bob Rowell's announcement was clearly expected to make his jaw drop, or at the very least elicit polite interest. Just recently, however, Jackson's manner with the Principal had lost any air of deference. He didn't know who Jimmy Tarbuck was, simple as that, and didn't see why he should be expected to know, or care.

Rowell smiled and sang softly, mellifluously, to the Santa Claus tune -

"*Jim-my Tar-buck is com-ing to town . . .*"

Rowell then chewed the stem of his glasses and stared hard at his young reformer. It was a trick of his, this shift from the playful to the intense, and the vulgar chewing of the glasses added nonchalant command. It might have been a mannerism left over from the R.A.F., Jackson considered, where command had been a simpler thing.

This morning Bob Rowell was trying to come across at his most urbane, but the affectation did not work because Jackson now understood Baker's Law about power at Coxcomb Hall. For all his ruses and pretences, Rowell could not pick up the telephone and replace *anybody*. His institution was bankrupt, in every sense. It was in its death throes and had been, by all accounts, since its inception. For some weeks Jackson had had a sinking feeling in his stomach. Something apart from the bowel-heaviness he had become used to on account of the appalling Hall diet, the endless brisket, tapioca, and suet.

The truth was he had made a mistake in coming here. Perhaps an irrevocable one. He was beginning to feel it in his belly and in his bones.

Well, he sighed. So be it. Jimmy Tarbuck, indeed.

On the other side of the desk Rowell cursed his luck for catching Tim Jackson in such a disaffected mood - just when he wanted to impart something really imaginative, really exciting. But he was prepared to be patient. One had to be patient with muscular Christianity. That was all. *'All things come to he who waits'* . . . or, *'They also serve who only stand and wait'* . . . and so on. Rowell knew that in the end he could be assured of Jackson's attention and generous support.

And, in the end, Jackson knew it too.

Jackson was frowning again. Quizzically, this time. Sighs and frowns for every occasion. All feeling expressed in sighs, frowns and raised eyebrows. By the time he was forty his forehead would be rippled with migraine.

He straightened in his chair: "You did say Jimmy Tarbuck, didn't you, sir?"

Rowell nodded. *They also serve* . . .

Rowell sat back and breathed in so deeply his Royal Air Force Club tie fell to one side, exposing strain on the buttons of his fresh Clydella.

He relaxed and started again.

"Jimmy Tarbuck is playing the pier, Tim." It was time to recall the first name. "He's playing all the piers this summer. Clacton. Scarborough. Skegness. There's even talk of him stopping at Mablethorpe - only Mablethorpe hasn't got a pier!" Rowell laughed loudly, too loudly, at his cruel joke at Mablethorpe's expense. "Mablethorpe!" He laughed again. "Then he tours the East Midlands. But, the point is, Tim - " Rowell leant forward and tapped his blotter - "the point is, he's playing here first. Before any of them." Rowell set down his glasses on his immaculate, leather framed, purple blotter. When Jackson still remained silent Rowell started playing with his glasses, lifting one stem over the other, rubbing the stems together. In a different mood it would have been suggestive, sexual. Rowell, even in his late fifties, was full of irrepressible libido. It was a source of pride to him.

He spoke down to his purple blotter.

"We're going to bring him here. To Coxcomb." He was in a world of his own now. "We're going to bring Jimmy Tarbuck to Coxcomb Hall!"

Rowell lifted his eyes from the blotter and nodded knowingly, cutting off any questions Jackson might have about bringing 'Jimmy Tarbuck to Coxcomb Hall', or bringing 'Coxcomb Hall to Jimmy Tarbuck' for that matter - because he, Bob Rowell, had considered everything, and was at least one step ahead. Then he lowered his head and stared out from under his brows, eyes shifting from side to side, as if he knew he had made an announcement that rendered him vulnerable, and he waited in this attitude a moment, for the storm to break on his bare crown, the scorn to break on his bare crown, the rotten eggs, the tomatoes, the brickbats, as it were. But again the gesture was lost on Jackson, who still didn't even know who Jimmy Tarbuck was. A famous popular singer, perhaps? Some awful, balladeering baritone? A wandering, solitary, *Black and White Minstrel*? Some worthless, sentimental millionaire in a lesser mould to Matt Monro or Mel Tormé, no doubt. This was the kind of trash Rowell got steamed up about, when all was said and done.

With that irritating thought Jackson took this opportunity to spar with Rowell, bring him down a peg or two.

"Jimmy Tarbuck? Here? At Coxcomb? Good grief!

You must be mad, sir!"

Rowell looked up.

"I knew you'd say that."

"The whole idea is quite barmy. Ridiculous."

"But you don't understand the context, Tim." Rowell leant back and picked up his glasses. "What I've got in mind is a Fete. Open to the public. A giant fete. A Grand Fete!"

Jackson relished the idea of Bob Rowell confiding in him like this. There was no one else with whom he could share thoughts of this kind – fantasies and dreams. No one at all. O'Donnell would have fallen asleep. Dr. White would have been thinking of his wife all the time (and who could blame him?) and Newlings and his kind were simply no use at all. Entirely incompetent. Couldn't do anything. Couldn't fry a sausage. Jackson was the only one with whom Rowell could share his dreams and schemes, and he knew it.

And suddenly Rowell could wait no longer - he was in full flow. He spoke in short, clipped sentences, as if he had a huge list of things to go through, and occasionally, to keep his rhythm, or jog his memory, he flicked his R.A.F. Club tie on the edge of the desk - a miniaturised gesture of command meant to sting, like the flick of a riding crop -

"Tarbuck will open the event. That'll be the big draw." Double flick. "I'm talking about the Whit weekend. We'll have a marquee. Everyone will be here. All the holidaymakers from Yarmouth. The miners, the factory workers, the fishermen, the miners' wives, the fishwives, their families, kith, kin, and so on – salt of the earth, Tim, from this marvellous country of ours." Single flick. "We'll have a beer tent. Plenty of beer. Local brews. Real ale. Drag them all in. Lots of stalls, rides and so on. Punch &

Judy, Fortune Telling, Magic, thrills and spills, Tim." Double flick. "Just like Yarmouth pier. But better. Or worse, if you like. But for a cause, Tim. For a cause!" At the mention of a cause he smirked at Tim Jackson, exposing his yellow, furry teeth - he knew the mention of a cause would drag Jackson in too, like a miner to a beer tent. "We'll have a bus – a sightseeing bus - to ferry them in and out . . . And we'll clean up - I mean, *clean up*! All kinds of rides - ghost train, horror train, love train, what have you. Scenic railway. Maze. A giant maze! A magical mystery tour. We'll have the Mayor over here too. The Mayor of Great Yarmouth, why not. Or if we can't get him, the Mayor of Gorleston. Baker will see to that. Knows all the Gorleston top brass, so he says. Staff out on the field. Buildings locked up, of course. All doors locked but plenty of colour through the windows - variety, activity, books, plants, displays and so on - all locked up, though, neat and tidy. Big push for that. And I want you to take charge."

He stopped to allow these details of The Grand Fete to sink in and provoke a response.

"The purpose of this Grand Fete, I take it," Jackson said in reply, after allowing a few seconds to elapse himself, a suitable period, he judged, for Rowell to begin to sense his utter ridiculousness, "the exact purpose of this Grand Fete, I take it, like any other fete, is to raise money, is it not?"

"Ten out of ten," Rowell nodded. "Straight to the top of the class, Tim. Filthy lucre."

"The Hall's finances are not really my concern, Principal. That's your area, is it not? As owner of the enterprise."

At this Rowell set back his chair with an angry jerk and got to his feet – filthy lucre was a sore point. He left his desk and went over to his tall, rotting sash casements. He stared out over the playing fields to the Vampire, to the misty woods and streams beyond.

"We're in a parlous state, Tim," he said. His glasses still dangled from his hand. "A parlous state. We need a cash injection. We need a good boost, a big boost."

"But how will this make money? Mr. Tarbuck will cost money, will he not? A lot of money. So will the marquee. The rides, the stalls. The maze. So will everything. Sounds a risky business to me, Principal, if you want my advice."

Rowell looked over his shoulder at Jackson.

"You don't understand." He smiled his yellow smile. "That's the trump card, Tim."

He continued to smile. Jackson hated Rowell's smiles. They were so full of rancid lust and insidious intent.

"Jimmy Tarbuck is an old boy!" Rowell declared. "He's an O.C.! An Old Coxcombian! There will be no charge! He's a millionaire, Tim! Good grief! Don't you know who Jimmy Tarbuck is?"

Chapter Nine

A Scent of Semen

Scenes such as those in the Games Room in front of *Dr. Who* on Wednesday evenings had dulled Jackson's sensibilities, and of course he had witnessed other more explicit acts, particularly after dark. The muffled cries of younger boys in older boys' beds had quickened his pace down the dormitory corridors a score of times. He could be satisfied, these days, that on his duty nights, at least - and he did many more than most - word was out that this kind of thing was no longer tolerated. So the scene before him now did not shock him in terms of its sexual openness. What did shock him was the thought, the deliberation, the planning behind it, the organization. The way Mrs. White's petite figure, all in black, moved from tree to tree with such assurance, pointing out which trees were to be used, which allocated to which pairs. There must have been enough boys here to make up a rugby team. In fact they probably were a team. The fittest and the strongest. But no, that was not true. They only looked powerful in their braced postures of restraint. They were, indeed, now he came to consider it, a motley collection of the most senior boys. How had they been chosen for this? Was it by age? By favouritism? By chance? Perhaps selection had been made on the simple criterion of who could pay. And there were some here, no doubt, who were paying for this with his money. Jacko's cash. Jacko's stash. They had taken money from *his* wallet, from *his* Harris Tweed, in order to pay for this treat. From the hideaway he'd chosen, Jackson could not see how much money had changed hands at the start, but there had been notes, and not just brown ten shilling notes. Green notes. Blue notes. Once the money had been counted out in front of Mrs. White, from Parsons' hand into Hallett's hand, and then replaced inside its bag, a brown paper shopping bag, the duty of actually making the payment fell to Hallett. He had done this with an exaggerated, supercilious grace, presenting the folded bag to Mrs. White with a mock bow. This posturing was to cover up, no doubt, his own nervousness and excitement for what was in store this chilly autumn evening.

After Jackson had tumbled to the clue in his Othello class, the rest of his detective work had been easy. He'd drawn the isolate Leery to one side. Not something suspicious in itself, because he often spoke to Leery, offering him advice about his work, praise for his sketches, cartoons - Spiderman, Hulk, Donald Duck - general counsel, encouragement, tacit sympathy. Leery had not known much, which was to be expected, but he'd overheard that there was to be another meeting on Friday afternoon in the woods, and that had been sufficient for Jackson.

In each pair each boy stood either side of his tree, his back to the trunk. Some trees were close together, some not. The trees had been chosen, Jackson deduced, not for their proximity but according to girth. When the boys had all been allocated their different trees they were told to take off their belts. The order was not given by Mrs. White herself but by Hallett, who seemed to be her second in the business, though the redoubtable Parsons had a role too, or thought he did, for he always stood close by. Parsons carried with him another brown shopping bag. It was impossible for Jackson to learn much from the bag, except that it didn't seem to be particularly full or heavy. More belts, perhaps. Spares. Parsons tried to look stern and unselfconscious, as if his duty were to ensure there were no breach of discipline, which was the wrong approach entirely. The only way to appear at ease in these extraordinary proceedings was to do what Hallett was doing - feign a humorous detachment. Anthony Hallett was the brains, Jackson decided. He had set it all up with Mrs. White. He had approached her and made her an offer, outlined what he had in mind, and she had agreed. The money had been irresistible. *His* money – Jacko's cash - had been irresistible.

It seemed important that Mrs. White never issued audible instructions to the entire party. By containing her voice she contained her presence, her mystique and power. The witch of the woods, indeed. She dealt only with Hallett and Parsons, and only whispered to them, never looked at them directly, so that sometimes they had to lean down to her. She was so petite! Such a small, dark, powerful figure, in her black corduroy trousers, black leather boots and three-quarter-length coat.

Everyone was in position.

Their belts were not to be used in the way some of the boys might have hoped, it turned out. On command each boy held his arms backward round his tree trunk. Hallett then slipped a belt around the boys' wrists and drew it tight, binding the wrists together, though not so tight that it hurt. Then Parsons had a function at last. He approached with his shopping bag. From the bag Hallett took a wooden peg - the peg Jackson had seen them examining in his classroom! - and squeezed it into the buckle, trapping the leather. The same operation was completed the other side of the tree. Once the belts were fastened in this way the two boys were secured to the tree, their arms pinned. But Mrs. White was not satisfied with this. This lady took no chances. Again, the deliberation and organization were extraordinary, and Jackson began to change his mind, to believe the unbelievable, that it was Mrs. White herself who had set up the whole enterprise, and that she'd had consultations with Hallett and Parsons in order to do everything to her specifications.

There was a distinct chill in the air this afternoon. Jackson wondered if this would not have some dampening effect on the boys' lust. Perhaps for this reason Mrs. White allowed them to keep their trousers on until the last moment.

Her technique was simple.

She approached a boy and felt him through his trousers. If he was already erect she undid the trousers, pulled them loose with her gloved hands, and then forced them all the way down with the toe of her leather boot, pushing them down tight so the trousers bound the boy's feet, rendering him more helpless still. She then stroked the boy through his underpants a few times. This was done with some judgement. Two of the boys climaxed with this preparation alone and she left them as they were, without exposing them further. For each of the others she took the pants down to expose the boy completely, then brought him quickly to climax with her gloved hands. No boy lasted more than about fifteen seconds, most only five or ten.

So the last pair hadn't long to wait until Hallett and Parsons released them. They cleaned themselves up as best they could, pulled up their trousers and resumed an air of casual dignity. Jackson noted that this last pair were the slightest and most ineffectual looking of the bunch, and he realised that they had been paired deliberately and given their orgasms last for good reason. It now fell upon these two to bind up Hallett and Parsons.

In fact all these precautions for her safety, though understandable, were quite unnecessary, and left behind a trace of paranoia with the patchouli oil. There was not a hint of rebellion in the group. They were quite overwhelmed by what had happened. They sagged and lolled against their trees, undressed, released, at ease, astonished by the swift and delightful novelty of this experience. What a difference, Jackson could imagine them thinking, from the mechanical pumping in their own beds each night, night after night, ad infinitum.

Anthony Hallett was last of all. He was pinned almost the other side of his tree, from Jackson's point of view, but Jackson could see Mrs. White at work on him quite clearly. To Hallett alone did she offer some words as she rubbed and fondled. And the rubbing and fondling seemed more protracted with Hallett, drawn out in stops and starts to prolong his ecstasy. Her expression was difficult to read, as she stroked and squeezed, rubbed and fondled. It seemed tense, or intense. Unsmiling. Whether she spoke just of arrangements for next time or said things of a more personal nature it was impossible to tell.

After his orgasm Hallett's blonde head fell partially into view, severed by his climax. Mrs. White said something more to him, smiled at last, and then made her retreat.

With her money.

Her money. Their money. Jackson's money from Jackson's paltry salary. Her ill-gotten gains. Wrapped in a shopping bag. Firmly clasped in her gloved hand. Off she went.

The entire operation had not lasted more than twenty minutes.

Jackson watched the boys help each other from their harnesses. They pulled up their trousers, did up zips or fly buttons, then left, subdued, in desultory fashion, hands in pockets, heads down, back through the woods, towards the Dell and the Quad and the Games Room, and the grey, trapped, petty, bestial lives that awaited them back at the Hall. While Jackson watched them go, one question above all preoccupied him.

How much money had changed hands in the last twenty minutes? He saw the confluence here of two inexorable forces, one relatively innocent, the other not quite so. He stepped out from his hideaway and glanced through the trees in the direction of Woodlands. A scent of semen hung in the afternoon air. Clara White was long out of sight, with her wad of notes, heading back towards Dr. White's tied cottage, with its blind windows and dark damp rooms.

That was where she lived, after all, with her unprepossessing, middle-aged, boring and incompetent husband. For a bleak moment Jackson saw the scene from Mrs. White's point of view, and found himself, to his surprise, uncensorious.

Chapter Ten

In a White Bathrobe

Dick Baker smiled his bland and affable smile, and winked and nodded, and joked and quipped. He was remarkable, Jackson considered, for his superficiality. Baker was virtually amoral, without scruple. Animal. How could he stand at ease in this circle - with Newlings and the venerable Dr. White himself - when he had betrayed both at the deepest and most personal level? How could he stand there, with his swelling paunch, with his winks and his nods, and make his conspiratorial jokes and cynical quips and asides, and so bond himself to these two, the stiffly unhappy Newlings, and the shaggy cuckold, Dr. White? Next lesson, when the good doctor went off to another titration, Baker would go to Woodlands, Dr. White's home, to enjoy intercourse with his wife. Maybe he was even thinking about that, right now, about the games they would play, while he smiled and nodded and listened to Dr. White. After their lust there would be much laughter at her husband's expense, no doubt, and laughter too about little Jimmy Newlings, and his pathetic enslavement to Clara, about his dwindling savings and self-respect . . . And still Baker smiled and nodded, joked and quipped to both of these men.

Jackson knew a good deal more about the lives of all three now, because he himself had become better acquainted with Clara White.

The theme of Baker's jokes today was an elementary deception he had practised on the unsuspecting Bob Rowell. Sometimes the Principal was too removed and aloof for his own good. It was now public knowledge that The Grand Fete was being planned, and Jackson had, for his own reasons, gone along with the thing in the end, and furthermore had assumed responsibility for much of the organization, for allocating staff their tasks and duties. Baker's richest vein of jokes came from the boast - quite true in every detail - that he himself had given Rowell the inspiration for the whole idea.

Baker was the staff's self-styled emissary to the outside world. It was a fact of life that the majority of the staff hardly ever left the premises of Coxcomb Hall. Some, like Rowell, not even in the holidays. This led not only to an extreme insularity of outlook, but also, on a more mundane level, to inevitable lapses in fashion and taste, which could expose the Hall staff to painful embarrassment when they went to Gt. Yarmouth, or even in the local villages, the local pubs. In itself this was a further deterrent to venturing outside in the first place, into their own era, the mid-sixties, into the upheaval and social change just beyond the glass-sharded walls of Coxcomb Hall. With their brilliantined hairstyles, military moustaches and shabby tweeds, these men might set off from the Quad laughing heartily together in the back of a taxi, but they became subdued and self-conscious on arrival in Gt. Yarmouth. In the spring and summer months of 1965, Yarmouth was crowded with holidaymakers, with young people who had, in the phrase of their times, 'let their hair down'. They strolled about in flared jeans and t-shirts, and carried transistor radios blaring harmonies from *The Beatles*, *The Yardbirds*, or *The Rolling Stones*. Just eighteen months before, on New Year's Day 1964, the first experimental edition of *Top of the Pops* had been broadcast from a converted church in Rusholme, Manchester, hosted by the winsome northerner and up-and-coming BBC celebrity, Jimmy Savile. In eighteen months this programme had become the opium of the nation; so intoxicating was it to the Coxcomb boys that the Games Room had to be locked up at 7.00 p.m every Thursday when it was broadcast. Such sea-changes in popular entertainment were discomforting, alienating to the Coxcomb staff, to say the very least, and to guard against the disturbing feelings they evoked it was the custom, tacitly agreed, always to visit the town in groups for solidarity. A trip into town had a curious side-effect on the collective psychology: when they returned to the Hall each found himself in a vicious mood, vigilant for the slightest infringement of the rules, and most severe in his beatings.

Excursions to Gt. Yarmouth were rare though, and Baker's role as emissary to the outside world was widely accepted without resentment, and his audience was happy to be regaled now, sitting in their comfy staff room chairs, near a blazing autumn fire, by Dick Baker's accounts of what was 'on' or 'in' or 'out' or 'far out' during break and lunch times. For his own amusement and aggrandizement, Baker ('The Gorleston Knowall', as everyone called him behind his back) often exaggerated things or even span out a lie or two, inventing colourful details to tantalize his armchair audience and inflame the envious spark in their eyes.

To Dick Baker, Rowell was the very worst kind of removed and affected homosexual, one who sought to hide, or by some awry logic qualify, his sexual preference with snobbish notions of class and taste and decadence - in this there was a quintessential Englishness, a 'dear boy' Noel Coward quality, that Baker utterly despised. He had taken great pleasure in leading Rowell up the garden path before, for the entertainment of his fellow underlings. And it was he, Baker, who had informed Rowell, answering an innocent enquiry about who was playing the Pier at the start of the season, that Mr. Jimmy Tarbuck was performing at the Whitsun weekend. He then added waggishly - a piece of sheer inspiration – that Tarbuck, with his own national television show this winter, was, of course, an O.C., an Old Coxcombian.

He had never anticipated this little pretence would have had the power to seize Rowell's imagination in the way that it had.

"Well, of course, Tarbuck is an O.C.," Rowell could be heard saying to someone or other around the echoey corridors, any day of the week.

"Didn't you know that Jimmy Tarbuck is an O.C.? Didn't you know that? Well, you know now!"

These were the refrains, set in lofty public school accents, which Baker was enjoying imitating for the amusement of Newlings and Dr. White this break time, as they supped their milky coffee and ate their custard creams and chocolate fingers and bourbons.

"What will you do when he finds out?" Newlings asked. Oh, how he wished he could have thought up and dared to execute such a jape!

"I'll say O'Donnell told me. From the records."

A gust of laughter at the very idea.

"The records! He'll deny it, I think." This from Dr. White.

"Then I'll say he was *drunk*."

More laughter here, in particular from the grey and furry Dr. White (not often to be seen laughing these days, it had to be said) at Baker's devil-may-care irreverence; not so much laughter from little Jimmy Newlings though, for whom the joke was too close to the bone.

All three were ghastly dinosaurs, Tim Jackson reflected, watching from his distant corner, and they deserved all the misery they caused each other, and some more on top of that, seconds, from anyone who sought more from life than the thwarted existence that prevailed here. With this reflection his thoughts turned once again to Clara White, and he sighed and walked across to the window where the biscuit table stood. He took a custard cream and stared out at the Quad, and beyond the Quad to the tuck box shed, the Dell, the woods, and Woodlands.

Jackson's sigh was not amorous. It was not accompanied by the fierce and conflicting emotions that Newlings suffered when he looked out this window to the Quad and the woods beyond. Jackson's sigh was one of weariness and sympathy, in equal part, being faced with a problem that had become as pressing as it was intractable.

"*'tis the strumpet's plague*
To beguile many, and be beguiled by one."

The lines came naturally to his mind, but he felt uncomfortable calling any woman a 'strumpet'. It implied the kind of outmoded assumptions Newlings, Baker and White would feel at ease with, but not him. And the insult was inappropriate for other reasons.

Because in the end, as he saw it, taking a rather broader moral view than some might have expected of him, Clara White was simply doing what was easiest in order to escape a situation that demanded extreme measures, and in a more enlightened age she might have been considered to be doing a kind of work, and very useful work - relieving the young men of their ungovernable urges, which might otherwise drag them into abusing one another. Here lay some of Jackson's sympathy. And furthermore he could not at all blame her for cuckolding her aging husband, nor for taking what pleasure she could from Baker, though he disapproved of the man. Her bleeding of the despicable Newlings was again something he could just about condone. None of these things spoke much against Clara White as far as he was concerned. No. 'Strumpet' was a gross and unjust term.

But that was only part of the problem.

"- and be beguiled by one."

He had called at Woodlands at a time he knew to be safe. He'd been to O'Donnell's smoky den to check the timetable and he'd found a period in the day when all of them - Baker, Newlings and Dr. White - were engaged and he was not. He called at eleven o'clock one Tuesday morning.

Clara was up, but not yet dressed in the austerity of her widow's weeds. Her appearance was really quite deceptive. She wore a freshly pressed man's shirt, a checked Clydella, one of her husband's work shirts. She wore the Clydella with its tails out over some scruffy green corduroys, and the shirt was buttoned only halfway up, and by every other button. It was quite exposing, not only of her cleavage but of her midriff too. On her feet was a pair of ancient, paint-bespattered sandals. Her dark hair fell across one side of her face unbrushed, and she wore no make-up of any kind. She looked as if she'd been caught in the middle of a decorating project, with the big shirt slipped on as an overall, except that it was far too fresh and pressed and clean. To Jackson, the borrowed Clydella, the careless sharing, was confusing: it gave an impression of intimacy, of matrimonial harmony and warmth, which was quite unexpected.

The impression was mistaken. Clara had taken the shirt from her husband's wardrobe because the clothes she wanted were soiled. She was waiting for Dr. White to wash them, which he was due to do that very evening. Tuesday was wash-day.

Until this moment Jackson and Clara White had known each other only by reputation and from brief encounters at the Sunday chapel services. Clara's attendance at chapel in recent months had become sporadic. She was now shedding the last obligations to Coxcomb Hall that her husband said were incumbent upon her, as his wife, living in a tied cottage within the grounds. Her absence from the Sunday service always provoked Bob Rowell into asking after her health - 'Is Clara poorly?' - forcing Dr. White into silly lies and ingratiating apologies.

When she had been a more regular member of the congregation, though, Jackson had noticed her friendly glances and smiles, which at first he had taken to be nothing more than polite gestures to welcome a newcomer. After a few weeks he had begun to imagine she intended more. Looking along the pews at the staff line-up, at Rowell, at O'Donnell, at Newlings, and at Dr. White himself, and at Eric Crampton, the ancient and effeminate geographer, with the strange, long-winded nickname – 'our fey and ancient queen' - and at the new musicman, the piano-tuning Egg Taylor, a bald and tubby buffoon who'd blown in from nowhere on a gust of fantastical lies about famous people he knew (such as Brian Epstein, manager of *The Beatles,* no less) and whose efforts to tune the Hall piano for assembly were so disastrous every hymn sounded like honky-tonk; and finally Pez Rankin, the lowly, shovel-bearded caretaker, who knew his place, two discreet and lonely rows behind the rest – yes, looking at this lot, Jackson could well imagine that, without flattering himself, he made an attractive catch in such select company. But in due course he'd heard the rumours about Baker and Newlings and Mrs. White, and from then he'd felt an aversion towards her. He did not feel obliged by politeness to respond to her hints and approaches. The thought of his name being mentioned in the same breath as Baker and Newlings was quite appalling to him. He only had to fall once, after all. In fact, he needn't fall: there need only be some malicious rumour. So he had kept clear of Clara White. He had taken to leaving chapel by the vestry, in order to avoid running into Dr. White and his wife on the walk back through the unkempt graveyard to the Hall.

Yet here he was calling on her. It was a considerable personal risk on his part, he felt, but he was duty bound.

They exchanged pleasantries at the door and she invited him deeper into Woodlands.

Far from a smell of fresh paint and the disorderliness of a household undergoing home improvements, Jackson was at once struck by the air of neglect, first in the dark and dingy hallway, and then in the kitchen, where a heap of dishes and saucepans waited to be washed up at the sink. There was that sweet and cloying smell of damp in the kitchen, the smell that draws the eye to rotting skirting boards and bubbling plaster. On the kitchen table was a paperback – *On the Road*, by Jack someone, or no one - face down, and a newspaper. The paper was a broadsheet, the Daily Mail, spread out at the entertainment section. Fred Bassett caught Jackson's eye. That cartoon sausage dog, so much a homely, sentimental emblem of the English middle-classes, was the last trace, perhaps, Jackson thought, raising an eyebrow, of Dr. White's fantasies of domestic bliss.

"Sorry to disturb you," Tim Jackson said, remembering his gentlemanly manners.

"Would you like tea?" Mrs. White returned in kind.

Mrs. White seemed not at all uncomfortable in her surroundings. She evidently felt no embarrassment about the mess, or about what might be seen as her personal slovenliness. When Jackson had rung the bell she must have been sitting here reading her novel or her newspaper, surrounded by all this sordidness, rather as if she were a guest here too. It was not her business. It was as if she might look around at any moment, in her unbuttoned Clydella, and agree with Jackson that the place had become pretty shabby and that something really should be done about it. A spring-clean. A decorating project.

"I'd love some tea," Jackson said. "Thanks awfully."

Thanks awfully struck a false note, and the atmosphere stiffened further.

Clara filled the kettle and put it on the electric hob. No electric kettle, Jackson noted. The water would take some time to boil on the ancient yellow cooker.

"So. To what do I owe this pleasure, Mr. Jackson?" Clara White asked the question from the other side of the kitchen table. She stood with her arms folded under her small breasts in a defensive posture.

Their eyes met, and, instead of the flirtatiousness that he had seen there before, or the melting warmth, Jackson found only a cool defiance. Without make-up her brown eyes were bald of lashes and brows, and her skin was pale and large-pored. Caught unprepared like this, her air of cool defiance impressed Jackson. It struck him that she already knew what he knew.

But what an extraordinary thought that was! That here he stood in the same room as the woman who went from tree to tree stroking and masturbating the boys for cash - and some of their payments, Jackson could never forget, had been made with his own hard-earned money. And he did not earn a great deal of money. Yet some of *his* money, *his* earnings, *his* cash, earned for services rendered to Bob Rowell and his dreadful institution, had found its way into this house, this Woodlands, and into Clara White's small and fearless, grasping hands. And she showed not the slightest sign of shame or regret. What effrontery.

Jackson's stare hardened too.

He had followed the progress of the meetings in the woods closely, half hoping that Clara White herself would bring the business to a conclusion, that she would become too anxious about the risks involved, or that some sense of propriety would in the end get the better of her. But that is not the way things had turned out at all. Instead, she had become more relaxed and secure in the company of the young men. There had arisen a humorous rapport with some of them, particularly with the sensitive and artistic Hallett. After the financial and sexual transactions were over, some boys stayed behind to share a cigarette with Mrs. White; and on the last occasion Jackson had seen them passing around what they called in the press a 'reefer' or 'joint' of marijuana, or hashish, which presumably had come from Mrs. White herself. Other, rather different acts of generosity had been forthcoming too. At the start, while payment was being made, boys could now buy more: an opening of her raincoat to reveal her naked breasts during their turn, or a prolonging of her caresses beyond the regular time allowed. The hard and suspicious air of the first meeting had completely disappeared. There was trust, there were smiles and mild laughter. There was flirtatious, teasing good-humour throughout. The boys still stood belted to the trees - but this was at least partly their preference, Jackson suspected, a gratification of masochistic whims. In time, no doubt, she would charge for that too. Charge, charge and charge again.

As far as Jackson was concerned, things had gone too far by a very long chalk.

He glanced away from Mrs. White's defiant stare for a moment and when he looked back into her eyes he knew that she knew he had been spying on the whole operation. And to his discomfort he discovered that it was he who felt embarrassed here, in the shabby kitchen. He found himself cast as a voyeur. He realized, with a hot flush, that his motives for this visit to her house could be seen as quite odious. She might be wondering if he had come to blackmail her into performing some sexual favours for him – To what do I owe this pleasure, Mr. Jackson? - or to threaten her in some other way, to extort some of her profits from her. That would explain her defensive posture and the defiance in her eyes. She was not about to give anything up lightly. Not her. It was a problem Jackson had not foreseen at all.

How could he explain himself? How could he come clean and retain some dignity and credibility? He felt the situation already slipping out of control.

The kettle had begun to make its first steamy noises.

"Look," he said, staring back at her with what he hoped was a disarming frankness, "I know what's been going on, Clara."

Clara's small round mouth puckered but the directness in her stare never faltered. She had detected his embarrassment and intended to use it against him.

"Know about what, Mr. Jackson?"

"About your meetings with the boys. In the woods."

She frowned. "Oh that," she said, and she went to fetch the teapot from the draining board. She removed from it the old teabags, which she dropped into a dirty saucepan, and took the pot over to the kettle without rinsing it first.

"And?" she asked, with her back to him, putting the new tea bags into the dirty pot.

"And?" Jackson echoed. "*And*, I think it has got to stop, Mrs. White!"

She glanced over her shoulder and smiled. There was warmth in her look now. It was the kind of look she had given him across the chapel several months ago. But different, without make-up. No coyness now, just frank and uninhibited. Jackson couldn't help himself finding the Clydella shirt, so open and loose, rather alluring. She wasn't wearing a bra. At the Hall Jackson had become, like all the others, a deeply frustrated man. But he had his faith, his fortitude, to sustain him, when men like Newlings went under, of course.

"Can I sit down?" Jackson was anxious that his animal excitement showed, even through his trousers.

"May you."

"May I sit down, please?"

She looked him over, letting her gaze settle a moment on his hips, then nodded her assent.

Jackson took a seat at the kitchen table. It was her seat. The paper was spread open in front of him.

Fred Bassett. Sausage dog.

"Look," he began again, "of course it has got to stop. What would happen if the newspapers - if the Daily Mail, for example - " he gestured across the cartoons and tv pages - there was a large picture of Stratford Johns as Superintendent Barlow, looking very severe indeed, standing at the door of a white Ford Zephyr, a trailer for *Z Cars* - "What would happen if the Daily Mail got hold of what you are doing? The police would be here. The Hall would be finished. You'd be finished. We'd all be finished. Quite aside from the moral question, the moral outrage, I should say, of what you're about here."

Clara White filled the teapot, even though the water had not yet boiled. She fetched cups and saucers, milk, sugar, stretching up to cupboards and reaching across the table with lightness and grace, setting everything out neatly, taking her time, lingering over her every movement, in her untucked, unbuttoned shirt, without her bra.

Jackson tried to drive his point home, re-addressing his earlier argument.

"Think about what you do. About what you have been doing. Just for a moment. Imagine it. Think about the boys strapped to the trees. Imagine, for a moment, what a picture that would make in the Daily Mail or the News of the World. For goodness' sake, Clara!" He was making an appeal now.

"Have you got a picture?"

"No!" Jackson's scruples were being squeezed hard here. "Of course not!"

She sat and poured their tea, then took her cup in both hands, warming her hands.

"You're giving me ideas," she said archly.

"I hope not!" Jackson couldn't help his response

coming out as yet another exclamation, and felt his foolishness. She was moving too fast for him. He was too easily shocked.

"Which is preferable, then, do you think?" she asked. "That I give those boys some relief, or that they get their relief preying on the eight-year-olds?"

Jackson had thought of this himself, of course.

"In some ways what you're doing is preferable, no doubt," he conceded. "But in some ways not. It certainly isn't the only other option. However - " with some regret he could see there was no point in indulging her interest in a moral argument: to her that was just a game - "that is, in a sense, irrelevant. What you think and what I think would not stop a newspaper ruining all of us."

"Would that not be a good thing too?" She smiled again. To Jackson it was frustrating that she should so coolly enjoy these hypothetical questions. She just did not care. It was obvious she had no intention of acceding to any demands he might make.

"For me, no. Personally I'd be unemployable. And for you too I suspect the position would not be altogether comfortable." Jackson gave her a knowing look – How would her husband like it? Wouldn't he kick her out? Onto the street? Into the Gt. Yarmouth red light district? Under the pier? But such sparring was not what he had come here for. There was business in hand. "Let's stop these idle speculations," he said. "We both understand that you don't mind much if this place goes to rack and ruin. It so happens that I do care. And that is why I am here with you today."

Clara White sipped her tea in silence.

"I am here to demand that you stop your meetings with the boys. You must leave them alone. Entirely. You must leave them alone."

Clara White looked at Jackson over the rim of her cup for a long moment, then she stopped drinking her tepid tea, stood up, and took her cup to the sink. She poured the slops into another dirty saucepan in the sink and upturned her cup on the draining board. She looked out the window into the woods that led back to Coxcomb Hall and all the bizarre demands of reality that it represented to her. It was easy enough to grasp, at last, that life came down to a struggle for sex and money, but what ridiculous pretences were involved in the pursuit of these humble ends. Sometimes it was as if those real objectives were not even in view, were not even there at all.

While Clara White stood there at the sink, considering the autumnal woods under leaden skies - such a damp, English, moribund scene - a tall, slim, blonde figure stepped from the bottom of the stairs into view at the kitchen doorway. His arrival, languorous but assured, was given away by a creak of floorboards. He was dressed only in a white bathrobe which stopped short well above the knee.

It was Whore Hallett.

Jackson couldn't contain his shock, and yet another exclamation.

"Good grief, Hallett! What on earth are you doing here?"

Clara White did not even turn from the sink. She stood absorbed in the black branches of the autumn trees, the faint breeze out there moving the tree tops against the November sky. A chilly breeze, it would be.

Hallett did not answer Jackson directly. He took out a packet of Players No. 6 from the pocket of his bathrobe. "I came down for a light," he said.

"*Hallett*!" Jackson exclaimed again, as if a blast of volume would shake the world back into its proper compartments.

"Clara?" Hallett said.

Clara White turned at last to look at the figure in the kitchen doorway.

"Have you got a light?"

Clara White hesitated, returned his look, then went to a drawer in the kitchen table and found a box of matches. She tossed them to Hallett, who caught them easily. As well as having artistic hands he was one of Coxcomb's few natural cricketers.

Hallett struck a match and lit a No. 6.

Jackson looked from one to the other, from the woman in the unbuttoned Clydella to the young man in the bathrobe. He could not work out where the power lay between them. As soon as he had seen Hallett he had jumped to the conclusion that Clara White had seduced him. She had been tempted by him and had given way to her temptation. But perhaps she had only given him what he had paid for. Looking at them now, at Hallett's poised arrogance, at the way he smoked his cigarette and tipped the ash on the hall carpet, Dr. White's hall carpet (would not Dr. White be back quite soon? - was he not, even now, approaching at his breakneck pace down the path?) and looking at the way Clara White returned his stare, unsmiling, expecting something from him which he did not seem prepared to give her, looking at this brief tableau, Jackson concluded that the power here rested with Hallett. But what hold did he have over her?

Hallett tossed the matchbox onto the table. It landed on the picture of the stern Superintendent Barlow, blotting out his face and torso, and the entire bonnet of the white Ford Zephyr.

Hallett turned his back on them and started up the stairs. Clara White went after him. She followed Hallett up the narrow staircase.

Jackson stood. His reflex was to leave immediately. He had seen and heard quite enough. But he couldn't resist lingering a moment to see if he could make out what was said between them now. He could hear Clara talking in a low undertone. Then there was an interjection, but it was from someone else, not Hallett. Someone else spoke. Another voice, a third voice - male, adult. There was someone else up there! A threesome? Surely not. Clara continued, and the third party answered. Yes. No. No. No. There was a longer muttering from Clara White. Again, a No, from the third party - in a definite and superior tone. His voice was distinctive. He didn't seem worried about Jackson or anyone else overhearing. Clara, on the other hand, seemed intent on not being overheard. Jackson knew that voice, the third party's voice, even from its monosyllables. He knew that voice.

And then there was a laugh - and Jackson knew that laugh too - at once high and menacing, theatrical in its vicious intent. He'd heard it penetrate down corridors, resound sharply in the Games Room, he'd heard it spin, like a blade, from the open door of the ghastly Prefects' Room.

Ossaf.

Jackson turned and left the kitchen and retraced his steps down the dingy hallway to the front door. What was this he felt? Pique? Envy? Humiliation? Dread?

He let himself out.

Chapter Eleven

Ossaf

When his aging but well kept Jaguar Mark ll, in British racing green, 2.4 litres, still capable of its maximum speed of 101 m.p.h., was stolen, Rowell was distraught. But he did nothing to help the police with their enquiries. The car was written off and he bought himself a second-hand Austin Cambridge, a pale blue rust-bucket, and pocketed the balance from his insurance. On the surface of things life returned to normal.

But beneath the surface of things everything had changed irrecoverably.

Several assumptions made by the police, and several depositions made by Rowell, had been false. Rowell had some pretty shrewd suspicions about what had happened to his car, but the consequences of trying to act on them were too unsettling and humiliating to meet head on.

There could be nothing more serious, in Rowell's book, than a failure to do one's Duty. It was a basic training in life. Duty gangs took care of every aspect of maintenance at the Hall, from cleaning ovens and urinals, windows and dormitories, to the cleaning, polishing, and routine maintenance of the Principal's car. This was a Duty which fell to only two or three of the very noblest and most trusted souls each year. That trust had to be absolute. Parsons was this year in charge of the Duty. Even a senior of good standing, with an excellent sports record and a good singing voice, such as Anthony Hallett, would not be picked simply because Rowell, on a whim, found something 'shifty' about him. (Rowell had seized this opportunity to snub the unattainable Hallett.) Head Boys, picked first and foremost for their disciplinary qualities, were seldom car cleaners, and with Ossaf every precaution had been taken to ensure he never came near the Principal's car.

To juniors new to the school the name Ossaf, one of the very first they learned, had a comical ring, rather like Christofalos, their most immediate threat. To begin with, at a distance, they might confuse the two in person because they were the only non-Caucasians at the Hall, and were figures of similar bulk. But there was danger in confusing Christofalos with Ossaf at closer range. For all his greed and bravado, his emptying of tuck boxes down his throat, his trampling of treasured belongings between the waxy duckboards, Christofalos was harmless. He was a braggart and a showman. His terror fizzed away with the spume of the Coke bottles that he ripped open with his bare teeth.

Colin Scott never wore his glasses in the Quad and easily mistook Ossaf for Christofalos from thirty feet away. There was the same adult corpulence and his hair was licked back in the same oily way. But as Ossaf came closer, approaching fast and zigzagging to cut Scott off, the similarity to the swarthy Mauritian disappeared even to the purblind Scott. By the time Ossaf was close enough for Scott to look up into his eyes, black slots pressed deep in a dark and furry face, it was too late. The animal reflex at this moment was to duck or run, but his mother's conditioning let him down again, kept him anchored to the spot. People were not to be feared in that way.

And then the pain. There was a momentary blackness and a crunch of cartilage, and a searing ringing and shaking throughout his top-heavy skull. Ossaf aimed for the ear, and with such force Scott was felled to the gravel. When Scott opened his eyes he saw Ossaf unclench his fist and release a sizeable flint above his bare shin.

This was a 'stoning'. Some suffered perforated eardrums on account of such stonings. The purpose of the assault, both random and routine, was to remind everyone of the grid that divided the Quad into pens of seniority for the different years. You could not see the grid but it was surely there, as if made of wire and concrete posts. All but the prefects shared the Quad during lock-out, the dead time between classes and tea when every building was off-limits, no matter what the weather. Some sense of order during lock-out was necessary. Those who would not listen or could not understand might endure repeated stonings: at least three boys (Leery was one) wandered out of kilter, off-balance, in their invisible segments or pens, on account of Ossaf's stonings.

Not only quick with his fists and knees and feet and forehead, Ossaf was also quick-witted, and would have done well academically had there been anyone to teach him and had he wanted to learn. But Ossaf's mind was like a piece of apparatus in the physics laboratory he liked to play with sometimes: his concentration was looped between two sprung spools that drew him first one way, then the other, without ever allowing him to reach a point of equilibrium and receptivity.

On the one hand he was infantile, in his continuous craving for pleasure and distraction, and on the other hand he was a very self-aware, sensitive and insightful young man. He was capable of shouldering immense responsibilities, but given to bouts of incapacitating moodiness, profound melancholy. The development of his mind had been circumscribed by the lethal shards of broken glass that topped the walls of Coxcomb Hall: he had spent literally more than half his life here. This fact in itself gave him infamy, but what established his preeminence - even among the neo-criminals - was his willingness to do things set aside as impossible by common sense and common scruple; to combine recklessness with cleverness, brutality with wit, and to carry out his monstrous acts with the ease, the coolness, the grace even, of the born thespian.

For Ossaf was a natural and talented actor. He was so immersed in his gift he was hardly conscious of it. His seamless performances made him a sublime liar and manipulator, a snakelike hypnotist of the easy prey around him. Rowell was correct in his suspicions. It was Ossaf who had plotted the theft of his car. Ossaf had gulled the innocent and trusty Parsons - keeper of the keys - into handing over his precious charge at the beginning of the car wash. The other car cleaners were already part of Ossaf's plot. It was a fine Saturday and Rowell's Jaguar had the most thorough lathering, waxing and polishing, inside and out, that it had ever had. It took all morning: no tar spot, no crusted loop of bird dropping, no dead insect on the radiator grille, escaped the car cleaners' devotion to their Duty that day. For hour upon hour the sensual curves of the chrome bumpers, the badged, convex, glittering hubcaps, threw back close-ups of the car cleaner's faces - acned, sty-eyed, treacherous. Windows and mirrors were polished, door locks and hinges oiled. Even the tiny hinges of the quarter light windows were oiled, and the excess oil wiped away with a fresh yellow duster.

This valeting was not for Rowell but for the pornographer Ray Hooley, or rather for his father, the north London fence, who had expressed an interest in Rowell's car. He'd demanded an inventory of valuables at Coxcomb from his blue-eyed, blue-movie son, and the Jaguar had been at the top of the list Ray had compiled. Hooley's father wanted the Jaguar, in British racing green. Every crook should have a car like that – they all had them on television. Ray Hooley consulted Ossaf and they entered an uneasy alliance.

From Parsons, through Ossaf, the car keys had been passed to Anthony Hallett. Fit and fleet of foot, Hallett rode the twelve miles to Gt. Yarmouth on his Dawes ten-speed to get duplicates cut. By the time Rowell sent a car cleaner to fetch Parsons so that he could put his beautifully polished Jaguar away, Ossaf was able to drop the enamelled fob in Parson's hands and send him back.

The theft of Rowell's car changed everything. It released a sum of capital into a system that had always conducted transactions in shillings, sixpences and threepenny bits. Suddenly everything was up for sale. Bicycles, watches, records, clothes, all manner of treasured possessions. Time was when money had only had importance within the community for cigarettes and illicit drink. But boys who had been used to having five shillings a week and living well, and living within budget, now needed five guineas a week. And they needed that money by Friday afternoon, without fail.

Ossaf was aware of the gambling for places in the Games Room each Wednesday evening. He had also learned how Clara White had barred him from the Friday afternoon sessions, how he had been rejected from the outset. The black boy, the darkie, had been ruled out, cut out, from the very start, by the white whore, by Whore White. This went deep, but the actor hid his wound. He would not stoop to challenge her proscription or bring it into the open by taking his proper place at the head of the billiards table. He would go to the sessions with Clara White when he wanted to go, not on the roll of Parsons' poker dice.

But Clara's rejection stayed with him every minute of the day, and he sensed his acts of terror, his sadistic punishments and random stonings, his dramatic turns, had all been made somehow irrelevant, passé performances, matinée performances, to scant, uninterested audiences, by this sexual sensation every Friday with a real, live, adult woman. He had no choice but to feign aloofness while he worked out his angle of attack.

Though relatives had removed Ossaf from Coxcomb on only two occasions since he was seven years old, and only briefly on each occasion, during these exeats they had imparted a sense of birthright. The second release had come when he was thirteen years old. A pair of uncles arrived one August afternoon and spirited him away for a fortnight at home in Jeddah. This was in 1960.

During the holiday he was taken to witness a royal occasion. The spectacle was held in an impromptu clearing in the business district, surrounded by modern office blocks, advertisement hoardings, every mark of the new prosperity of the middle east. A throne had been set out under awnings, chairs and forms under sunshades, all upon a royal red carpet. Ossaf and his uncles arrived before the main crowd and had a good view, standing about forty feet from the royal enclosure.

The event was the execution of a pair of young adulterers. The beheading of the man, kneeling at mid-distance, some twenty feet from the royal carpet, in the dust, was very quick, almost over before Ossaf realized what was going on. A casual touch on the shoulder and the prisoner lifted his head just enough for the executioner to slice it off with one stroke of his scimitar. The executioner then turned his attention to the young woman, who was also kneeling close by, but who had been unable to see what had just happened to her lover because she was hooded, though she must have heard the low sigh of satisfaction from the crowd. In the next few minutes it became obvious that beneath the hood she was also gagged, and her execution was the more affecting for this.

An assistant took away the scimitar and passed to the executioner a wooden stave. The executioner raised the stave above his head and delivered some twenty blows to each shoulder of the woman with all his strength. When he had finished they cut her loose and she sagged and collapsed in the dust without a sound. A truck backed up and emptied stones in front of the crowd.

The doctor in attendance interrupted the execution three times in the next hour before he was able to pronounce the young woman dead.

Ossaf had begun to lash out when he was a junior,

when cornered and brought to bay by racial taunts. In puberty he established himself as a terror and such taunts had stopped, been silenced completely. But by then his retributive justice had begun to assuage a sexual need, and in time his lashing out became simply lashing - he did it for the pleasure and excitement alone.

His accusations and summary sentences, his talk of the strictures of sharia law, became part of a rehearsed performance. But added to this was another piece of theatre which came about by pure chance. It perplexed those who thought they knew him well and made him incomprehensible, insane even, to the terrified victims of his assaults.

Ossaf had studied Richard lll for an 'O' level examination. There was never any question of Ossaf or any of his classmates ever sitting a public examination successfully, but Rowell ran a few exams anyway to show his curriculum ended somewhere. The teacher who tried to present the play to the class – Mr. Wills, fresh from university - stayed but a few weeks. During his brief tenure he gave up a disastrous reading of the play with Ossaf's class and managed, at his own expense and with Ossaf's assistance, to hire a copy of Lawrence Olivier's 1956 film, then only seven years old. With this film Mr. Wills' problems with his class were over.

Ossaf was an actor who had never been on stage, never even seen a theatre, and the only outlet for his passion was an intense interest in film of any kind. He ran private film shows for himself during the holidays (locked up in Mr. Crampton's projection room) and public shows for the whole school in term time. His lonely private screenings during holidays were not all of classic performances: at least half these films were just sex films, blue films, brought in by mail-order, but from these he gained a comprehensive knowledge of sexual acts and practices - heterosexual, homosexual, sado-masochistic and bestial – that stood him in good stead. He gained this carnal knowledge without once, in all his hours in the darkness of the projection room, in all his time at the Hall, in all of his eleven years of incarceration there, he gained this knowledge without once being caressed, kissed, or even touched with affection by any other human creature. His carnal understanding, coloured in the manner of its learning, was assimilated into his vicious persona, his seamless performances, so that he was at ease talking to anyone, even the pornographer Ray Hooley, on any sexual matter. From his blue films, the virgin Ossaf acquired sexual maturity.

He paid for his pornography habit from the proceeds of the public events he organized for the school in the dining hall. The films for these shows were old and cheap and the choice was narrowed further by Ossaf's personal taste, but they were always profitable because attendance was mandatory. Some of the juniors, sitting cross-legged on the greasy parquet floor, found it hard to stay awake during Ossaf's films, which were always romantic and very boring to them. Once the lights were put out, many juniors, like Colin Scott, were only kept awake by their vigilance for the cockroaches that strayed down from the kitchen serving hatch. Throughout the film, throughout every chase and duel and love scene, Scott's eyes were trained on the foul-mouthed hatch and this ragged moustache of insect life.

For general entertainment this year Ossaf had so far screened two complete flops - *Arabian Nights*, 1942, starring Leif Erickson and Sabu; and *A Night in Cairo*, 1933, with Myrna Loy and Ramon Navarro. He had tried to rescue the season with an expensive modern hit -

Spartacus, 1960, with Kirk Douglas and Tony Curtis – but everyone had already seen it, except Ossaf.

For Mr. Wills' lessons on Richard lll, Ossaf took the class to the Geography projection room, where the Bell & Howell unit and stand-alone screen were kept. Crampton, the aged effeminate geographer - 'our fey and ancient queen' - had surrendered a key to Ossaf years ago in return for some peace and quiet in his decrepitude. Ossaf ushered the young Mr. Wills and his class into the darkness of his private theatre.

There they watched the Technicolor Olivier classic, with its star-studded cast of Richardson, Gielgud, Claire Bloom, Stanley Baker et al.

The quick-witted Ossaf absorbed the language easily but Mr. Wills insisted on interrupting the film with explanations to the slower members of the group. When, after Act l, he asked Ossaf to stop the film yet again in order to explain some genealogy and historical background, Ossaf lost patience with his teacher and caused a disturbance. He overturned a form with a deafening crash. If they were going to make sense of the thing, he told Mr. Wills, they had better go back to the beginning and watch it again without further interruption. Mr. Wills was pleased and surprised by this passionate outburst, despite the violent gesture. The class then had to sit through the opening sequences several times, at Ossaf's insistence.

He took away a copy of the play, and as the film rolled on from lesson to lesson, Ossaf learned whole speeches and soliloquies. By Act lll he was learning entire scenes in advance of the lessons. He mouthed or muttered the words along with Olivier as Richard's cues came up. When the film had finished and they returned to the classroom, he delivered his speeches and soliloquies in full to the rest of the class, imitating faithfully the sharp, clipped tones of Olivier. No one dared laugh. He would storm into the classroom at the beginning of a lesson, banging the door against the wall:

> *"They do me wrong and I will not endure it!*
> *Who is it that complains unto the King*
> *That I, forsooth, am stern and love them not?"*

For Mr. Wills, the sight of Ossaf, this large dark boy with unshaven jowls and greased back hair, with those cruel eyes pressed so deep into his face, the sight of this boy bursting into the classroom with his theatrical entrances, blasting out Shakespeare - for Mr. Wills this was at first a triumph, an inspiration, and then something tragi-comical at which he could not even smile. He tucked his text under his arm and clapped.

"Bravo . . . Bravo, Ossaf . . ."

In return he received the white flash of a rare grin from Ossaf, his most promising and his most menacing pupil.

For a while Mr. Wills indulged Ossaf's enthusiasm, lending him his personal copies of Othello, Macbeth and Julius Caesar, volumes he was never to see again. And then the truth came to light. As soon as Mr. Wills, Rowell's only young graduate on the staff, discovered how Richard lll was used elsewhere around the school, he packed his bags and left unpaid.

With the opening lines above Ossaf might launch an assault on the tuck box shed, sending the door banging and flapping and spraying his words in a staccato burst over the shelves. The juniors, feasting at their boxes in the semi-darkness, stared down at him in terrified bewilderment.

Egg Taylor

"They do me wrong and I will not endure it!
Who is it that complains unto the King
That I, forsooth, am stern and love them not?"

They understood well enough that they were
accused, but had no idea of what crime. They understood
Ossaf was a tyrant, but had no idea why he picked on
them, why he wanted their bare flesh to pinch and stroke
and flog. The Shakespearean English, the references to the
King, and on other occasions to the Lord of Ely, to
Clarence, Hastings, Rivers and Grey, dumbfounded them.

"Chop off his head, man; somewhat will we do.
And look when I am king, claim thou of me
The earldom of Hereford, and all the moveables
Whereof the King my brother was possess'd."

He made impossible demands of them:

"My Lord of Ely, when I was last in Holburn
I saw good strawberries in your garden there;
I do beseech you, send for some of them."

Ossaf strutted close to some cringing ten-year-old
and thrust his dark face, his brilliantined head of hair, so
close that their breaths mingled:

"Why, madam, have I offer'd love for this,
To be so flouted in his royal presence?
Who knows not that the gentle Duke is dead?
You do him injury to scorn his corse!"

To hear one of his fellow juniors called 'Madam' or 'Lord' by Ossaf might cause some friend, perched high on a distant shelf, to titter. Such amusement was short-lived. This was just the kind of provocation Ossaf waited for. With a few sharp movements the tittering boy would be pulled from his perch and marched out the shed. He was taken, like a chicken from its hutch, to the larder of the prefects' room, where he was stripped and his white flesh whipped. And after the beating, in a ritual no one understood except Ossaf, and he only in part, the boy would be made to embrace his torturer, his dark and oily tormentor, and to hold him, and to feel Ossaf's erection pressed against him, and to thank him for his punishment.

Such thanks were necessary, Ossaf explained, with a smile, turning to his chip-toothed, acned, sty-eyed and scrawny brethren, under the precepts of sharia law.

Chapter Twelve

Cinéma Vérité

Newlings' sessions with Clara White had taken an awkward turn. Her mood when he was there had always been brittle, likely to lapse into teasing or mockery at any time, and he was used to living with her contempt. In fact, he enjoyed her contempt, and he'd always worried that this was too obvious to her. Part of him wanted, quite literally, to be trampled under foot. One fantasy, which he still could not broach, involved her wearing stilettos and treading on his erection, rubbing it into Dr. White's damp, beige, bedroom carpet. As yet he found the fantasy too embarrassing to discuss, and he knew that her price for indulging him would be outrageous.

But Clara White's moods had now changed. The teasing had gone, and with it her confidence. She took his money with indifference, almost as if - and this is where Newlings began to suspect something – almost as if the money were no longer hers. One Wednesday, when the session was over and he'd brought up her customary cup of tea, she said to him, while he stood there still in his underwear:

"Tell me about Ossaf."

Newlings found his wallet, sat down on the bedside, and took out twenty-five pounds.

"See," he peeled back the empty sections of his wallet. "You leave me with nothing again. Nothing."

She folded away his money and tucked it under the pillow.

"Tell me about Ossaf."

"Ossaf?" Newlings frowned, as if trying to remember who Ossaf was, then slipped from the bed and put on his trousers. "Chief scourge and gangmaster." He pulled his buttoned shirt over his head. "A sadistic martinet." Newlings' sexual insecurities made him add, while pretending to look about for his tie - "Why on earth do you want to know about Ossaf?"

"What's a martinet?"

"Very strict disciplinarian." Newlings stuck out his weak chin to say that, and knotted his tie very firmly: "From the Marquis de Martinet. Introduced new drills to Louis XlV's regiment. Died 1672 at the siege of Duisburg."

"So Ossaf is strict. What else?"

"Ossaf . . ." Newlings repeated the name with some weight as he squeezed his feet into his shoes with the laces still done up - he had not long before the good doctor's return for second break: it was a tight schedule they ran here, a very tight ship they ran - "Ossaf . . . is a brute. Rowell uses him to keep the Duties going - cleaning the kitchens and so on. It's his last year, thank the Lord. Don't go near him, is my advice. I have absolutely nothing to do with him. I would advise you to take a similar course."

Clara noted Newlings trying to pass off personal cowardice as boxing clever. Newlings had confirmed her worst fear. All the masters, of course, would be just like the craven Newlings, or weaker still. Ossaf was beyond their control.

Clara said nothing more. She was sitting up in bed with the yellow candlewick tucked firmly across her breasts, drinking her tea. At the end of their sessions she always insisted Newlings make her a pot of tea, and when he'd gone she offered the slops to Dr. White for his elevenses.

"I must be going," Newlings said, looking back at her in bed, drinking her tea.

"Au revoir!"

He blew a kiss and was gone.

Then Jackson too brought up the subject of Ossaf in a muted but heated exchange with O'Donnell in the staff room. Jackson was advising headmaster O'Donnell, in no uncertain terms, that Ossaf must be brought to book, that he seemed more than ever beyond control. There had been another incident involving a junior trapped in the Vampire. Trying to escape from the engine cowling, the boy had taken a very nasty cut across his back, from some projecting lug or bracket. Jackson had just returned from the hospital where the boy had needed half a dozen stitches. The doctor in casualty had wanted to know how the accident had happened. *It had not*, Jackson said in a fierce undertone, *been easy! . . .*

Sipping his milky coffee and dunking his custard cream, Newlings listened to Jackson's story from a few paces away.

What had actually happened was far worse than Jackson's account. The boy had been naked in the cowling. His clothes were fifty yards away in a heap by the rugby posts. Ossaf's game had been to challenge the boy to come out and run to get his clothes. While he made his descent, and while he ran for his clothes and struggled into them, he would be a target for Ossaf's vicious catapult. This was no home-made contraption of wood and rubber bands. It was an expensive weapon from *Gun & Game*, a field sports shop in Gt. Yarmouth. The worst of the trial for the victim was the descent from the cowling without a stitch of protective clothing. The boy did not dare descend blind, slowly, with his back to Ossaf, but neither did he dare to expose his genitals and his face during the moment when he braced his weight to make his jump. This fellow was himself a tough and brave little boy, and there were no tears. He had been in such scrapes before. At first he had tried to out-wait Ossaf, because it had begun to rain. But this tactic had only provoked his tormentor into shelling the cowling from the outside. The stones made such a terrifying din on the fuselage the boy panicked. The thought of a stone flying into the cowling and ricocheting all around, maybe smashing him in the eye or in the teeth, was too much.

Despite his reputation for doing the unthinkable Ossaf would never have fired a stone into the cowling. He had begun shelling the Vampire to drive the boy out in the same way that a beater beats the woods in a pheasant shoot. And sure enough, after the seventh stone, his prize, the naked boy, with bloodied flank, had begun to slip out from the womb or anus of the Vampire.

At which point, before the fun could really start, Jackson arrived, drawn by the noise of the stones on the fuselage. He had been on a smoking patrol in the far woods. He came running at full pelt in the drizzle across the field, as if trying to make a try from the halfway line.

"Mr. O'Donnell," Jackson whispered, almost as breathless as he had been after the rescue, "Mr. O'Donnell, headmaster, with all due respect, you cannot condone this kind of thing." Jackson spoke in whispers, his head steady, lowered to one side in his hawkish way, but he did not appear calm at all. He seemed excitable, and therefore weak. Any show of feeling was a show of weakness. A lack of self-control signified, unmistakably, a lack of control over the boys themselves. A self-discipline problem was a discipline problem. There was an indissoluble link. It was a mark of total personal and professional failure.

Recently things had been getting on top of Jackson. There was too much going on just beyond his or anyone else's reach. Despite all his selfless Christianity, he now feared as much for his future as for the principles at stake. There was a shadow over his fate. He knew very well that his career would be ruined if the truth of this place ever reached the wide, sane and merciful world beyond its shard-topped walls.

"Headmaster, you cannot let this pass!" he said, and his coffee cup trembled in its saucer with his emotion.

"Boys will be boys, Jackson."

"And this boy is nine years old! He has six stitches in his back. He was naked and he was being assaulted with a dangerous weapon!"

O'Donnell cleared his throat of smoky phlegm and

squared up to his young interrogator.

"That's not Ossaf's story."

Jackson winced. "*Ossaf!*" Jackson whispered the name to the floor with unbridled contempt. He was flushed and beside himself with anger.

"Ossaf is our Head Boy, Mr. Jackson," O'Donnell cautioned, safe now that he could adopt the admonitory tone, following Jackson's show of temper. "He is in a position of absolute trust."

"Headmaster," Jackson began again, looking up to meet O'Donnell's eyes. He was being forced to say something he had not planned to say. "Ossaf is up to something. Something dangerous, perhaps. He spoke to me in a most opprobrious way. I think there is reason to question the trust you have in this boy. He is intelligent, cunning, cruel and deceitful. He is a tyrant, a bloody tyrant, to the juniors. Everyone knows it."

"That is not my view," O'Donnell said. "Nor is it the view of the Principal." With that, as if Jackson had shown a grave error of judgement in expressing his opinion so excitedly and without supporting evidence, which was true in a way, O'Donnell walked off to have a quiet word with Baker, who had, yet again, been AWOL for several days, abandoning his classes to O'Donnell's care.

Jackson's cheeks and ears were quite red. His shoulders drooped and his suit sagged on his athletic frame as he stepped over to the Quad window. A curl of dark hair had fallen across his forehead.

After some embarrassing scene, or some humiliating, torturous lesson, when a member of staff needed to be alone with his thoughts, needed to restore some personal dignity after total exposure and degradation, the Quad window afforded him a few moments respite.

Respite from the expectant faces, the raised eyebrows, the half-raised coffee cups, from the encroaching feet, encircling eyes, and ensnaring conversations of colleagues ravenous for his suffering. It was an unspoken law of the staff room that this vantage point was reserved for those who'd had quite enough for the moment, who needed to retreat and regroup, pull themselves together, before they could face the world again.

So Jimmy Newlings was both crass and selfish to approach Jackson at this moment, whatever the burden of his curiosity, and break the unspoken law.

"Mr. Jackson," Newlings began. "I've been meaning to ask. How go your reforms of the prefect system? Duties and all that. And the dreaded Ossaf!"

Jackson sipped his cold coffee, swallowed, pursed his lips. He turned to the dried up History master. Skin flaked from Newlings' cheeks and forehead. His eczema was bad today. It had been bad all week.

Out of my way, chrysalis! Jackson wanted to cry aloud, and with that push this husk of humanity from his path and sweep out of this primeval pit and down the stairs and across the gravel Quad to the distant drive, and out and away from all this misery and folly. Oh the hell of earning one's living! If only he had become a minister!

"Ah, Newlings."

Jackson smiled at his colleague. He ignored Newlings' question. He had his own question to ask, and he could pull rank.

"Good to speak to you. The Grand Fete. A maze, wasn't it?"

Newlings had done nothing about designing and organizing the construction of The Giant Maze or The Grand Maze for The Grand Fete. The maze was going to trap the smaller children while their parents went about wasting their hard-earned wages. The Grand Fete was to be a genuinely family event – or rather, it was to have all the attractions Rowell imagined a family event should have for the working-class holidaymakers whose money he sought to grasp and filch. A big day out for everyone, he had said, but he meant, A big day out for hoi polloi. Jackson had allocated Newlings and Baker the task of designing and constructing The Giant Maze, among other less onerous projects. Neither had done anything about these responsibilities. Neither had lifted a finger. Jackson knew that the initiative would lie with Jimmy Newlings. Baker would get nothing done without prodding, and who better to prod him than Newlings, who was so much under Rowell's thumb that he actually lived beneath him. Jackson had pitted Newlings' cowardice and tenacity against that evasive and oafish slider Baker, and Newlings knew this had been the plan. Very clever and very unfair.

"We've got a few ideas," Newlings said.

"A few ideas?" Jackson lowered his hawkish face again. "Well, we need more than a few ideas, Newlings." He looked into Newlings' red-rimmed and watery eyes. It was true what they said. The crapulous habits had taken hold. There was a lingering look of booze about Newlings all the time these days. It hollowed his thin features and pulled at his eyes, made them bloodhound, hangdog. And the lingering smell too, of course, the scent of O'Donnell's after-shave, as it were.

"We need more than a few ideas now, Newlings," he repeated. "We need a maze. A first class, giant maze. Don't underestimate the time it will take to construct, especially given that Mr. Baker - " Jackson glanced over Newlings' shoulder at the plump, robust Crafts Master - "has not been enjoying the best of health, it seems."

Foolishly Newlings turned to follow the direction

of Jackson's gaze, which gave the latter the opportunity he needed to put his cup and saucer down on the table behind and take his leave.

"Excuse me," he said, cutting Newlings, and leaving him standing there by the window without an answer to his question.

It was a week before Newlings came across the next clue, but he failed to take it in.

Clara White was sitting astride him in her jeans on the yellow candlewick with her shirt open and pulled back from her shoulders. She was allowing him to stare up at her naked breasts, but not to touch them. The nipples of her breasts were bristling in the chill of the Whites' draughty bedroom, and as always Newlings mistook this for arousal. The room was warmed only by a double bar convector heater at the foot of the bed. Already, Clara White noted, Newlings had begun to froth at the corners of his mouth. Lying flat on his back didn't help, perhaps. Today they could have only what she called 'passive sex', meaning no effort or contact on her part and the minimum contact from him. There had to be these dedicated rest sessions, she said, in order to sustain the eroticism of full intercourse, otherwise he would become too easily satisfied by her. Newlings found the meanest sexual favour, such as her permission to let him undo a few buttons of her blouse, deeply arousing, and could not imagine ever reaching the state of satiety she spoke of, but she was insistent. And insistent too that he pay the same for the 'passive' as the 'active' sessions, and that she should dictate which came when.

This morning, however, just for a moment, he was distracted from her body by something above on the blotchy ceiling. He thought it was just a damp mark of some description, near the light rose, but at a second glance he saw it was not a mark but a hole. A crack of an inch or so spread from the rose into a jagged triangle of missing plaster. It had not been there before, as far as he could remember. A thought was about to frame itself in his mind about this hole when Clara leant over him and pinned him by his forearms to the candlewick, and then lowered herself to allow her small breasts to come close to his face, but not so close that his tongue might come out from its frothy slot to touch her flesh.

For Clara, things were not going according to plan. She had wanted to keep this session subdued and to keep her body unexposed. But now she found herself obliged to fake the scene and give away much more than she'd intended. It had become imperative to get Newlings onto his front. She lifted herself again and locked her elbows so that her chest was directly above his face, but high out of reach.

"You are so beautiful," Newlings muttered.

"Turn over."

He was accustomed to such commands and often this led to the most exciting moments in their passive sessions, often to the climax itself. He obeyed, and rolled onto his front.

"Undo your trousers. Pull them down."

Again Newlings did as he was told, undoing his grey, shiny slacks and pulling them down awkwardly, at first without and then – so boldly! - with his underwear, to expose his bare buttocks. Clara took a pillow from her side of the bed, covered Newlings' head, and held the pillow firmly there with her left hand, so that he could not move his head or see anything at all. She knelt at his side and reached between his legs. Newlings lifted himself so that she had access to his cock, which she drew down between his hollow thighs. She quickly brought him to a climax from this difficult position. When she had finished she looked up to the ceiling, to the light rose, just in time to see the glint of the lens as the camera was withdrawn.

She despatched Newlings, insisting, irritably, that she would have to put the candlewick, which had only just been cleaned, into the bath to soak, before Dr. White returned for his elevenses.

At this stage Clara still thought she and Anthony Hallett could stay ahead of the game. She had her anxieties, her suspicions, but she'd had those before, when she'd started the sessions in the woods, and her fears had proved unfounded. Those sessions had continued without the slightest threat or hint of any danger. Quite the contrary, they were harmonious, good-humoured, and she had prospered by them enormously. She enjoyed, she thought, a trusting relationship with the seniors, particularly with Hallett and Parsons, though the latter seemed less involved these days. (Parsons had missed the last two sessions: the rumour was he'd gone back to his divorcee on Hemsby Lows, who did not charge.)

Ossaf, though, whom she had met only once, had worried her immediately. His easy white smile and pressed black eyes had struck her as unfathomably treacherous. His manner with her was unctuous and insincere. He had an adult sophistication and assurance, and yet there was something missing, something discordant about his whole performance. It was as obvious as the gentle down on his unshaven cheeks, yet she could not name it. The performance was too varied, too calculating and concealing. He stood with his hands tucked up to their thumbs in his blazer pockets, and with the blazer drawn forward to disguise his middle-aged corpulence. But those neat, dark thumbs never relaxed. They pressed or squeezed their pocket seams in a prehensile way, the surface twitchings of a manic restlessness beneath. And for all his sophistication he had not yet learned adult habits of hygiene: the sweat of his fat was pungent but he wore no deodorant. And he had a horrible, dry, high, vicious laugh. Something once heard, never forgotten.

Here is a very horrible boy, she'd thought, from the start. But she'd met him face to face only once, with Hallett, and had no desire to see him again, so her understanding of him remained as it was, which was what they both wanted.

Chapter Thirteen

Investments

Some of the cash from Rowell's Jaguar had gone as seed money, venture capital, for a scam far more daring than the theft of the car itself. Even those most closely involved, such as the pornographer Ray Hooley, did not understand the scope of the arrangements planned or in place. The car had netted some six hundred pounds. Ossaf had spent a quarter of this on a cine camera - a Practica, the best available. He had reasoned to himself that the purchase of the camera was the gamble, and to buy cheap only increased the risk.

His first film had naturally been of the group

sessions in the woods. For the moment that was kept in the can. Besides Hooley and his father, Ossaf was the only one who knew about it. The film of Newlings and Clara was produced in effect by Hallett, but very much directed by Ossaf. Clara had been led to believe that with such a film she could at last gain access to Newlings' savings. Ah, those savings. That pot of gold. The silver lining. The treasure chest. The source of so much anxious scheming, dreaming and tittle-tattle, and such swollen glances and baleful asides. But a third film had already been made before the film of Newlings and Clara had been shot, which takes us back to the Tuesday morning when Tim Jackson visited Woodlands.

Very soon after they became intimate, the infatuated Hallett had approached Clara with an unturndownable deal. He'd been offered, he told her, thirty-five pounds - which would all be Clara's, of course – "Oh it will all be yours, Clara, of course. That goes without saying" - for full sexual intercourse with her, on film. He'd said they could sell the film to Hooley's father and his London friends, who would then put in orders for more films, and for much higher prices. He knew how the idea would please and excite her.

Much of what he said was perfectly true, but when Hallett had talked of 'more films at higher prices' he was merely following Ossaf's line, and Ossaf wasn't thinking of Clara and Hallett in a variety of Kamasutra positions, as they so luxuriously imagined, nor would he have approved Clara's fantastical price lists. Ossaf had in mind a variety of second-hand ideas from his lonely holiday screenings, bisexual and sadomasochistic scenarios, which he kept for the moment between himself and the Hooley family - a family secret. Hooley senior's curiosity had been aroused by the film of the group session in the woods and he was impatient for ideas of what he called 'a similar standard', 'original merchandize', 'top drawer material'.

As Clara was attracted to Hallett anyway, and had already enjoyed intercourse with him several times, the thought of adding thirty-five pounds to her savings, and maybe opening up a new income stream, was an attractive lure.

The plan as it was put to her by Hallett had the right blend of infatuation – "Yes, of course all the money will be yours, Clara, my love," he reassured. "Don't worry" - conceit and presumption, to convince her she was dealing with lambs, not wolves. She had gone ahead and made passionate love to Hallett on the yellow candlewick, giving herself away completely, turning in a good performance, and Ossaf had shot the film himself, keeping his objectionable presence out of sight in Dr. White's loft. She had collected her money beforehand, as at the sessions in the woods. This was a detail Ossaf had insisted upon in order to build trust. The more trust, the more exposure, he had privately surmised. And it had worked. When Hallett had asked, after they'd undressed each other down to their underwear, and stood a little goose-pimpled in the chilly bedroom, to make love naked on top of the candlewick, Clara had complied without demur, even though it meant she would have to strip off the candlewick afterwards and put it in the bath to soak.

The net was closing but Clara could not see it. Ossaf, with the thought of his exception from the sessions in the woods ever-present in his mind, had enjoyed filming Hallett and Mrs. White. He liked manoeuvring Mrs. White into position, into various positions, from behind the scenes. He enjoyed his manipulative, voyeuristic, pseudo-Iago role - *Would you, the supervisor, grossly gape on?* he asked himself, smiling, as he lay down in Dr. White's loft and set the Practica in position - *Behold her tupp'd?*

With the Hallett/Clara film in the can he had moved on to the much more important and ambitious project - the film of Clara and Newlings. He had instructed Hallett to ask Clara about Newlings, about how much he paid, what he liked, and so forth. Then he told Hallett to inform Clara that she was being abused - outrageously abused. This was Ossaf's most audacious deception. He told Hallet that Clara White was the victim of a simple and long-term conspiracy. A conspiracy plotted and sustained by none other than Baker and Newlings themselves.

He put this to Hallett at a private meeting in the gymnasium. Freezing cold, with its permanent scent of hormonal sweat, rotting plimsolls and medicine balls, the gym was a very private place. He beckoned Hallett to a bench in the far corner.

"I have news about your beloved," he said, wasting no time.

Hallett stalled and frowned.

"Sit down."

Once Hallett was beside him Ossaf slid closer. Recently, he told Hallet, both Newlings and Baker had been overheard saying things about Clara White – inappropriate things. Hallett looked suitably curious and alarmed. Ossaf slid closer still. They had been gossiping about her, Ossaf said, even laughing about her, behind her back. They had been boasting, saying very personal things, sometimes between themselves, sometimes more publicly, in the corridor, in the staff room, in the toilets, wherever . . . This was difficult news for Hallett to listen to, as Ossaf knew it would be. Ossaf began to enrich and embellish the gossip with intimate details and, as he put it to himself, to rub '*this young quat almost to the sense!*'

Hallett tried hard to dissemble but it enraged him to hear the things Baker and Newlings had said about Clara's body, now that he had intimate knowledge of her body himself, of its lovely curves and endearing blemishes. In the conversations Ossaf invented, Newlings and Baker had made fun of Clara for her small breasts, her broad hips - *'Quite a nice little craft, and pulls very well,'* Baker had quipped, to Ossaf's script, *'but no top deck and too broad in the beam . . .'* (In fact, Ossaf had borrowed this line from one of his more innocent holiday screenings: *Carry on Cruising*, with Sid James and Dora Bryan, 1958.) He also recounted how both Baker and Newlings had sarcastically scorned Clara intellectually for falling for their tricks and devices. Ossaf was very persuasive in this vein, seizing the opportunity to insult Clara's intelligence in front of Hallett, and thus further diminish Hallett's adult experience, which he could not equal, and which made his endless hours of raw and twisted celluloid sex so base and worthless.

The idea that Newlings was her abject victim, Ossaf continued, and that he was desperately parting with his hard-earned savings because he was so alone in the world, was really so wide of the mark it was quite ludicrous. The truth was that both Newlings and Baker thought Clara cheap, dirt cheap, and easy - *'better value and more convenient,'* Ossaf whispered viciously into Hallett's ear, squirming deeper into his Iago role - *'better value and more convenient,'* he repeated, *'than a whore under Yarmouth Pier!'* Anthony Hallett stood up at that, and all but wrung his hands in anguish. Oh yes, Ossaf went on openly, loudly, still seated. Oh, indeed! The theatrical echo of his voice in the freezing gym made him speak more boldly, richly. Baker and Newlings' antagonism and rivalry was all a sham. Nothing but a sham! he declared.

From the outset they had been collaborating to use Clara, and to abuse her, and to take her as often and as cheaply as they pleased. They were nothing but lying misers and everyone knew it now - except Clara White. And Dr. White. And Anthony Hallett.

Hallett stepped away and Ossaf called after him, taunted him. This ruse of theirs was the staff room joke! he threw in. And he knew all of this – and here was his trump card - from the Principal himself! From Lord of the Manner Bob Rowell!

Even when passed on to her in much diluted form by her young lover, Clara considered these revelations too poisonous to be believed, especially from one as naive and besotted and jealous as Hallett. But unluckily for her the period in question coincided with Baker showing a swaggering arrogance towards her that aroused suspicion. Then Ossaf pulled off a masterstroke. He had a minion temporarily pinch Newlings' wallet, and he filled it with cash from the sale of Rowell's car, over two hundred pounds, and he gave this to Hallett and told Hallett to show it to her. Hallett himself was both fascinated and appalled. He had never seen so much money in his life. Clara looked at the money. Counted it. She knew it was Newlings' wallet. She knew it only too well. The ocular proof.

She handed the wallet back to Hallett with a firm, cold expression. Her bald brown eyes were still and stolid and she said nothing. She looked away, her mind burning with vindictive plans and schemes. She wanted Newlings at her mercy now!

His precious hoards. His long-term investments. His secret laughter. His wallet – *See? You leave me with nothing again. Nothing.*

The idea had then been put to her that she needed something tangible against him. With a film of Newlings, for example, doing something gross, indecent, obscene perhaps, she could not only drain him at her own rate for as long as she liked, she could do so without having sex with him any more. (Then she could move on to Baker, Ossaf hinted . . .) The immediate threat would be to show the Newlings film to the seniors and the staff in the geography projection room, to which Ossaf had unlimited access. This would bring more than sufficient pressure to bear on Newlings. He would be destroyed, ruined by such an exposure. It would open a whole new vein of scorn and humiliation, and Dr. White, who had been treating Newlings more and more as a confidant of late, actually visiting Newlings' rooms for long evenings of confabulation (Oh, this was common knowledge, Ossaf said - it had been going on for months), Dr. White, Clara's husband, would probably try to kill, to murder Newlings. In short, screening the film would be the end of Newlings, and he couldn't fail to see it, whereas she, Clara, could just pick up her bags, cut her losses and go, still with her pockets full. But it would never come to that, in Ossaf's opinion. Newlings was a spineless man. He'd never take the brinkmanship. With just the threat of the film she could drain him. She could bankrupt him.

For this film with Newlings Ossaf had wanted a scene of sadomasochism and he told Hallett how it should be played. It would open with Clara tied down, spread-eagled on the yellow candlewick. Enter Newlings, who would immediately force her into fellatio. After which, various as yet unspecified pleasures would follow, involving reversals of the sadomasochistic roles. This film would mainly be for Ossaf's personal delight but it would also, he thought, meet the needs of Hooley senior's 'top drawer material'. Hooley junior was keen to advise on the details of the cinematography, when Ossaf outlined his idea. Ray Hooley, a fresh No. 6 dangling from his lips, squinting in his own smoke, bragged that he had taken part in just such a film himself, when he was only fourteen, with a woman of forty-five.

"Hooley," Ossaf told him, when he'd finished this boast. "I underestimated you. It turns out that you too are nothing but a whore. From this day I shall call you, Whore Hooley."

But Ossaf's dream project was never realized. The problem was Whore Hallett. Hallett would not deliver. He refused point blank. And once he was in the soft and pleasant presence of Clara, in the swirling scents of her bewitching patchouli oil, he could not bring himself to broach anything even remotely similar. She would not accept being at Newlings' mercy in any way, he told Ossaf, and besides, it was all too much a reversal of what Newlings had come to expect, and would therefore make him suspicious.

So the film had gone ahead on different terms, with Clara keeping her clothes on as far as possible and having a very limited part. Nonetheless she had found the business stressful and awkward. She was sure Newlings had noticed the hole in the ceiling, and was adamant that no similar arrangement could be made for Baker, who was far too wily for such a trick. Besides, Dr. White had noticed the hole too and said he was going to see Pez Rankin about some plaster to plug it up.

Chapter Fourteen

I Dream of Jeannie with the Light Brown Hair . . .

"No! No! No! *No!*"

Rowell rapped his baton so hard it slipped from his hand, dropped to the floor, and rolled under the lectern.

After the first bar, or even after the very first note, the puny Scott boy, Colin Scott, was the only one who seemed attentive and to know what he was doing. A harmony could not be prepared in isolation, and yet it was surely because Scott was dedicated enough to practise alone, singing away to himself in the woods or the rubbish pit, that he was so good. It was a dismal reflection on the entire junior choir.

Rowell lifted his head. He looked grim but patient. He rapped a knuckle on the lectern.

"Once again, after three."

Obediently the faces looked up at him and awaited his signal.

Rowell's choir was for treble choristers only. Once a boy's voice began to break he was sent down from the choir stalls in disgrace. But even in the carved stalls of an early Saxon church, under the shining strip lights, in their obedient rows, in their clean white surplices, in their fluted ruffs, and even though none of the boys was more than eleven years old, there was no innocence about Bob Rowell's junior choir. Above the ruffs and pure linen surplices, on which Rowell had spent so much of their parents' money, the faces of the little boys, all framed by square, cropped, military haircuts, executed in the darkness of the barber's van, were tired and drawn. So many of their eyes were infected with sties, and all had a bluish underscore. Many boys - far too many, so many it drew attention to itself - had teeth that were chipped or missing, and this horribly distorted their features when they were in full song with mouths open wide. It made them look, in their surplices and ruffs, like a row of pallid broiler chickens that had spent all their short lives under artificial light - scrawny, malnourished, de-beaked.

Under the strip lights of the Saxon church and their white light of truth, the *Coxcomb Hall Boys' Choir* looked like what it was: a collection of impoverished, ill fed, abused little boys, compelled to dress up and sing to please their lascivious master.

Rowell offered them the opening lines again, an example to follow, head up and in full voice:

"I dream of Jeannie with the light brown hair,
Borne, like a vapour, on the summer air!"

As he sang he looked to a stained glass window above the altar, Christ in Gethsemane, and his dewlaps shook with the cadence of the lines, the longing in them. And as he sang he let his concentration drift from the demands of the exacting job in hand, to a memory of the previous summer, to an incident which had actually been the inspiration for the current rehearsals. He saw in his mind's eye Johnny Cussack, blacked up and with his boater on, set at that rakish angle, he saw and heard him singing the lines, and he heard again, following his own voice like a descant, the exquisite melancholy leant to the words by his one-time protégé. Rowell had driven his Jaguar all the way to Glasgow to catch *The Black and White Minstrel Show* at the end of its summer run. This adventure, a spur of the moment thing, an expensive whim, had led to one of the most satisfying evenings of his life. Rowell had steeled himself to go backstage after the show to congratulate John Cussack, and had been received warmly for his pains. On seeing his old mentor from the R.A.F. Cussack had stood up from his dressing table at once. In the crowded, busy confines backstage Rowell was slow to recognize his protégé, who was still blacked up but without boater and negroid wig. Cussack's head of expensively cut, auburn tresses, disguised him further in his minstrel's make-up.

Cussack, tenor star of the show, threw open his arms:

"Bob Rowell! For goodness sake! Welcome! Welcome! *Welcome*, sir!"

Cussack turned to his fellow stars and starlets, lifting his arms high in theatrical appeal, inviting them to share this moment of surprise reunion, but his fellow stars and starlets seemed otherwise occupied. Dai Thomas, also still blacked up and white lipped, was slumped in a stuffed chair, de-wigged and exhausted. His boater lay in his lap. Silver-haired and portly, a stiff drink in one hand and a cigarette in the other, he looked – apart from his make-up - like a relic from some gentleman's club of a bygone era. He ignored Cussack and Rowell. He didn't seem to know what was going on. He seemed stupefied by drink and fatigue.

"But I owe this man everything!" Cussack declared, putting an arm around his old R.A.F. choirmaster, Bob Rowell. He beamed first at Rowell, then at the stars and starlets at their brilliantly lit dressing tables. Some of the ladies, all busy removing make-up, turned and forced curt smiles. Close up to Cussack's face and body Rowell could feel the heat from the performance just finished. Beads of sweat bubbled the black greasepaint, and the white lipstick that stretched wide round Cussack's rather mean mouth had dribbled to halfway down his chin. John Cussack had a weak chin.

"*Bob Rowell*!" he declared again, apparently too surprised, or just too exhausted to think of anything else to say. "Welcome! Welcome! *Welcome,* sir!"

After a stiff but tepid gin, supplied with some reluctance by Dai Thomas, Rowell had left, not wishing to overplay his backstage reunion, and had checked into the chilly Royal Northern near the station.

Now, in the little Saxon church, with just three weeks to go before he was due to enter *Coxcomb Hall Boys' Choir* for the preliminary rounds of the 1966 *BBC Look East Christmas Carol Competition,* held earlier and earlier every year to give the lesser choirs more time to lift their performances to BBC standards, with just three weeks to go it was worth recalling that summer evening, despite the sense of alienation it brought to the rehearsal. It was indeed worth remembering, and so Rowell raised his head and sang out the lines again and again and sang them resoundingly, his eyes closed, dewlaps and jowls trembling with sentiment, his own baritone filling the poky church with the secular refrain:

> *"I dream of Jeannie with the light brown hair,*
> *Borne, like a vapour, on the summer air!"*

Then he stared down hard at the boys in their surplices and ruffs.

"Choir! After three. One. Two. Three!"

Thus the rehearsal laboured late into the evening. The carols themselves came last. Rowell left these as something to look forward to, a light reward after the harder stuff, knowing that *Away in a Manger, Hark the Herald Angels Sing* and so on still had charm for the boys, reminding them of the warmth of Christmas at home just two months past.

Rowell was also using the preparation for the carol service to begin rehearsals for an altogether different event. The Grand Fete. It was his plan, which he had shared with no one at all, not even Tim Jackson, to have half his choir black up as miniature *Minstrels,* and dress the other half in girly costumes, so that he could present his very own *Junior Black and White Minstrel Show!* at The Grand Fete. The idea was to be unpublicised, a wild novelty that couldn't miss with parents and public alike. In his weaker moments Rowell imagined that he might even upstage Jimmy Tarbuck himself.

But first he must enjoy some early success in the preliminary rounds of the *BBC Look East* competition. That would give his secret enterprise the lift it needed, and on the waves of that success he would float the idea with Tim Jackson. He was quietly confident about all of that.

Indeed, in his fantasy, he had already leapt ten months ahead to enjoy the cream tea he would give the choristers in his plush red apartments, when they watched the carol service together on his television. And afterwards, a few of the younger boys (he had already marked them out: the heavenly Christopher Hallett and two of his sweet young friends) would be detained for special voice training, which would involve them stripping down to their underpants so that Rowell might caress their childish throats and chests and nipples, and make them sing out louder and shriller until he was quite, quite satisfied.

Chapter Fifteen

The Giant Maze

Other preparations for The Grand Fete, lacking Rowell's passion, were not quite so advanced. Dick Baker had at last begun work on some sections of the Giant Maze, but he had left his chipboard constructions outside the Craft Shacks in the Quad, and they'd already been rained on several times and were covered in bird droppings. They might rot there before they were even painted. Ossaf had been deployed to help with all projects, to harness his Duty gangs into lifting, carrying, hammering, painting and so on. Ossaf had accepted his new responsibilities without complaint, as always, but these jobs brought him under the authority of Tim Jackson, and as yet Jackson had said nothing to him.

On Rowell's impatient direction he reported to Jackson one Saturday lunchtime.

Unlike O'Donnell and Rowell, Jackson had no office, no bolt-hole. He was obliged to do all his work, for his lessons and his reforms, from his prefabricated classroom. Jackson was at his desk, head down, seizing a rare moment of peace and quiet to get a spot of marking done. Around the edge of his desk was a wall of beige exercise books that he had hardly begun to breach.

Despite the severe February weather he'd wedged his door open to allow some ventilation after the morning's classes. (It was the suet, he as sure, that caused such appalling wind.) He sat hunched up, marking in his overcoat. A drop of mucus had gathered at the tip of his Roman nose. He did not pause, or even lift his head from his work, when Ossaf came up the wooden steps and stood in the doorway, blocking the light, awaiting Jackson's attention. The interruption was unwelcome.

"Yes?"

There was no reply. When Jackson set down his fountain pen and turned to see the dark, stout figure of Ossaf, with his oily hair scraped back from his face, with his glinting smile, he felt a flush of adrenalin around his temples. Ossaf stood in his habitual attitude, with his hands pushed forward in his blazer pockets, his prehensile thumbs fastened down the seams. But it was the boy's smile that drew the eye. It looked as if he could hold that smile for hours without the slightest strain, yet it was not a grin or a grimace but still a smile. His glistening white teeth were small and even, and they pointed inwards at an impossible angle, as if set in multiple rows like a shark's.

It was a difficult moment for a man of Jackson's sensibilities. Here was the scourge, the gangmaster, the sadistic menace, who had gone unpunished, despite his own direct intervention and appeal, after the incident down on the rugby fields. Jackson looked back down to his desk and removed his reading glasses.

"Yes?" he said again. He cleared his throat. It was absurd to be unsettled by this boy, for that is all he was. A boy. No more than seventeen or eighteen at most. But so devilish!

"Sir," Ossaf began, his voice clear and resonant, not at all that of a deferential schoolboy. "Sir," he repeated,

> "*'tis death to me to be at enmity.*
> *I hate it, and do desire all good men's love.*"

Jackson could not help the beginnings of a smile himself - but he stopped it. He thought there was a personal flattery here, as he was English Master, and well known, not to say despised, for his passion for his subject. But Jackson was under a misapprehension. There was no flattery here. Ossaf was in role now and could remain in role indefinitely, just as long as he could hold his smile. Neither the line nor the smile signified any assumptions about Jackson's affection for the text quoted.

"Who sent you, Ossaf, and why?"

Jackson was crisp and he spoke down to his desk, to the beige wall of unmarked books. With his coolness he wanted to make it clear to Ossaf that he had not forgotten the incident with the catapult. He had not forgotten the naked boy, his back bleeding, running in the rain to the heap of sodden clothes on the touchline.

Ossaf stepped forward into the room. His steps were loud on the suspended floor. When he stopped he seemed about to snap his heels to attention in fascist salute. Jackson looked down. Those heels of Ossaf's spotless, Clark's Oxford toecaps - heels buffed to a gloss by some poor fag or slave, some poor Colin Scott . . .

As Ossaf replied to Jackson his prehensile thumbs came off the seams and pointed like tiny pincers.

"The Principal thought I might be of assistance with preparations for The Grand Fete, sir."

There was a pause.

"Did he now?"

When Rowell had mentioned some weeks ago that Jackson could "use Ossaf" to assist, Jackson had been dismissive. He wanted nothing to do with the slave labour of the Duty gangs. He had come to realize, though, that Rowell had no intention of providing any other source of labour from outside the Hall, and colleagues like Baker, Newlings and O'Donnell could only be relied upon to do nothing at all. Jackson had undergone a change of heart on this issue, and Rowell might have had the cunning to appreciate that; he may, indeed, have timed this visit from Ossaf to perfection. But Jackson's change of heart was not driven by the motives Rowell would have imagined. Jackson thought of it this way: if he took some supervisory role over Ossaf and the Duty gangs, he gained entrée to the prefect system, and thereby leverage for his reforms.

"Firstly, then, Ossaf," he said, sitting there at his desk in his overcoat, dangling his reading glasses by the stem, much in the manner of the Principal himself, "firstly, then, collect from Mr. Baker the plans for his Giant Maze. See to it that all sections of the maze are completed. When the construction is finished, have it painted green. Green as the grass. Have Rankin transport the sections to the field. Set it up near the Vampire."

Jackson had mentioned the Vampire deliberately, but this did not in any way discomfort Ossaf, who bowed and withdrew without another word, having received his orders. There was something of the manners of his homeland in his bow, more proud than deferential.

It is a strong mind that is not impressed by the exercise of power, and Jackson was impressed, when, on a pre-breakfast jog the next morning, he came across a vast green structure that partially obscured the grey and gloomy Vampire. The maze was complete, and painted. It was set out on two cricket pitch tarpaulins to protect the wooden base from the dew. Jackson stopped to take a look at it. The side panels were some four feet high, plenty high enough for the intended clientele, and the channel was about a yard wide, sufficient for the happy little souls to pass each other on their way to more confusion and dead-ends. Angle brackets and regular rows of battens across the top secured the walls. A wooden sign saying 'Wet Paint' and 'No Entry', in neat calligraphy, was fixed across the entrance on a piece of string thumb-tacked to the sides. In his mind's eye Jackson could see Anthony Hallett's blonde and handsome head bent low, putting the final touches to the painted sign, and Ossaf's dark thumbs pressing home the tacks. That would be the sum and total of Ossaf's part of the labour, no doubt. However, here was The Giant Maze. It was complete, to all intents and purposes. Finished. Just like that. And they were only in February. There were more than three months before Whitsun, when The Grand Fete was scheduled to take place. If the attractions could be finished by Ossaf with this kind of efficiency, then there was nothing to worry about. But what was the human cost? Which poor innocents had been bullied and whipped into making and painting The Giant Maze with such speed and industry?

Tim Jackson walked about the structure. There was certainly a good deal of it. It measured thirty paces each side. A mass of chipboard in 4' x 8' sheets. Tons of the stuff. Gallon upon gallon of green paint too. Where had all the money come from? Brackets, battens, screws - it all had to be paid for. He made a mental note to ask Rowell about that. If finances were really in such a parlous state, how could they afford this lot, not to mention all the other apparatus for the Fete? Looking across the top of the maze, with its woven battens fanning this way and that in every direction, like some vast green raffia mat, he tried to pick out the pattern of the thing. It took him a little while. It was a fiendishly complex design. He couldn't imagine Baker or Newlings ever devising such a labyrinth - Hallett's contribution might have been more than just the calligraphy.

Well, it was done. Now it would have to be covered up and left here until Whitsuntide, then moved to its planned location at the far end of the colts' rugby pitch. As he jogged off towards the woods the other side of the games fields, Jackson imagined the flat and yellow grass that would be left behind when the thing was moved. That would be unsightly. Perhaps that is where they could put the portable toilets, he thought. With Ossaf's dramatic demonstration of what was possible, Jackson began to feel differently about The Grand Fete. Perhaps the thing could be a success. An understanding of Ossaf's power had informed Rowell's fantasies all along; now Jackson shared Rowell's understanding, if not his motivation.

Perhaps the Fete could be a turning point, it really could be what Jackson had secretly hoped - an opening up, an airing of the place to the outside world. And perhaps, afterwards, there could be no return to the closeted perversity of the present regime. After putting on the pretence of being a civilized, normal, even colourful and happy place, it might be impossible to slip back into the barbarous misery to which everyone had become accustomed. The Grand Fete could be pivotal to all their lives, and to all Jackson's schemes for reform. Now he was jogging past the colts' field, where The Tunnel of Magic was to be constructed, linked to The Giant Ghost Train, and The Tunnel of Love and The Great Sleuth's Trail. Until now Jackson had thought these preposterously ambitious ideas, but glancing up he could see already in his mind's eye children laughing and shrieking on fairground rides, their colourful cars and chrome safety bars glinting in the blue Whitsun sky.

Chapter Sixteen

Beauty and the Beast

The raucous cries of triumph and the howls of dismay fell silent on Ossaf's entrance. Parsons' old, yellow, bone dice, 'Parsons' bones', were left where they had fallen in the centre of the torn baize.

Three nines on a pair of Jacks. A full house. Someone had just got lucky.

Ossaf was in his cape. He was at his most dangerous when he was in his cape. Beneath it he could hide any number of vicious surprises, not least the metal catapult from *Gun & Game*. His cape was, in fact, the academic gown of the young graduate, Mr. Wills, who had introduced Ossaf to Shakespeare, and then so woefully regretted it. It was one of several items of clothing and personal property Ossaf had stolen from Wills before Wills' shameful departure.

Ossaf swept up to the billiards table with his cape

billowing behind him, like a headmaster descending on some folly or abuse. His attention fell on the dice, and on the leather cup, tucked in a corner pocket. The symbols of the ritual from which he'd been excluded.

> *"Since every Jack became a gentleman*
> *There's many a gentle person made a Jack!"*

He span about, seeking applause for his wit from the fawning cowards around him, all of whom, every one of them, at some stage of their short lives, had been beaten into submission by Ossaf. As a dreamy junior Parsons had been poked and thrashed by Ossaf with a cricket stump for the crime of staring in the shower, staring at Ossaf's plump black nakedness, at his shrivelled cock and scrotum, in the cold shower. Cup-eared Parsons, though seventeen year's old now, slipped to the rear, behind fellows less likely to fall victim to Ossaf's wild and violent outbursts.

Ossaf snatched Parsons' leather cup, gathered up the dice, and dashed both skin and bone to the ground -

> *"THIS IS THE FRUIT OF WHORING!"*

There was a dramatic silence, which Ossaf held by glancing from face to face of the assembled company, noting in particular those who had slipped to the rear. Suddenly, taking all of them, except a few bright prefects of the very inner circle, by complete surprise, Ossaf began to laugh his high, theatrical, maniacal laugh, and as he laughed his glance darted about the faces of the seniors, and each face in turn smiled in relief and began laughing too, and Ossaf nodded at them when they laughed, approving of their laughter, until all were included in this orchestrated, empty merriment -

"All those who love me, follow!"

Ossaf span about on his shiny toecaps and led the posse of seniors from the Games Room back outside into the freezing Quad. Without turning to see who had followed and who had not, who loved him and who did not, he led them across to the teaching block. They went upstairs to the geography projection room, where the frail Eric Crampton showed films from Shell (*Shell Presents!)* and Unilever (*Unilever Presents!*) all year round on the Bell & Howell projector, instead of teaching geography. The previous week Crampton had celebrated his seventieth birthday in here, sitting on the polished benches with O'Donnell and Newlings, the only staff who'd turned up to share his bottle of cheap red wine. He'd apologised for the wine but explained to his guests that he was still penniless, he could afford nothing better. "I shall die in harness!" he quipped, as he refilled yet again the plastic cups of his thirsty friends, and he smiled wanly at them as he stooped and poured, hoping they'd say that he wouldn't. "Of course you will, Crampton," O'Donnell assured him, lighting another Gold Leaf, quaffing more wine. "You fey and ancient queen."

Ossaf unlocked the door and opened it.

Inside, sitting side by side on the back row of the forms facing the screen, sat two adult figures. They were Clara White and Anthony Hallett. Their faces were pale and their eyes anxious, but Mrs. White was trying to put on a show of indifference, even boredom.

Though the light was on in the projection room, Ossaf now directed proceedings with a black rubber torch, which he fetched with a flourish from a belt clip under his cape. Now he was an usher in the cinema guiding the seniors to their seats. On a signal with the torch to the projectionist's box at the back of the room, the lights went out and the film began to roll.

For a few jerky seconds there was nothing but a shot of a well-washed blackboard. Then a hand and arm appeared, the hand grasping a new stick of chalk, and the upper arm covered in the folds of an academic gown. The hand was Ossaf's small dark hand. It began to move eerily across the board, leaving words behind it in a faltering, gothic script:

BEAUTY
AND
THE BEAST

There were titters from some of the seniors, which gathered confidence at the end when the hand slipped with comical melodrama all the way down the blackboard.

A few more seconds passed. The film became flecked with white scratches and dust marks, like an ancient silent movie. Then abruptly there was a full colour exposure of Dr. and Mrs. White lying reading, under their yellow candlewick, in their double bed at Woodlands.

"*What?*" A gasp from Clara White, from the back of the projection room.

Dr. White had his glasses on and was reading a book by Denis Wheatley - *The Devil Rides Out*. This shot lasted until he turned the page, and then was replaced with a shot of the same bed, made up and with no one in it or on it. This empty shot lasted considerably longer than it was meant to, as the cameraman waited for the subjects of the film to climb the stairs and enter the room. Then the sound equipment detected footsteps and the next moment the black head of Clara White could be seen, and behind her came little Jimmy Newlings. There was a roar of approval from the audience at Newlings' entrance. Clara and Newlings sat awkwardly together on the side of the double bed and then Newlings tried to undo Clara's blouse, but she slapped his hand away. Loud titters from the audience at this. She undid her blouse herself, and without hesitation removed her plain white brassiere from beneath it so that, before Newlings, she sat with her naked chest exposed. Newlings reached forward to touch her breasts but again he was slapped away. At this point the first word of the film could be heard. It was a quiet, strangled, agonized "*Please*" from Jimmy Newlings.

"*Oh please!*" someone mocked from the audience. "*Please please me!*"

On the screen Clara White replied to Newlings: "Take off your shirt."

Newlings stood and undid his shirt and removed it, exposing his pasty skin and hairy shoulders.

Groans of revulsion from the audience.

"Lie down." Clara White was brusque, impatient.

Newlings lay down across the bed, his body now in full view of the camera. His chest was flat and his lower ribs stuck through his thin white skin. His was unmistakably the body of a starving animal. No pity came from the audience, only more titters and whispers. But these were cut short when, for an infinitesimal moment, Newlings' starving eyes seemed to meet his audience's eyes down the barrel of the camera, and for that moment the audience looked down not just through the camera, but through Newlings' eyes as well, into the endless tunnels of anxiety and unhappiness they'd gouged with their own bare hands.

Then Clara White leant across him and the moment passed. She told him to roll over and then covered his head with a pillow. She told him to undo his trousers. She helped him pull the trousers and his underpants away from his buttocks and crotch, and then, as he arched, she reached between his legs to draw his erection out from beneath him. Disgusted laughter came from the audience, and gathered pace and force when Clara began to rub him to his climax. The audience moaned in crude imitation as Newlings gave muffled voice to his ecstasy. The film lasted just long enough to see his body go slack and silent, and then some numbers flicked up in reverse order and there was the clatter of the celluloid flapping on a full reel.

Applause, at first uncertain, became hearty.

The lights did not go up straight away. With typical thoroughness Ossaf waited until his projectionist had replaced the film with the one that Mr. Crampton had set up for his first lesson in the morning. A check was run on this film to make sure it was cued to the right place. This entailed everyone having to sit through the wobbly orchestral soundtrack of:

Shell Presents!
The Bessemer Blast Furnace

With the check completed the lights went up.

Ossaf stood before the screen, his hands crossed in front of him, holding his heavy black torch.

"No one," he announced, "will say a word about this to our fey and ancient queen, nor to any of our very noble and approv'd good masters, until I say."

There was a moment's silence, and then all were released from old Crampton's projection room to carry on with the evening's diversions.

Chapter Seventeen

Counsel of Despair

Newlings had never seen Dr. White so distraught. His eyes were wild and full. He needed help.

"You are my friend, Newlings."

Again the good doctor sat with his back to the casements of Newlings' living room windows, and again his furry hands lay limp and curled on the rosewood table. Newlings looked down at the good doctor's hands. They were yellow-nailed, chemical-stained, aged claws, lying lifeless on his polished rosewood table. They too asked for help, in their curled up way, but Newlings thought only of the scratches those horny nails would leave, and the chemical residues of the day that might leak from the good doctor's anxious palms onto his French polish. These thoughts pressed on Jimmy Newlings while he tried to summon pity to his expression, and find new platitudes and words of counsel to offer his colleague, the veritable

Science Master, the good Dr. White, old Whitey.

"You are my friend, Newlings."

Newlings had been caught off guard first by the smell of drink, and then because White had refused to speak his business. White had insisted they go up to the second floor and enter the safety of Newlings' apartment before he broached his complaint. Strong fumes had overtaken Newlings on the stairs, as Dr. White laboured over the second flight, a couple of steps behind. Old Whitey was in a man-size bubble of alcohol vapour - noxious, flammable, hazardous. Newlings had been trying to have a night on the wagon and to him the smell was quite overwhelming. His dried out system could have scented alcohol at twenty paces. He led the way slowly, trying to give himself time to compose what he would say if Dr. White made some open accusation. The man was sodden, saturated, and if he had now somehow discovered – through that blabbermouth Baker? - that his confidant of late, good old Jimmy Newlings, had been having sex with his wife, every week, for all this time, what might he not do? He might assault Newlings. He might have a weapon concealed about his person. A knife, scissors, a screwdriver, anything would do. He might have taken something from his labs - a phial of acid, in the face, in the eyes. Anything was possible.

But in the event White had been humble and apologetic once inside Newlings' warm apartment, with the door closed behind them. The rooms in this part of the Victorian wing were the only ones in the whole of the Hall with effective central heating. In looking after himself Rowell had been obliged to look after those who lived in the apartments surrounding him. Rowell, Newlings, Jackson and O'Donnell were the only staff who slept warm at night. In Dr. White's and Crampton's tied cottages there was no proper heating whatever. Eric Crampton moaned all year round about hypothermia.

Standing there recovering from his climb up the stairs, with the door shut behind him, Dr. White felt keenly the warmth in Newlings' rooms. He sniffed the warmth. It was so warm it made his clothes feel damp. He took a deep breath and inhaled the warmth, and when he exhaled the warmth his fumes lifted and expanded, ballooned outward and upward, inflating further his man-size bubble of vapour. Dr. White stood there staring at Jimmy Newlings' carpet and thought of his heating bills, he visualised them, saw how they unfolded from their guilty buff envelopes, unfolded in his horny schoolmaster's hands, and how they perched on his fingers and spread their proud red wings and soared off into God only knew where - his heating bills were in the stratosphere these days! They had trebled from last year. Because Clara was living there, and keeping herself warm all day. That was all. But good grief those bills were terrifying. They were ruinous. They took all he had. They came in angry, rabid, successive bites from the Eastern Electricity Board where Clara – Oh bless her! Curse her! - used to work! . . . Even so, while little Jimmy Newlings lived here with all this warmth for free, and added to his savings each month . . . Every evening, as soon as he got home, Dr. White lit a log fire and switched off the blow heaters and bar heaters that Clara always left on, every day, all day, all over the house. Even in the bedroom upstairs the bar heater was always on. Permanently. Why? What for? Oh, what was that bar heater on for in their miserable bedroom? And yet there was so much wood - they lived in the woods! – but she never bothered to make a fire. She never even bothered to clear out the grate. She never even fetched in the logs. She never opened the bills from her very own Eastern

Electricity Board. Such a lazy, slatternly wife he had married. Fit for nothing but reading books. Oh, such a desperately unhappy marriage!

Much of this kind of domestic detail had come out tonight in Whitey's initial and unreasonable rant against Clara, which was broken up here and there with maudlin, self-pitying confessions about his own inadequacies. He told Newlings that he'd not been home this evening. He'd taken a lift from Baker into Hemsby and they'd been to the pub there, The Feathers, where he'd drunk himself into what he now called a 'more stable state'. Baker refused to bring him back – "Waste of bloody petrol," he'd said - so White had to ask the publican to phone for a Yarmouth taxi – more ridiculous expense that he could not afford!

With his heightened sense of smell Newlings could sniff the smoky comforts of supper and cigars at The Feathers. To Newlings old Whitey looked bloated with indulgence. Full of bad blood and food and booze and wind. The sunken cheeks of his beaky face were now puffy, shutting up those watery eyes.

"But you see it's worse, Jimmy . . . You see, my wife . . "

Newlings felt himself blanch.

"What's happened, Whitey?" Newlings gently solicited. "Is she poorly? Has there been an accident?"

White hung and shook his head.

"She is not ill. It is me that is ill. I am sick. I am very sick. Sick of it all."

"You are *drunk*!" Newlings declared, giving up his sympathetic manner and damning the good doctor for his indulgence.

But what had Baker said in his car on the way to The Feathers? What had Baker told White? Or in The Feathers, after a few drinks, perhaps, Baker squeezing one more round out of Whitey before he'd spill the beans - Oh, just one more round, Whitey! Come on. Dig Deep! - before he'd talk turkey to the good doctor, before he'd tell him what he craved and dreaded to hear. Or in the gravel car park, maybe, just one last loose remark, thrown out the lowered window of his frog-eyed Sprite, before he sped off and left White waiting for his taxi. What had Baker said? That blabbermouth!

White lifted his head and looked at his host.

"Clara has been having an affair, Newlings."

"Clara?" Newlings stared at White. "Don't be ridiculous! Clara is the very soul of honesty!" Newlings shook his head. "Dear oh dear, Whitey. You've got yourself drunk and over-excited again. Pull yourself together. Good grief! You don't know how lucky you are! Lovely wife. Lovely house. I'll make some coffee, then I'll send you on your way. Back to your lovely house and your lovely wife! Clara will be worried sick about you!" Newlings rose and went to his kitchenette. As he left the table he heard White mutter behind him:

"I know it all now. I know she has . . . I know it all now . . ."

Once out of sight in the kitchenette Newlings braced himself against the drainer and tried not to panic. Some self-control was called for here. He must get rid of White as soon as he could. If he were implicated, if he were accused - what then? Then deny everything, of course. Be affronted. Outraged. Is this how you repay me, Doctor, for my hospitality and kindness? Shout and swear at him and send him on his way. Kick the old bugger out into the sobering, cold night air. But what had that braggart Baker said? Before the pub, perhaps. In the car, in the noisy confines of his rattle-bag, frog-eyed Sprite, on the dark and lonely lanes to The Feathers? What had he said?

Never mind that. Above all, Newlings had to get the good doctor out of his apartment. Even if he were not accused, the longer the conversation went on the more likely he was to make a slip of some kind, to say something which would tip old Whitey into precipitous suspicion and, no doubt, precipitous action. Precipitous suspicion, precipitous action, precipitous suspicion, precipitous action, suspicion, action, suspicion . . .

Filling the kettle, he called out from the kitchenette:

"Clara's a lovely woman, Whitey. She doesn't deserve this, you know. You are a lucky man. Stop behaving like some lovesick schoolboy. Pull yourself together!"

This kind of posturing was not easy for Jimmy Newlings, who could hardly pretend to be a man of the world, but from the safety of the kitchenette he could carry it off well enough.

When he returned to the living room with two mugs of boiling black Nescafé, Dr. White looked up at him with a lopsided smile, a smile sunk at one corner into squiffy cynicism. The expression looked exaggerated, unnatural, wounded, as if he'd had a stroke. Such was the depth of ill feeling now in White's watery eyes, Newlings imagined that he was capable of stringing him along here, of allowing him to pretend all he liked, only to deliver the crushing revelation that he knew all about his mornings with Clara, knew every detail of what went on, of how much he'd been paying, even. That Baker had told him everything in the car. It was a most disquieting idea.

"You are naive, Newlings," Dr. White said, accepting his mug of boiling Nescafé, clutching it for its warmth with his old, numb claws. "I'm sorry, but you are naive, my friend. Where women are concerned, that is."

With his head bent to his mug, and with his eyebrows raised, the good doctor sipped his scalding Nescafé, then repeated his judgement. "Where women are concerned, you are naive. That is a fact, Jimmy, my friend."

Newlings fetched some coasters and put them on his polished table and set his own mug on one of them. This business relieved him of the obligation to reply. He sat down again with White and sipped his own Nescafé. Such a hot, tart, unpleasant drink.

"You need to go home and get a good night's sleep, Whitey."

"Hear me out, old boy. Hear me out. Then I'll go."

"But I don't want to hear you out, Dr. White," Newlings asserted, his tone firm and clipped. "You are drunk." Newlings shook his head again in disapproval. "Just look here a minute. Look at me. Leave your coffee . . . You are drunk and you are going to say something you'll regret. Like that other time, remember? Think of tomorrow morning. Think of the staff room. Think on that. Sober yourself on that prospect, old boy. So just drink your coffee and go. Say no more."

But White was too far gone to respond to such reasoned appeals.

"You're the only friend I have, Newlings."

"Nonsense! You get along with O'Donnell? Rowell? Eric Crampton? Don't you? With Jackson? Baker? With that new musicman – Egg Taylor? Great chaps. Stop feeling sorry for yourself. You have plenty to be thankful for, Whitey. I've said so before. Plenty. You should remember that sometimes. Lovely house, lovely wife . . ."

Dr. White had stopped listening after the name Baker. When he heard that name he seemed to tighten up, he shifted in his chair, his eyes lost focus beneath their unspent tears and wandered loose and blind over

Newlings' features, searching for a memory, a connection. Newlings looked down, unable to bear it, and saw that the good doctor wasn't using the coaster he'd provided. His scalding mug of Nescafé sat on the bare rosewood of his antique table, on his French polish.

What had happened? Had Baker alluded to him, to Newlings, made some hint, some oafish joke, whose punchline Whitey was now beginning to decipher? In his mind the question had a rhetorical air. Suddenly it seemed inevitable, given Baker's character, that the secret would be spilled sooner rather than later, spilled casually, recklessly, like so much gravel from The Feathers car park, as he sped away in his rag-bag sports car.

Again Dr. White sipped his scalding black Nescafé, head lowered, eyes open wide, cheeks drawn in. Right now he looked like a man in his late sixties, early seventies, as old as Crampton or O'Donnell. He put the mug down again with shaking hands on the rosewood. The heat of it was at last getting through his numbness. Newlings didn't know what to say next. He did not know what might be precipitous. But he had to speak.

"Look. You better be getting home, old boy. Clara will be worried to death about you."

"Will she?"

"Of course she will."

"Will she?"

"I don't want to hear any more about this. Quite frankly."

White gave him a baleful look. All the earlier sentimentality had gone. He seemed grim and full of dark intent.

"Don't hide from me, Newlings."

"I'm not hiding from you. But you are drunk, Whitey."

"I know I'm drunk. I'm drunk for a good reason."

"Well, I don't want to hear about your good reason."

"But it is a good reason. A very good reason. And you're going to hear it."

"I don't want to hear it. Drink your Nescafé and off you go."

Then, strangely, bathetically, the danger passed.

An equilibrium was suddenly achieved in White's psyche between his drunken recklessness and his bourgeois repression, causing an air lock, forcing him to suffocate in his own wretchedness. He needed to be outside again, he needed space to choke and breathe. He did not finish his Nescafé, and when he stood up from the polished table he spilt some of it.

"Thank you for your coffee," he said, "and for your counsel. I shall go. You are right. I must get home. Must get to bed."

Newlings stood and escorted his guest to the door.

At the open door, feeling the cold draught coming up the stairs, White stopped and turned and spoke through his teeth at Newlings. There was just one word.

"*Baker!*"

And then he was gone, stumbling fast, too fast, down the stairs to the front door.

Chapter Eighteen

The Tunnel of Magic

"Where is my car?"

For all his wit and manipulation Ossaf did things that on the face of it were childishly impractical at times. His preparations for The Grand Fete were coming along far too fast. Several rough wooden constructions were now standing out in the winter weather, where they would rot and fall apart before they were ever put to use. The cheap, ¼" chipboard would not withstand snowfalls and storms, and even if it did, it would look shabby and decrepit by the Whitsun weekend. Only The Giant Maze had been given a protective coat of paint; all the rest was brown and bare. And the latest pieces were only nailed together, rather than screwed and bracketed. The Tunnel of Magic, already half made at the far end of the colts' rugby pitch, was the flimsiest and most pathetic structure of all.

Everyone else could see failure in the making. To

the Duty gangs who slavishly assembled platforms and sections of tunnel during lock-out, or during their few free hours on Sunday afternoons, it was plain as day. But of course they could say nothing. They lifted and hammered, and sawed and sweated in doomed silence, like prisoners of war labouring on their own gallows. The only words above the hammer blows were Ossaf's, as he strolled among them with his hands in his blazer pockets, his prehensile thumbs twitching on their seams -

"We all must make sacrifices for The Grand Fete!"

It had become a refrain.

Anyone else would have conceived preparation for The Grand Fete in separate phases, and construction of the various parts would have been completed according to a simple schedule. There would have been deadlines, contingency plans, a place for everything and everything in its place, and it would all have come right around Whitsuntide. But Ossaf's imagination did not work in this way. His mind in some ways was like an infant's, or an idiot's. Novelty was everything. He had never learned to think of his actions as taking place in a habitual, temporal world.

Looking on, the masters of Coxcomb could see the day, not too far off now, when Ossaf would leave. It was such an obvious assumption people would not even mention it, except to express their relief or satisfaction. But Ossaf himself did not see things in that light. For him the world was only as it was now and he thought and cared no more about it, and did things only for their immediate gratification. It pleased him to execute Jackson's instruction to make The Giant Maze, so he re-organized his Duty gangs and made them construct and paint it, and told Rankin to deliver it in sections to the corner of the field where the Vampire stood. It interested him to make

The Tunnel of Magic, which Bob Rowell had mentioned to him in passing, and to install that at the far end of the colts' rugby pitch, and so there it was.

Bob Rowell, explaining things to himself in an ordinary, adult, if rather sanguine way, imagined The Tunnel of Magic and The Giant Ghost Train nearby were working prototypes which could be dismantled and stored: he had already earmarked a place, an outbuilding to the rear of his garages, where the apparatus could be kept weatherproof until spring. He did not want to know any more about it. He did not want to interrupt or interfere with Ossaf's work in any way, not when it was all going so well. He assumed Rankin had some supervisory role, as he did in the holidays, and he certainly didn't want to get involved in any discussions about how the jobs were being done - drills, nails, paint pots, things of that order. If the jobs were being done at all, that was more than good enough for Rowell, upstairs in his third floor apartments. He would come down at the end to suggest final touches and improvements, and to make sure, with Rankin and Baker, that things were reasonably safe, but apart from that he had no interest in Tunnels of Magic or Love, or in Ghost Trains, Mazes, Sleuth's Trails and Scenic Railways. They were a means to an end, The Grand Fete, at which Jimmy Tarbuck would preside as master of ceremonies, and at which Rowell's junior choristers would do their damnedest to upstage the illustrious Tarbuck with their very own, *Junior Black & White Minstrel Show!*

For Ossaf, though, The Tunnel of Magic and The Giant Ghost Train were ends in themselves, and that is why he went about designing and building them as soon as Rowell had mentioned them. And contrary to Rowell again, he had not the slightest interest in the success or failure of the project in part or as a whole. One day he might care about that, for some arbitrary reason, but right now the overall design, the grand design behind The Grand Fete, had no significance for him.

Like Tim Jackson, but for different reasons, he did not even know who Jimmy Tarbuck was.

Ossaf's mind had been moulded on the playing fields here, under the shadow of the de Havilland Vampire. His psyche was circumscribed by the shards of glass on the perimeter walls, his moods clouded by the wintry weather preeminent in all seasons. His fantasy was populated only by boys and masters, and confined to what might be thought of as various 'sets' or 'scenes': the draughty tuck box shed, the Vampire's cockpit and watery engine cowling, the Dell, and the dark woods, thickets, and misty streams of the grounds of the Hall. All of which had a kind of dramatic artifice for him, as if they were part of a derelict film lot, where he moved from set to set playing out his roles and spinning out his plots - there was nothing real beyond this. He had been outside these confines so seldom since he was seven year's old he scarcely conceived of a world beyond Coxcomb's walls, and desired nothing from it nor any further knowledge of it. For him the world was just this small, grey, walled place, this scepter'd isle, this England.

But of course, at times, there were other moods.

As yet The Tunnel of Magic was nothing more than a chipboard construction some thirty feet long nailed to 4"x 4" timber frames, and The Giant Ghost Train which was to adjoin it, wasn't even half built. Neither had any rails. The problem of rails had stumped Ossaf, but that had not stopped him constructing a carriage of sorts. This was based upon a bogie wheel contraption, a basic trolley, abandoned long ago in Baker's workshops. Two narrow, ornamental benches, borrowed from the netless tennis courts, had been bolted to the chassis, and the whole thing had been painted gloss black. On its bogie wheels, with its high wrought iron seats, it was a cranky, top-heavy, antique looking device, like some experimental carriage from the dawn of steam railways. It did not move easily in the dewy grass of the rugby pitch, even when drawn with ropes and straps by a pair of senior Duty gangs, even with Ossaf leaning forward and all but screaming at them from his wrought iron seat – "Heave! Heave! Heave!" He rocked to and fro on the seat. "We all must make sacrifices for The Grand Fete!"

Now, in the twilight of a late February afternoon, on the rear of these two wrought iron seats, Ossaf sat in his black Crombie overcoat, something else he had stolen from the hapless Mr. Wills, his collar turned up against the cold. He was alone, sitting to one side in the rear of his open carriage. There was the wooden Tunnel of Magic in front of the rugby posts, and his carriage some twenty feet back, squaring up to the loneliness of its unlit, untracked journey ahead.

For once the weather had been clear all day and the air was crisp. There would be a frost. Ossaf sat still as the dead on the rear seat of his black carriage, in his funereal Crombie. His dark eyes, deep and hard as jet in the soft, downy fat of his face, did not look ahead at the tunnel, but instead looked up, up, up, to the very tops of the winter trees bordering the playing fields. The uppermost branches and their stark twigs were clear against the dimming sky, black filaments in the blue February air. In the distance a tractor could be heard from the fields beyond the woods, the sounds of its engine rising and falling when it turned in the headlands, then settling to an even pitch as it dragged its way back.

Rooks cawed over the woods.

"Light thickens, and the crow makes wing to the rooky wood . . ."

Stuck fast here on the wrought iron seat on this late afternoon Ossaf did, in this mood, have a very acute sense of time, of seasonal time. The bare winter trees, so black and damp against the cold blue sky, and the distant sound of the tractor ahead, brought a sadness to him, a recognition that the world carried on without him, beyond the sharded walls, after all. The tractor turned in the headlands without him, the rooks cawed, the frost came and went without him, the sky went dark as it had done for billions of years, over trees that had come and gone for millions of years. He sat alone on the wrought iron seat of his carriage, at the far end of the playing fields, staring above The Tunnel of Magic to the winter tree tops, to the uppermost twigs, and he sensed here his absolute aloneness, his mortality, and his mood was tranquil and deeply melancholy.

He was not aware of the large, flapping figure of Dick Baker coming towards him across the fields from the direction of the Vampire. He did not hear him when he began to shout.

"Ossaf! . . . Ossaf!"

The trees and the sky, the smell of the woods and freshly turned soil, absorbed Ossaf's senses to the exclusion of Baker's wild and breathless cries.

"Ossaf! Ossaf!"

Still a hundred yards or so away, Baker began to wonder if the figure he took to be Ossaf, sitting on the bench seat of the strange carriage, was really a human being at all; if it was not some monstrous effigy or some artefact of black magic to be used in the The Ghost Train or The Tunnel of Magic, just propped there on the seat and left out in the weather. The figure was so rigid and lifeless.

With this in mind Baker paused and stared, then he advanced again through the dew at a slower pace, and stopped his shouting, saved his energy, until he had come close enough to see the figure clearly.

Ossaf was conscious of someone approaching through the long grass behind him, but he did not turn. Ossaf feared no one, and at this moment did not welcome the company of any other human soul. Baker had to walk right up to the carriage and lean over the wrought iron tennis bench to make out, in the gathering dusk, the dark skinned Ossaf in his black coat.

"Ossaf! It is you! Answer me!"

Ossaf turned and looked across at Baker from his wrought iron seat. Baker was wild. He was in his bright yellow Paddy Hopkirk rallying anorak. His shoes and ankles were soaked.

Baker was about to ask what the matter was. Ossaf looked so curious sitting out here on the carriage in the dusk in his black coat. What was going on? But another concern, more pressing than Ossaf's mood or welfare, displaced this curiosity.

"Ossaf! Where is my car?"

Ossaf turned to face ahead once more. He did not answer, but nodded towards the tunnel.

Baker looked into the empty mouth of the tunnel. He frowned. He gaped.

Ossaf climbed down from the carriage, alighting on Baker's side so that Baker was obliged to step out of his way.

"You had no right . . ." Baker began, but his words trailed off as he stepped towards the tunnel. He stared in but could see nothing. "Ossaf!" It was getting so dark. He turned back to Ossaf.

"Ossaf! Wait! Wait here!"

But Ossaf was already twenty yards deep in the dusk, walking back in his Crombie coat through the dewy grass, back towards the bleak linocut of the Victorian wing.

Baker hesitated, then ventured into the tunnel. Once inside, a few feet in, he could make out a dim silhouette of his car at the other end. But the shape did not look right. He withdrew from this end of the tunnel. "Ossaf! Come back here!" He ran at a loose jog, rally anorak flapping, to the other end, and started his approach from there. The boot of his car was visible about ten feet into the tunnel. So far so good. Baker's mind leapt to the conclusion that he'd been the victim of some practical joke and the car had been parked here out of the weather in this stupid shed Ossaf's gangs had constructed. He made a mental note never, ever to entrust the cleaning and polishing of his car to Ossaf's Duty gangs again, no matter how junior the boys.

But alas, the car was not as it should have been at all. When Baker came level with it he discovered that the front of his Austin Healey was transformed. The wings had been unbolted and removed and now stood propped, lights upward, against either side of the tunnel. The frog-eyed lights stared up at the roof boss-eyed. The bonnet was on the floor, crooked on something - the battery. Around the engine, wiring stood erect all over the place: cut, yanked, undone. The engine itself looked shrunken, naked, pitifully small and powerless.

Bob Rowell was reassuring.

"We'll look at the whole thing again in the morning, Dick. In the morning it will all look much better, much different. Stay here the night. In the sick bay. Matron will arrange it for you, Dick."

"You're finished, Rowell."

Baker was in an emotional state. He was furious, inconsolable, and he looked a mess too. The collar of his yellow rally coat was all skew-whiff. His trousers were wet and the turn-ups had collapsed around his ankles. His shoes and socks were soaked through and covered in grass cuttings and seeds.

"Ossaf will be here in a minute, Dick," Rowell continued. "Then everything will be explained, you'll see."

"Finished."

Rowell found himself treading on tiptoe with the despicable Baker, because, on the face of it, Ossaf had quite overstepped the mark, and in doing so had put Rowell in a tight spot. Baker was loud and clear - he wanted to call the police. He was going to call the police. Rowell had strong feelings about having police officers on the premises. The idea of a squad car, two squad cars maybe, in convoy, rumbling across the playing fields to the curious tunnel - and what about that tunnel? The Tunnel of Magic? How could that, or The Giant Maze, be explained? Where were the Health and Safety Certificates? - to discover Baker's dismembered sports car – well, it was all too fraught with difficulties. He found himself having to treat Baker with a quiet affection and respect he could not easily pretend. From here Baker could cause real mischief, could threaten Rowell. Indeed, he had already done so. This was painful, given Baker's contribution to Coxcomb, where he had never been anything but an irritant.

At the back of his mind Rowell had another idea, though. He could not quite believe things were as they appeared. He could not quite believe that Ossaf would ever have put him into such a compromising position. Such treachery was no doubt in his nature, and deeply rooted there, but it most certainly was not in his conditioning in regard to Rowell. Nothing like it had ever happened before. Rowell's interests were always at one with Ossaf's. If Rowell fell, Ossaf fell. Loyalty was mere self-interest, no virtue attached. That had always been their tacit understanding. And Ossaf was much too smart to get himself into a tangle with a buffoon like Baker. No, there was more to this. Ossaf must have something up his sleeve, Rowell considered, and that is why he wanted Ossaf here in his study, with Baker, right now.

"I'm sure Ossaf can explain, Dick," Rowell murmured again. "I'm sure he can put everything right."

Baker was not insensitive to the discomfort that Rowell was trying so hard to cover up. He knew how much Rowell hated police involvement in any aspect of life at the Hall. Even when his own car was stolen he hadn't pursued any proper enquiry.

"Be sure of one thing, Rowell," Baker warned. "Even if he is able to put my car back together, which I very much doubt, I shall not be content with an apology from Ossaf. I want a full enquiry. It is high time this place had a thorough going over by the proper authorities!" He repeated that. "The proper authorities! We're in a parlous state!"

Rowell nodded, and remained silent. Yes, Dick. He met Baker's glare full-on, but, he hoped, not defensively. He sustained his equanimity. How galling it was, though, to hear Baker on such a high horse, as if he'd ever cared . . .

There was a soft knock at the door.

"Come in!"

Parsons opened the door just wide enough to duck his seal-eared head inside the Principal's study. In fact the gap was so narrow his ears caught between the jamb and the door. Extraordinary that he still did that, Rowell noted, after all these years.

"Ossaf is here, sir," he said apologetically. "He was over in Mr. Crampton's room all the time, sir," he added.

"Tell Ossaf to come in." Rowell wrinkled his nose and winked at Baker, as if to say, *Now we shall get to the bottom of this, Dick, don't you worry!*

Parsons withdrew. Ossaf entered, opening the door wide with ostentatious confidence. He turned and closed the door, then approached the Principal's desk. He stood to one side of the desk, facing Baker, so that an allegiance was established between himself and the Principal. He stood in his accustomed pose, with his hands buried in his blazer pockets, his thumbs fastened down the seams.

"Ossaf . . ." Rowell's gaze remained on Baker. "Mr. Baker would like to know what you have done to his car. Explain yourself."

Ossaf stared straight at Mr. Baker too.

"Mr. Baker's car is required for The Grand Fete, sir."

For a moment Baker looked incredulous. But then, instead of expressing his outrage, he half closed his eyes and took on a tone of infinite weariness and superiority: "What on earth are you talking about, Ossaf?"

"It is needed for The Tunnel of Magic, and also for The Giant Ghost Train, sir."

Baker's high, smooth brow rippled all the way up to his hairline.

"As a generator, sir," Ossaf explained, "for the lights and effects - the ghosts, the ghouls, the vampires, the mummies, the werewolves - "

"You are talking about my car, boy!" Baker exploded. "My personal property! Have you gone mad?"

"Sir," Ossaf said, and he glanced at Rowell, then back at Baker, "it is for the Fete. We all must make sacrifices for The Grand Fete, sir."

"I don't care a damn about the bloody Grand Fete! I care about my car! You have stolen and vandalized my car! And now you are going to answer to the police, *young man!*"

The emphasis on 'young man' was clearly meant to bring Ossaf out of his adolescent fantasies and his flouting of school rules into the adult world of legal authority. This subtlety put the conversation on quite a different footing, but not in the way Baker might have expected. What Baker didn't realize was that in adopting such a contemptuous tone with Ossaf he quickened a reciprocal contempt, a loathing even, that was just as strong, or stronger, but – unlike Baker's open scorn – was quite indiscernible. Baker was up against the full strength of Ossaf's acting talent.

Baker was the only member of staff who had ever stung Ossaf. Years ago he had made a remark when Ossaf was a new boy in exactly the contemptuous tone he'd adopted now. "You know what your trouble is, don't you, boy?" he'd said to the tubby but fierce little darkie. "Your trouble is you haven't got a personality." There was a terrible truth in the remark that Ossaf could never forgive Baker for laying bare. It was a truth with which he had never been able to come to terms. He could not meet it. It cast him out and left him searching blindly for a role, a cause.

But now, in response to Baker's contempt, Ossaf only bowed, in his mock-ceremonial way, and turned to Rowell, whose face remained set, still the model of equanimity.

"Mr. Rowell," Ossaf said, "there is something I wish to show Mr. Baker and yourself." Ossaf turned back to Baker and took a breath:

   "*'tis death to me to be at enmity, sir -* "

   "Oh shut up, Ossaf!" Baker was quite beside himself now. "We don't want your cod Shakespeare here! We don't want that here! We don't want it anywhere! You're a bigger peasant than all of them – than Pez Rankin himself! - did you but know it! And you're about to get a very rude awakening, boy!" With this Baker got to his feet. "Having heard what your Head Boy has to say, Mr. Rowell, I should now like to telephone the police. I shall use your telephone right here, if you don't mind, and if you do mind, I shall use a different phone. It's all one to me. But you will not stop me. That is not within your petty power, Mr. Rowell!"

   Rowell looked grave, but his confidence was very high and his eyes remained squarely on Baker, even though looking upwards now. He had heard what Ossaf had said. He had felt Ossaf take control.

   "What is it that you wish to show us, Ossaf?"

   Ossaf said nothing but executed again his small bow to Rowell and turned back to Baker, who now stood bearing down at him from his superior height, and with all the gravity of manhood.

   "After Mr. Baker has made his call, could we please go to Mr. Crampton's room." It was not a request. "I need Mr. Baker's opinion on a film we are showing tomorrow evening."

   "Not tonight, thanks, Ossaf," Baker drawled, his weariness and superiority returning. He ignored the Head Boy's bizarre digression. "After I have made my call, we will be talking to the police. No films tonight, thanks, Ossaf. Nice thought, though." He returned to Rowell. "And after I have talked to the police, Mr. Rowell will pay for me to take a taxi home to Gorleston. I shall not return to the Hall until my car is repaired and delivered to my doorstep. And all that is going to cost Mr. Rowell a very pretty penny!"

"What is the film about, Ossaf?" Rowell asked. His gaze had dropped from Baker. He knew the game was over and the game was won. He polished his glasses, then folded them and set them square on his immaculate purple blotter.

"It is a blue film, sir," Ossaf replied.

"A blue film?" Rowell looked up at Ossaf. "You mean a sex film, I take it?"

"Yes, sir."

"But is it suitable?"

"Yes, sir. Highly suitable."

"Well, what is it about?"

"In this film Mr. Baker penetrates Mrs. White via the anus, sir. Intercourse lasts about eight minutes."

"Eight minutes!" Rowell said, and he looked askance at Baker. "Baker! Why are you always rushing into things?"

Chapter Nineteen

Cabin'd

The rogue element, the humorist and cynic, the spoiler of O'Donnell's quietude, the irritant in Rowell's bed of leisure, was now, as Ossaf put it, cabin'd, cribb'd, confin'd, bound to saucy doubts and fears. He was an honoured guest of the sick bay, and of Matron's devoted attention. Dick Baker now attended all his classes. Dick Baker now helped out with the Duty gangs. Dick Baker now did what he was damn well told.

If he didn't, his film would he screened and he would be thrown to the wolves. Life for Baker at Coxcomb would become intolerable. But there was not only the fear of that ruinous personal humiliation - and a murderous Dr. White - Dick Baker now faced financial ruin. Bankruptcy.

Homelessness. How was he to wriggle out from beneath the mountain of debt he'd accumulated since joining Coxcomb's establishment, if he were forced to leave it? Who would pay the mortgage in Gorleston? Forced to leave without a reference, his picture in The Gorleston Gazette, then The News of the World – a blue film star, a corrupter of the flower of the nation's manhood. Who would listen to his defence? He could see the pictures in the newspapers of the bailiffs turning him out, of him standing with his bags outside his very own front door. He could see the gauntlet of his long and empty street, and the net curtains rippling and twitching one after the other all the way down, tugged by ancient, arthritic hands - There he goes. That porn-star bloke. He's finished. Good riddance. Never liked him anyway.

One way or another prospects no longer looked good for Dick Baker, and the change had a marked effect on his health. At Rowell's insistence he'd been holed up in the sick bay since Ossaf had taken his car. In just three weeks he'd lost all his idle plumpness. His neck had slackened, leaving an ugly wattle, and his sandy hair had become dry and brittle and had begun to fall out in handfuls. He suffered continuously from what he called, with a painful grimace, "gut rot". The brisket, tapioca and suet did not agree with him. But when he grumbled about this to Matron, who was actually quite devoted to his care, she only brought him something she had laboured over herself in her own quarters, something she had slaved over for hours and hours on her Baby Belling hotplate, stooping, stirring, peering into some lumpy discoloured sauce, crying into her pot of lovelessness and misery more tears of frustration at her own drunken incompetence, and adding this and that until she'd created something quite inedible.

"Take that bloody muck away, you old crone!" Baker shouted at her, wasting what little energy he had. "Get out of here! Leave me alone, d'you hear? I'd rather starve to death."

It was as if Dick Baker had been diagnosed with a terminal illness. To anyone who'd listen he cited a host of ailments that changed from day to day. But people avoided Baker now, erstwhile emissary to the modern era. Baker was depressing. Baker was a bore.

There was still one person who cared, though, and one place where he was still welcome. At Woodlands, every Thursday, he could twitter in his hypochondriacal way to his heart's content, because Mrs. White looked forward to his visits more than ever, even though she no longer found his company amusing or physically pleasurable.

They remained in the kitchen with a fresh pot of tea and an ample supply of buttered toast, jam, and expensive biscuits, sweet comforters for the sickly Mr. Baker. Clara White took some trouble to look as unattractive as possible, but after Baker's first visit as internee she realized such precautions were unnecessary. His libido had collapsed with his health. He had no appetite for anything more than buttered toast and biscuits. Fundamentally, Clara observed, when the chips were down, Baker was just like all of Rowell's lackeys – infantile. All that worldly mockery and cynical indifference was tough as eggshell. Well, the egg was now pricked and blown. He ate his buttered toast and his biscuits with a sulky greed Clara found hard to forgive. She tried to ignore the butter dribbling down his chin, the crumbs floating in his tea.

The way things had turned out, Clara needed an ally and Baker was the only candidate. Newlings was out of the question, and she had considered but in the end dismissed the sanctimonious Tim Jackson. She was better off with a lapsed reprobate than an earnest prig.

Her concentration was focused on one target – the boy Ossaf. Ossaf had now become, for want of a better word, her procurer, her pimp. His revenge for her initial snub was now complete. Clara was not squeamish about such language and would not have objected to his role, if the relationship had not been so one-sided and exploitative. Now he took half the money she charged the boys, and half the money Newlings paid her, and she knew very well that it was an arrangement whose terms could only worsen.

For his part Baker had a fatalistic view of the whole business: there was nothing he, she, nor anyone else could do except let things run their course. They had to wait for Ossaf to make a mistake, have a change of heart, or to get bored, or for Rowell to exert some irresistible pressure on his slave, though it was impossible to see quite how he could do that, or why he would even want to try. Ossaf had a lucrative business now, Baker said enviously, and a business plan to go with it that could project well into the future, even after he'd gone. He had grown up a bit. Perhaps he was saving up a nest egg for his departure, he said bitingly to Clara.

It was true that Ossaf had begun, at last, to see things in temporal terms - to understand that we live, we earn, we die - but notions such as business plans and nest eggs were just the stuff of Baker's jealous fantasy.

Ossaf was busy selling new films, or rather ideas for new films, to Hooley's father, who had bought both the Newlings and Baker material, and was now impatient for things of a more extreme nature. In fact he had begun exerting pressure on his own son to obtain more high class and top quality material. This put the loafing, long-haired

Hooley, once so striking and original and adult with all his dreary pornographic talk, under the virgin Ossaf's command. Ray Hooley had become anxious and withdrawn. Besides the powerlessness of being trapped between his own father and Ossaf, he also suffered the weekly humiliation of never making the cut for the sessions with Clara White. Every Friday he was left behind to 'beat his own meat', as those who went off to the sessions liked to put it. Now he went about unshaven, his sideburns untrimmed, and he chain-smoked all the time. All the worry made him careless; he'd only escaped the barber's van on its last visit by hiding in the woods, starving in the woods, till after dark. But the pressure from his father remained constant, relentless. Hooley's father knew he was in a race against time to get stuff out. Coxcomb could not last.

But no matter what pressure he put on Ray Hooley, it could not reach Ossaf. At the moment it seemed Ossaf was content to take what he was paid for his films, and from Clara White, and breeze along while the going was good. How long that would last before news broke to the world outside, or before Ossaf himself leaked the news to the authorities, or sold the story to the papers, was anyone's guess. As Baker pointed out, Ossaf was not a predictable fellow, and it was upon his whimsical actions that everyone's future now depended.

Baker's fatalism was easy to understand because it was partly informed by his relationship with Clara White herself. Baker had been betrayed by her and she could not very well cover that up. That knowledge kept surfacing between them, bobbing up in their conversation like a message in a bottle. Whenever she suggested that he should actually do something, go out of his way to entrap Ossaf, to further some plot she had conceived against their mutual enemy, Baker's eyes steadied on hers, and their grey irises cooled and hardened. Why on earth should he help her now?

She had been trapped by her own greed and they both knew that. Ossaf had fished for her and he had caught her. She was obliged to admit to Baker, in order to regain some trust, that she'd fallen for the story of his conspiracy with Newlings, and she'd believed all Ossaf's tales about Newlings' savings. Those savings! Baker chuckled dryly. At one point Ossaf's intermediary – Anthony Hallett - had hinted to her that Newlings, years ago, had had a win on Ernie, "a massive windfall on the Premium Bonds!" A win so large Newlings would not discuss it under any circumstances, not with anyone at all, a win that had redoubled in shrewd investments in property, oil and gilts. Those savings! Clara had heard so much about Newlings' savings from both Baker and her husband, and in a curious way from Newlings himself, because he was always so guarded on this subject, that of course she'd believed what she wanted to believe, and she'd fallen for Ossaf's line that she could only prise open Newlings' shell and scoop out his pearl of great price by blackmail. Then Ossaf showed their film and she was trapped.

The fact that Ossaf had done that, seen that through, shown that film, scared Baker. Baker believed all Clara's confessions, and believed they explained why she was taken in by Ossaf, but this only confirmed his worst fears about Clara's character. Clara White, he'd decided, had turned out to be a pretty nasty piece of work, and no mistake. And to think that once upon a time he'd entertained his own fantasies of domestic bliss with this woman. That had been madness, looking back. Oh, where life led you when you followed your cock. She'd turned out to be so nasty she was her own nastiest enemy. The witch of the woods, the bitch of the woods, indeed. It was as obvious to Baker as it would have been to anyone else - except Clara White – that, on the contrary, blackmail could never have been the way forward with little Jimmy roll-your-own.

Well, Baker considered, what an ironic and expensive miscalculation. Anyone could have seen that, as far as Newlings was concerned, the slightest softening, the lightest show of affection from her, the smallest gesture of respect, would have opened whatever treasure chests and bank accounts he possessed like a cry of open sesame, and he would have poured all he had into her precious lap. Love, kindness, tenderness, or a mask of the same, had been all that was needed.

But Baker could not see that the move from prostitute to blackmailer ridded Clara of the obligation to have intercourse with Newlings – an irresistible temptation. To have done things Baker's way would only have deepened that hateful relationship. But, whatever the right and wrong of it, Clara knew only too well now that falling for the blackmail idea had not been the height of her folly. She was too embarrassed to confess to Baker that earlier on she had imagined that Ossaf, being what he was, a boy of eighteen with no knowledge of the world, could not only be outwitted, but could be seduced if necessary, codded and coddled if necessary - so that he might surrender, in part or in whole, his share of the pornography spoils to her!

Oh, such vague, vain notions, so wide of the mark. She could see it all so clearly now. What had she been thinking of? With Ossaf there were no promises to fulfil, only threats. She had been tricked, duped, gulled. Half her income now went to Ossaf. And what for?

To Clara this was the deepest cut of all. Instead of

the money accruing somewhere, being hoarded somewhere by Ossaf, as in Baker's barbed jibe about a 'nest egg', so there remained the possibility it might be regained and used for its original and worthy purpose - to change a life, to provide escape from a life - instead of that, the money that she earned, the money the boys' bobbed from their parents or stole from the pompous prig Tim Jackson, or from the broke and defenceless Crampton, or from the penniless Rankin, or from the fantasist Egg Taylor, who, according to Baker, had just told Rowell he couldn't stay much longer because of the terms of his new contract, which he was expecting any day now from Brian Epstein, manager of *The Beatles*! - instead of that money, so hard fought for and won from these fools, being hoarded in some secret place where it could be imagined in all its finery and shining glory, in all its treasure chests - instead of it being kept somewhere – anywhere! - it was squandered on whatever Ossaf needed for The Grand Fete - it went on chipboard, nails and paint!

But at the same time, in Ossaf's childish profligacy, Clara found grounds for hope. Someone with such puerile ambitions must be outmanoeuvrable at one turn or another; it was just a question of finding the right time and place. News of such an opportunity was what she sought from Baker on his Thursday visits, over buttered toast and biscuits. But there it was again: *She had betrayed him.*

Ossaf had paid her a bonus, twenty-five pounds, a pony, to give in to Baker and let him have that 'special kind of intercourse' she'd so long denied him, and then another twenty-five pounds on top of that to do it quickly, before the good doctor got around to fixing the hole in his ceiling. Fifty pounds! It was the last time she and Baker had had sex. Now she was no longer intimate with Baker, and was out of pocket too. Baker came here and drank her tea but gave her not a penny. And he never touched her or held her any more, and sometimes she needed to be touched and held by someone who liked her, or who had once liked her, just as any other human creature needs to be touched and held and comforted from time to time.

The conversations on Thursday mornings were often trying. Baker was usually morose, and when he did speak, he was often cryptic. This morning he said, after she'd played mother and poured his tea and added milk for him:

"We are to be part of The Grand Fete."

Clara said nothing. She did not understand.

"We are to be part of . . . The Tunnel of Love."

It was a gloomy joke.

Baker took a biscuit without asking, bit it, ate it, and watched Clara sit down the other side of the kitchen table. He watched her pick up her teacup and cradle it in both hands for its warmth.

"What do you mean?"

"Hallett is painting us in."

"Anthony? Anthony Hallett? Are you sure?"

Baker nodded. It was indeed true.

At that very moment, high in the Art Loft, a garret above Crampton's projection room, complete with sloping ceilings and leaky skylight, high in the Art Loft Hallett was at work, under Ossaf's direction, on the interior effects of The Tunnel of Love. Ossaf sat hunched on the corner of a table under the sloped ceiling, his head on one side, judging the works in progress. He was eating monkey nuts, and discarding the shells all over the yellow linoleum floor. Hallett showed him the first canvas, and they compared it to the original image projected onto the whitewashed wall. This image was a still from the film of Newlings and Clara. It was from early in the film, when

Newlings lay on his back on the candlewick. Hallett's canvas concentrated on Newlings' face alone, triple life size. Newlings' expression of eager anticipation had been brought forward to orgasmic ecstasy. His features were hacked, flattened and spread about in cubist chunks of colour. Newlings was still recognizable, and that seemed to be a clear intention, but the distortions and the primitive use of colour – bright green for the saliva spots – gave his face the mock terror of an African mask, chiselled out of fear and lust. But at the same time, with its slanted, red and watery eyes, the mask had a sad-clown aspect. The portrait bound together Newlings' crapulous ruin with the sexual weakness that had led him to it. Under the skylight Hallett and Ossaf inspected the picture and seemed to agree that it was satisfactory.

Ossaf nodded and shelled a monkey nut.

Hallett set Newlings' head to one side and crossed the loft to the slide projector. He operated the projector manually and brought up the next image. He adjusted the focus then came back and took up his second canvas. On the wall now was a still of Baker and Clara during anal intercourse. The image was mainly of their two bodies, with both faces averted from the camera. On his canvas, to get around the problem of the hidden faces, Hallett had broken up the natural attitudes of the bodies. Ossaf liked this effect so much he demanded that Hallet actually break Baker's neck and reset his head so that his face leered round at the viewer. Then he demanded Hallett rotate Clara's head, doll-wise, to offer her witch's lust directly to the viewer too. Instead of hair Ossaf wanted Clara's head alive with medusoid snakes, the longest and thickest of which he insisted should be elongated penises. It had hurt Hallett to paint his sweetheart in this way, and he knew Ossaf was forcing him to do this for his own vicious reasons, but Hallett had avoided his hurt, and outwitted Ossaf, by taking things even further than Ossaf specified, so that Clara as a person hardly existed for him in the painting. Then Ossaf became so carried away with his effects he told Hallett to heighten the sex and violence of the painting even more - to add details like smashed teeth and bloodied lips, spills of blood and pumped excrement, and pints of semen jelly splashed across Dr. White's buttercup candlewick.

Ossaf shelled and ate another nut.

Hallett seemed deep in thought.

"They'll need a lot of light, of course," he said tentatively. No one ever asked Ossaf for anything. It was an unspoken rule by which the balance of power remained unquestioned. "I mean, there will have to be good lights in the tunnel, I think. Don't you?"

Ossaf nodded. "Baker's headlamps," he said. "Full beam."

Hallett looked from the canvas to Ossaf, and his eyes narrowed in admiration.

"We'll need more than these." Ossaf gestured dismissively at Hallett's grotesque artwork. He slipped off the table and walked to the door, crunching his discarded shells underfoot. He opened the door then stopped and turned.

"Roast them in sulphur," he said. "Wash them in steep-down gulfs of liquid fire!"

Chapter Twenty

Second Opinion

"The question of Dick Baker . . . In all fairness one assumes, at least one can't quite believe . . . "

On his purple blotter the light refracted through Rowell's dangling glasses, tracing the circular ruminations of his mind, while he stared into space. He was at his most indifferent, leisurely and evasive. He couldn't see what the fuss was about. He had both Tim Jackson and Dr. White in his study, petitioning that for the sake of the community at large, and 'in all Christian decency' (from Jackson), something should be done about Dick Baker. Rowell was frankly surprised. He really couldn't focus on this. It seemed the least of their worries. Baker was far less a nuisance now than he had ever been. A few weeks ago he had motored in whenever he pleased, in his rattle-bag sports car. Not any more. Those days were over, and not before time. Now he attended his classes by day and was tucked up in the sick bay by night, under Matron's tender care. Rowell was quite at ease with the arrangement, and O'Donnell was positively delighted. It had taken years off O'Donnell, who never left his office these days.

But White and Jackson, earnest emissaries, the shaggy cuckold and the young do-gooder, were saying things about Baker's health that, if true, were more than a little disturbing. It seemed that since he had taken up residence in the sick bay, Baker had actually become sick, both in body and mind. Matron tended to him with dedication, his presence there had given her a new sense of purpose - she'd evidently come off the bottle, to some extent - but, by all accounts, the more closely she tended to him, the worse he became. "Whatever diet she's put him on," Jackson observed, "it's no good. She's starving him to death." Dr. White concurred, in his pompous but understated way: "There is not much of practical benefit from that quarter." But these two, Tim Jackson and Dr. White – Dr. White! Good heavens! It was most unusual for Dr. White to complain about anything! – Tim Jackson had brought him along to lend seriousness to his cause, no doubt – but these two senior members of staff were even more worried about Dick Baker's mental balance than his physical health. His mental balance. Now, what on earth was that? What could that mean? Tim Jackson complained that Baker had fallen into a pit of apathy so deep he'd dragged down the morale of the entire staff room with him. There was a certain professional obligation, wasn't there, he argued, laboriously, to cheerfulness, or if not cheerfulness then at least to stoicism, a degree of politeness, a willingness to communicate with one's colleagues. Baker had given up on all of this. The effect of his apathy was all the more marked, Dr. White put in, because he had once been so affable and hail-fellow-well-met, so full of jokes and stories. Dr. White went on to claim that it was "like having a dying man in their midst". No mincing of words now from old Whitey. And physically, Baker looked sick, very sick indeed, Rowell was plainly advised. His skin was slack and ashen and he'd become so very thin. Last week Dr. White had been obliged to help him out of one of the armchairs after long break. Baker hadn't the strength to get out of it himself for his next lesson. Then over to Jackson again, who became rather graphic, rather vulgar. Just yesterday, according to Jackson, Baker had become incontinent before their very eyes. He'd jumped bolt upright on the lesson bell, but then stood weak-legged as a drunk, and as he stood there a dark shadow had spread around his fly, and some urine had escaped his trouser leg and trickled onto the staff room carpet.

"Did anyone clear it up?"

"Not to my knowledge, Principal. But that's hardly the point."

"Did he defecate?"

"No, Principal."

Rowell sighed, relieved. Then he chuckled.

"He wouldn't, would he? Not on our diet!"

"The point is he needs a doctor, Principal." Jackson's voice was grave now.

Rowell dug his heels in at the very thought of a real live doctor on the premises.

"Can't you tend to him, Doctor White?" he asked, turning back to White, shutting Jackson out. "Just for a little while."

"A medical doctor, Principal."

"But Matron - "

"With the greatest respect, Principal," young Jackson interrupted again, accompanying his interruption with one of his irritating, downward glances of impatience, "the case is now beyond the scope of Matron. Matron could be doing more harm than good. She's not feeding him properly and she could be administering completely the wrong medicines. Certainly they are not noticeably efficacious."

Rowell gave Jackson a hooded glance. "Not noticeably efficacious, you may say, Tim, but - "

"Principal, with the greatest respect - "

"We'll give it another week, Jackson!" Rowell declared, taking charge, leaning forward, drawing things to a close. "Dick's confidence has taken a knock, that's all. He'll soon rally. He'll bounce back. He's that kind of fellow. Great chap."

Jackson looked to Dr. White.

"I could take him to Yarmouth in my car, Principal," Dr. White volunteered. "Or I could call for an ambulance, if you prefer. I do think it is necessary to get Baker to a doctor. It may be that he is contagious. There could be an outbreak, and that might be disastrous."

"An outbreak? Whatever do you mean? An outbreak of what?"

"It's difficult to say. Further down the line the virus - if it is a virus - could mutate."

"Good grief. Is that your scientific opinion?"

Dr. White blinked. "That is my scientific opinion."

Rowell looked hard at the beaky Dr. White. He was a cuckold and a fool, but he was not to be put off. The contagious aspect was not something Rowell had considered, and it cast the matter in a different light. Urine on the staff room carpet, and no one had cleaned it up. Just as well then, perhaps. But suddenly there were risks, however remote, multiplying beyond the question of Baker's personal welfare, like the virus itself. An outbreak. Of what, though? Whenever Bob Rowell looked at Dr. White all he saw was a shaggy cuckold and a fool. That was all he saw. To listen to the man, let alone take his advice, seemed the purest folly - there was the contagion, surely. However, if White were prepared to take the matter into his own hands - such altruism for one's colleagues, indeed! - then who could argue with that? So be it. Highly charitable. Highly commendable.

"Very well," said Rowell with a sigh, putting on his glasses and gathering up some red and angry bills, final demands, from his desk. "We'll do it your way. Doctor White will take Baker to the hospital and we'll have him checked out. A second opinion. Jackson will organize cover for Doctor White's classes. Doctor White will go forthwith."

"I think it's for the best," Jackson said sententiously, as he and Dr. White rose to take their leave.

Jackson thought, closing Rowell's door with this victory under his belt, and smiling at the good Dr. White, that he had cemented an allegiance with a man he would never have previously considered an ally. He was pleased to find himself in agreement with the good doctor, and to have helped bring off their little philanthropic gesture. But in all of this he was deluded. Dr. White did not return his smile. He had agreed to assist out of pure self-interest. He had offered from the very start to take Baker to the outpatients' department of Gt. Yarmouth General Hospital in his own car. Jackson's concern for Baker's health had handed Baker to him on a plate. To avoid any aggravation with Baker, Dr. White asked Jackson to go and tell him what was happening, and to escort him to his car, while he set the work necessary to cover his absence himself.

Baker was most agreeable to being taken to the hospital, until he heard he was to go there in Dr. White's car, then he had a sudden change of heart and became recalcitrant. However, in his weakened state, against Jackson's muscular Christianity, he could not alter in the smallest detail what had been decided. In twenty minutes Dr. White, with Dick Baker beside him in the tiny passenger seat, started up his polished, beige, Fiat 850, and motored down the drive through the woods.

"What's all this about?"

"Some of us are anxious about your health, Baker."

"Matron is tending to me."

"Matron may not know what's best. That's the Principal's opinion."

Baker gave a dry and knowing laugh.

They were at the gates. The lowly Rankin opened the gates to let them pass. He must have had his instructions from Rowell.

"Thanks, Pez," Baker muttered to his closed window, with an effete wave.

They pulled out onto the main road. For a mile or so nothing further was said. Dr. White had the excuse of being preoccupied with the traffic, with all the cars drawing up so quickly behind him and overtaking his tiny Fiat in such a hurry, but actually this silence in the car worried him far more than the traffic. They had twelve miles or so to go until they reached Gt. Yarmouth, and during that time he had to make his move. There would never be a better chance than this.

But still the silent miles went by! Baker seemed content to look out the window at the watery landscape and enjoy put-putting along without further conversation, and this indifference made the job all the harder for Dr. White. Eight miles slipped away with hardly a word and suddenly they had only three miles to go before they reached the town. The hospital was on the outskirts. It had begun to rain quite hard. Dr. White slowed the car. A lay-by came up on his left, a quarter of a mile ahead. He indicated, slowed further, pulled in and stopped his Fiat behind a lorry carrying a heap of scrap metal.

"What's up, Whitey?" asked Baker. "Hmmn? Water on the points? Never buy foreign. Let that be a lesson."

Dr. White had already stopped the rattling engine behind them. He removed the ignition key. He turned to Dick Baker.

"What's the matter?" Baker asked. "Are we lost?"

"Baker," Dr. White said. "I think we need to have a chat."

Baker drew in his sunken cheeks, frowned in an over serious way, and tried to summon some of his old, sardonic humour to his expression. He had a pretty shrewd idea what was coming next and he had no appetite for it. Certainly he could not cope with any physical threat, though he thought that unlikely from the good doctor.

"I thought we were going to the hospital, Whitey. I thought this was a mission of mercy."

"We are going to the hospital. Have no fear. But there's something we need to discuss first."

Dr. White glanced down, bit his lip, glanced forward again at the truck of scrap metal, bound for the docks, no doubt. The docks, the open sea, the stormy weather, the Hook of Holland, the wider world, away from these intensely personal concerns, which must be brought to the light of day, here in the cramped cabin of his Fiat 850.

"Oh, do let's get to the hospital, Whitey. I'm feeling rather rough, you know."

"Not just yet, Mister Baker." Dr. White said, and he

gave his passenger a sharp look. "Not just yet. I haven't finished."

"Finished what? You haven't started anything." Suddenly Dick Baker knew how to deal with this. Dr. White's hesitation had given him the breathing space he'd needed. "I thought your job was to get me to the hospital, Whitey. Here we are, stuck in a lay-by, and I feel I'm going to have a relapse. I need a toilet, man. I mean I really need a toilet badly. Or your seat is going to get rather badly stained."

"It's about my wife, Baker."

Dr. White looked as steadily as he could into Baker's grey and slippery eyes.

"Well, what about your wife?" Baker replied. "Is she sick? Is she as sick as me?"

The beaky face of Dr. White had gone quite pale and his lips were dry. He could have been seventy again, more than seventy, and he looked far sicker than his passenger.

"You have been . . ." Here it came. He was going to say it. The actual words. They had to come out. To be disgorged. "You have been *fucking* my wife, Baker! Behind my back!"

Baker frowned quizzically. An eyebrow lifted, a corner of his mouth lifted, in a consummate expression of understated astonishment and incomprehension.

"Behind your back? What?"

"I said . . . that you have been *having an affair* with my wife, Baker."

"Have you gone mad, Whitey?" Baker laughed. "Look at me! You old fool! Look at the state I'm in! Really, Dr. White! Whatever next!" Baker laughed harder, more brazenly, more directly into the good doctor's face. "You better come along and have a check-up while we're

207

about it, Whitey! Now would you please get me to a toilet? Would that really be too much to ask? Or I'm going to make an awful stink in here. An awful mess of your lovely little foreign number."

Dr. White looked forward again through the windscreen. The lorry was pulling away, exposing a tall wet hedgerow of hips and haws, and beneath that a bright new litter bin. Litter, it said. Rubbish. Had he got it all wrong? He frowned, staring hard at the bin, and the hedgerow of hips and haws behind. Had he got it all wrong? Was he going mad? He did not know what or who to believe. He replaced the key in the ignition and started the car. He put on the wipers. As he pulled out into the traffic Baker said, with gentle charity,

"Best we forget this ever happened, Whitey, I think. Don't worry about it, old man. Eh?"

Now the confrontation had taken place, Dr. White felt calmer. He did not feel that he'd made a terrible fool of himself, as Baker wanted him to. No, no. The main thing had been to release those words to Baker into the open air, the words that had been caught up in his breast, pressing, turning, fluttering, like baby birds, or bats, or tics, or slithering winged parasites - what a relief to let them out after such a long gestation!

From here he had a place he could return to in his dealings with Baker. The business had been opened up, that was the main thing, no matter in what circumstances, and that made White feel calmer for the moment, which was about all he could hope for. In recent months his life had been dominated by one tyrant emotion. When not in Woodlands, he had got used to living very much on the edge. The slightest upset to his plans, the slightest provocation or aggravation hurled him into a torrid rage.

When he couldn't find what he wanted in the shops

– and how he loathed doing the shopping, again and again and again; it was so shameful! When he dropped his change or his car keys. When a test-tube broke or a flask was upset in the labs. When he discovered a hole in his shoe as he walked - so very briskly, head down - the damp path back to Woodlands. It was with him, the rage, from when he woke to when he slept again. It had become a self-stoking, fiery torment. He no longer needed the causal chain that led link by wretched link back to his miserable marriage. His anger was right there at the surface all the time. He had thought, in his scientific way, that it would do him good to dissipate the feeling, as if it had some quantitative mass, as if his psyche were a cistern that could be emptied and refilled and emptied again. But, through trial and error, he found this to be a false hypothesis. For several days he had taken himself off deep into the woods and smashed branches against the ground, thrashed branches against tree stumps, bent saplings until they snapped, uprooted smaller saplings and whirled them round and round and cast them high into the trees, using their clumps of earth and roots for momentum. He heard them crashing through the fragile winter trees with satisfying violence, disturbing crows and pigeons and making invisible creatures scuttle for cover all around. And last Friday not just invisible creatures but visible beasts – a dozen or so senior boys took flight at his disturbance, went scattering, running for their lives, not fifty yards from where he stood. Smokers, he presumed.

It had done no good. There had been no finite mass to dissipate after all. The feeling remained, swollen and tight inside his chest. All the violent exertion did was make him out of breath, and frighten him with a sharp pain around the heart. Heartburn was all it was, he prayed, but oh, oh such heartburn.

This meeting with Baker had done some good, though, it had done some little good, he repeated to himself, comforting himself, as he drew in at the district hospital car park, his sick passenger all but forgotten at his side.

Chapter Twenty-one

Disabused

One Monday evening in early March Bob Rowell opened a letter that confounded him. The letter had arrived by the afternoon post and, noting the postmark, he had set it aside to enjoy at the end of the day with his customary pot of tea and plate of shortbread.

The writer of the letter informed him, quite unequivocally, that Jimmy Tarbuck was not, after all, an O.C., an Old Coxcombian. The news gave rise to long forgotten stirrings in Rowell. He stared at the letter in his hand and shifted from buttock to buttock in his antique captain's chair, and the chair creaked sympathetically in the silence of his Principal's study. With this letter before him - so light and so elegant, with its blue italic script in fountain pen, such an educated script, on headed stationery – with this letter before him Rowell felt weak, vulnerable, under attack. And the world of Coxcomb Hall diminished, withered all around him. Its remoteness from the realities of life was laid bare. Its web of pretensions, which in the end were his own pretensions, had been broken and the fallen gossamer clung all around him, fastened him to his antique chair.

After the initial shock Rowell was furious. Baker's illness made it impossible to chastise him or damn him in others' eyes, besides, he would look a bigger fool himself for so doing. But it wasn't just Baker who was to blame. There were others. There was O'Donnell. There were the records. Notification might have come months earlier from O'Donnell. O'Donnell had given his personal assurance that the records had been checked and on more than one occasion.

Oh yes, O'Donnell had said, and he'd nodded, and looked into the distance, to the woods and misty streams, or to the ground, where he scraped the gravel with his scuffed and worn-out toecaps. Oh yes – he exhaled a sigh of whisky and Gold Leaf - There's absolutely no question about it, Principal. It's in the records. Tarbuck's an O.C. all right. To the core.

But actually there had been little to gain from trying to find any information from the heap of collapsed suspender files in O'Donnell's office, and O'Donnell had never even bothered to look.

The news that March Monday eventide had finally reached Rowell via Mr. Tarbuck's theatrical agency in London. A Mr. Huggins had responded in writing after several letters and phone calls from Rowell had elicited no response. Mr. Huggins' letter was terse and to the point:

Dear Mr. Rowell,

So, it was not a joke.

Please understand that Mr. Tarbuck ***never*** attended Coxcomb Hall School, if there really is such a place, and so he cannot be, therefore, as you say, an *Old Coxcombian*. Indeed, he has never even heard of Coxcomb Hall – I asked him - and neither have I, and nor has anyone in this office. Cranleigh, yes. Caversham, maybe. Coxcomb Hall, no.

There seems to have been a mistake. I am very sorry.

We would be grateful if you did not trouble this office again on this question or on any related enquiry. We are all very busy.

If you wish to book an evening of *'The Jimmy Tarbuck Experience'* we would be happy to send a scale of fees and we will see what can be arranged.

Yours very truly,
John Huggins M.A. (Oxon.)

The original story put about by Dick Baker that Jimmy Tarbuck was an Old Coxcombian had been the very inspiration of The Grand Fete itself. Without that story Rowell would never have conceived of such a thing. And now, with no light of Tarbuck's stardom beaming on his enterprise, glowing at the end of The Tunnel of Magic or The Ghost Train, without that light the whole thing took on a dark and dilapidated aspect. It took on an unmistakable aspect of failure, in fact. Already there were problems, according to Rankin, with the maze. Some juniors had broken into it and had got themselves lost. In their frustration they had knocked down a line of panels to escape. The slow voice of Pez Rankin, with its long Norfolk vowels, echoed in Rowell's mind -

"Whaat's to be dun, Mr. Rowwell?"

A light railway, hired from Gt. Yarmouth fairground at enormous and as yet unpaid for cost, had now arrived for The Ghost Train, and a rail-road chain gang of seniors, complete with chants and songs handed out and led by Ossaf, had begun to assemble the track on one of the rugby pitches. Rankin could no longer mow the grass.

"Thaat's gettin long now between the tracks. Whaat's to be dun, Mr. Rowwell?"

Rowell left his desk and crossed to his rotten casements. What was to be done? The sports field, once a pleasant and open landscape, with its series of magnificent white rugby posts – Oh, what rugby posts! What posts and what pitches! They would grace any public school in England! Any Cranleigh or Caversham or *Rugby*, even! – the rugby pitches were now marred with Ossaf's shabby constructions and his incomprehensible plans. The Vampire had once had a distant power, a mystique, squatting there in the corner of the field. Its presence had been reassuring, protective, and, for Rowell, commemorative. Now it was somehow part of the shabbiness of the preparations for The Grand Fete. Its wings sagged and it looked more lopsided than ever. Its camouflage was peeling. Its roundels were scrappy and incomplete. It looked like a dull, dead target.

Rankin had told some garbled story about an

obscene painting hanging up crooked in The Tunnel of Love or Magic or on the front of The Giant Ghost Train itself. What did this mean? What did it bode?

"Whaat's to be dun, Mr. Rowwell?"

At times like this Bob Rowell did what he always did.

Between the rotting casements of his long sash windows was a unit of mahogany shelving containing row upon row of popular long-playing favourites: *Nina and Frederick, The Singing Nun, The Ink Spots, Light Operettas*, and, of course, the albums of *The Black and White Minstrel Show* and *The Cliff Adams Singers*. Most precious of all were some albums featuring John Cussack as a solo artist. It was one of these favourites – *John Cussack Sings* - that he now removed.

Cussack's clean shaven, smooth and smiling face, topped with its youthful bouffant, stared out gratefully to Rowell from the colour portrait. Rowell removed the record in its dust-sleeve, removed the dust-sleeve itself and blew away some imaginary dust, then set Side A carefully on the turntable of his Ferguson stereogram. He turned on the stereogram and went to pour himself a drink while it warmed up.

Directly below, on the second floor, Newlings too was pouring himself a drink, and one for his unexpected guest. The evening had not quite drawn in and Dr. White stood at one of the casements of the second floor looking out across the sports fields. He stood at the very same place where, a floor above, Bob Rowell had stood a moment before.

As White took the tumbler of whisky mac from his reluctant host he gestured to the field. "What on earth's going on down there, Jimmy?"

It was Dr. White's new habit to use Newlings' first name. Newlings was not comfortable with this, nor with any of White's manoeuvrings towards a closer friendship. He stopped at the window and followed White's gaze. A line of boys had appeared, perhaps fifty or more, and they were passing tuck boxes from one to the other down a line to the nearest rugby post, where the boxes were being stacked by a team of seniors into a pyramid around the base of the post.

"What on earth is all that about?"

Dr. White's tone was light and playful. He wanted to share a moment of puzzled amusement with his friend Jimmy Newlings, before he got down to the business of his visit, which was to tell Jimmy all about his trip to the hospital with Dick Baker last Saturday morning. He had felt very much better since that trip, but he wanted to face the truth head on, pure and simple, the scientific truth, now that he knew what the truth was, and he needed someone to witness that confrontation in order to make it real. He had said as much to his host, friend and confidant. Trying to deal with the truth alone, trying to meet it, face it, wrestle with it alone, would no longer do – that way madness lay. There was a definite purpose to this visit, then, and he had no intention of overstaying his welcome or of enjoying too much of Jimmy's whisky mac this evening. Besides, Jimmy was far ahead of him already. The sour odour of whisky and Stone's ginger was strong on Jimmy's breath, and, to be honest, Dr. White didn't care to spend too long in Jimmy's company when his new friend had had too much to drink. Jimmy tended to become uncommunicative and sullen, a bit defensive, prickly - a bit of a bore, in fact.

"Something to do with The Grand Fete, one presumes," Newlings answered indifferently. "Some new sacrifice for The Grand Fete . . ."

At this moment, from the Ferguson in the living room directly above, came the pure, liquid sentiment of John Cussack's voice, poured into the finest Irish brogue:

"Danny Boy! The pipes, the pipes are calling!"

And with the refrain could be heard Rowell, singing along with his protégé, trying to keep up, from glen to glen, from vale to vale, across the mountain side.

The crow's-feet around Dr. White's eyes creased with amusement and conspiracy – old Rowell singing the *Londonderry Air!* - but Jimmy Newlings was not amused and did not smile or respond in any way to the good Doctor. He was only tolerant of his guest this afternoon. He wanted no further overtures to a closer relationship with Dr. White Esquire. Each visit brought the same tension for Newlings, the same question lurking beneath the surface for the first fifteen minutes of conversation. More often than not White was in such an abject and confused state when he called it remained unclear what his purpose was in coming at all, and these introductory minutes could be very wearing for Newlings, ducking and weaving through the conversation, trying not to give anything away while remaining solicitous towards his guest, trying to keep a clear head when he'd already had far too much to drink, and all the time finding White's company, in his cramped bachelor apartment, crowding and burdensome and tedious in the extreme.

Friends? Not really. No thanks. Not by a long chalk.

This evening, though, the good doctor's mood was light and transparent and there seemed no immediate cause for concern. All the more reason, then, that Newlings hoped his guest would drink up and go. Newlings needed his isolation these days. Time was when he would have welcomed any visitor to relieve his loneliness, but now, mainly because of the drink, he preferred his own company above all others'. He spent his days with a faint pain behind his eyes, an alcoholic headache which never quite faded before his evening session began. Other symptoms were taking hold. A lack of appetite, a sourness in the pit of his stomach, that taste on his breath which no amount of boiling black Nescafé or boiled sweets could quite displace.

Worst of all, his sleeping patterns had gone. Frequently he awoke in the early morning to find himself still fully dressed, lying on the sofa. Or he awoke because he'd rolled off the sofa and fallen heavily onto the floor. His sleep was fitful and he remembered too easily his dreams, which had become nagging in their insistence to be understood.

In the most familiar dream he was a boy once more, a lonely, only child at his mother's home in Filby, on the Norfolk Broads. He had paddled his ancient second-hand canoe to the other side of Filby Broad. There was peace at the other side, in the lee of the wind, peace from the longings of his lonely boyhood. A moorhen emerged from the bulrushes, swam close by his canoe, dived beneath it, resurfaced the other side and disappeared again. The child Newlings sat completely still with his paddle across the green canvas decking, the bow of the canoe locked in the rushes. Black drips from the ends of the oar returned to the blackness of the water. In this perfect, remembered stillness, Newlings was tempted to lean to one side and roll, infinitely gently, into the welcoming darkness of the water, to join the black moorhen down there beneath her blacker water, but when he succumbed to the temptation his old canoe capsized too soon every time and tipped him onto the thin, damp piling of his living room carpet.

The images of the dream were as clear as the early morning landscape that he saw when he picked himself up and stepped uncertainly to the window. He drew the curtain, and steadied himself there, holding onto the damp pleats with a trembling grip. The mist lying on the long reaches of grass, the higher layers of mist pinned up briefly by the white rugby posts and the winter trees - all this was no more real or true than those remembered images of boyhood revisited in his subconscious. His gentle suspension on the water was an image, exaggerated and prettified, to be sure, but true to the peace of mind he had lost decades ago, and could never regain.

Newlings was not an evil man, whatever that might mean. He had fallen into the ways of paedophilia out of chronic and insupportable frustration, aided and abetted, led astray, by Rowell and the temptations of the boys in his charge. As soon as help of another kind was at hand Newlings had taken it, seized it, and now he was stuck fast in the charms and spells of the bewitching Clara White. Either way it was a question of enslavement. For most of his life he had wrestled with notions of self-denial, trying to ignore the ungovernable impulses of the flesh, and on and off, in his youth, he had tried to lend stricture to his self-denial with scripture, but that had never held good for very long. He knew too much history, had too strong a sense of evolution, and had been for too long persecuted by so many godless boys, to be much convinced by religious notions.

But no one gives up hope, sister of faith, ever, and Newlings had always held at the back of his mind the notion that, if he made enough money, he could not only buy his liberty from Rowell's thraldom but could also become, with his independent means, a quite eligible bachelor, one whom some other lonely creature - a divorcee or widow perhaps, down on her luck, looking for help and affection - might be tempted to care for, and even to cherish. A few years ago, when the position of matron had been advertised, he had naturally held out some hope that he would meet that companion sooner rather than later, and he had been bitterly disappointed at Rowell's selfish design to employ an ancient, sexless and incompetent crone, someone who brought with her her own pitiful baggage of inadequacies and unhappiness. Similarly, when he saw Dr. White venture out into the world, and not so very far, and return with a lovely young bride, he was again hopeful that at some point in the future he too could strike out beyond the sharded walls and find someone with whom to share what remained of his existence. He had tried advertisements in newspapers and magazines, but as soon as his correspondents learned of his circumstances all but the most adventurous, or the most desperate, lost heart.

The few who had actually come out to see him at Coxcomb always happened to be working-class mothers, separated, lonely and poor. Naturally he only arranged such visits in the holidays. For some reason he couldn't understand, for their trips to see Newlings at 'The Hall', every one of these women adopted the dress and manner of the working class as represented by contemporary British cinema, or British television. After the second or third such visit, he genuinely wondered if such women were play-acting, having fun at his expense, because their style of dress was so extreme, and their accents were so bold and so similar. Every woman wore high-heels, and was tight-bloused and chubby-cheeked, and her blonde hair was stacked high in a beehive, in the style of Barbara Windsor, or a seamstress from *The Rag Trade,* with Reg Varney.

They always came by taxi, and Newlings always paid for the round trip in advance. "Had a lovely ride out here, fanx. Fanx for that. Don't know what I'd 'ave done, really. Very grand here, int it?"

They minced around his rooms on the second floor of the Victorian wing, touching his things, stroking his things, and filling the air with their fancy scents as they flitted about. Newlings hated their restlessness, their poking and peering and shameless assessment of his heirlooms, and the way they kept passing by his long sash windows in full view of anyone outside the Victorian wing. Whether Rowell or Rankin or even Ossaf ever saw these blonde, bright creatures passing Newlings' windows or not, somehow Rowell always got wind of such visits and put in an overbearing and discomfiting appearance, all lathery smiles and yellow teeth -

"Ah! And who have we here, Jimmy? Delighted to meet you, my dear . . ."

After an hour or so, and some tea and cucumber sandwiches, and maybe some sherry - which induced, with the stress and anticlimax of the visit, terrible headaches for Newlings – these women went back in their taxis to Gt. Yarmouth, or to Gt. Yarmouth station, to their broken homes and errant children, and they never, ever came back.

But the truth was Jimmy Newlings could have accommodated his visitors elsewhere, and this is where he had failed to make a decision in life. Had he really wanted to make his circumstances more appealing he could have moved out of the Hall, but he was too jealous of his savings to do so. He had never boasted about money but there had arisen, thanks to Baker and others, this myth of his personal fortune. It was true that he had saved in earnest and had made shrewd and successful investments, but this was not the whole of Newlings' story. What Baker and the rest did not know was that for twenty years, since the death of his mother, he had rented out the furnished cottage she had left him in Filby as a holiday home. He had set aside the proceeds from this income in oil shares every year. This, and not his savings from Rowell's pitiful salary, had been his most lucrative plan to date, and he had never told anyone about it.

Alas, it was this capital that he had now started to draw on to pay Clara White. The thought of this dissipation of his assets, and with it all hope of one day finding companionship, was the thought that troubled him so much that he'd sought solace first in single malt, then in the new supermarket brands, and finally in whisky mac. By giving in to Clara's demands he was literally ruining himself, and he knew it.

"Jimmy, I feel you're the only one in this shithole I can trust, old man."

White was uncharacteristically foul-mouthed this evening, and it seemed phoney, borrowed, part of Baker's manliness. In the same way, he slugged back the last of his whisky mac and grimaced before sitting down, uninvited, at his host's rosewood table, whose French polish now bore so many scars and blemishes from White's earlier and humbler confessionals.

"I'm just a good listener, Whitey," Newlings said, with a worn out chuckle. He took a seat himself and smiled. "So, what's the news?"

"I took Baker to the hospital the other day."

"Ah, yes . . . I heard about that. Is he all right?"

"I don't know. There were some tests. Results not due till Friday."

"I see." Newlings smiled again. *Come on, man! Get it over and go! You ass! You cuckold! Get it out and get out!*

"I took the opportunity of saying a few words."

"About what?"

White looked down, tucked in his chair.

"Oh." Newlings feigned surprise and frowned, as if Dr. White had been unwise, reckless. "Whitey? I really think you should forget about all that, you know. Do yourself a favour."

Dr. White twisted his empty tumbler on the polished table. "He denied it, of course."

"Look here," Newlings leant forward, the very soul of reason, a frank and sincere friend. "Hadn't you better just leave it at that? You've cleared the air. Now put this bloody business behind you, once and for all. Forget about it. You're in danger of making a fool of yourself. In front of everyone. Not just me, you know."

White looked at Newlings and smiled. Newlings smiled back.

"Not that simple, Jimmy."

Newlings' smile withered. "Why not?"

"There's a canary."

"A canary?"

"A mole. A whistle-blower."

Newlings leant back and frowned. It was odd how White's mood seemed to have changed since his last visit. It was as if the idea of Clara's betrayal no longer affected him. Instead there was a sly triumph in his manner, as if he now held all the cards, as if he thought he knew all there was to know about Clara and her shenanigans. The scent of danger returned to Newlings, stirring up tired adrenalin with whisky mac. The atmosphere became charged once more. Again Newlings found himself in the uncomfortable and wearing position of having to guess, of having to go back and reconsider White's every move, looking for clues for what he might be up to. Again there was the fear. Was this going to turn into an ugly scene? A violent scene? The knife? The screwdriver? The phial of acid? In the face? In the eyes? Exhaustion with it all made Newlings bold:

"So who is your mole?"

There were several names Newlings could imagine coming back. There was little love lost between Baker and most of his colleagues. O'Donnell, or sly old Crampton, for example, or even the lowly Rankin - each was capable of such a betrayal, if only to alleviate the boredom of their captive lives. But the name that came back surprised him.

"Ossaf."

"*Ossaf?* Good grief! Ossaf?" Newlings had to hide his relief. "You don't trust him, do you? Above your colleagues?"

At this moment the volume of the stereogram was turned up in the apartment above for one of Bob Rowell's particular favourites. In fact the opening bars were sung as a clear duet between the tenor Cussack, and the baritone Rowell.

> *"I dream of Jeannie with the light brown hair,*
> *Borne like a vapour on the summer air!"*

But Newlings' mind had begun to race again. Ossaf. He had always taken care to keep his distance from this boy, who'd been a menace ever since his arrival. In recent years, under Rowell's patronage, Ossaf had become a law unto himself. And it was not only the power he held over his henchmen and Duty gangs. His influence was more insidious. He was far, far too clever for Rowell to control. He had outgrown Rowell long ago. Coxcomb Hall had been his devil's playground for years, to all intents and purposes. It was common knowledge that he bore Baker a grudge, but what he could have intended by betraying him like this, at this particular moment, was the burning question. Newlings detected implications, ramifications, for him too. But why? Why should Ossaf mean him harm? He'd always kept out of the boy's way, let him do what he liked. He'd always run away.

Dr. White took an envelope from the inside pocket of his Harris Tweed. He took it out slowly, reluctantly.

"Here."

His hand was trembling and the long white envelope exaggerated the tremor when he held it out across the table.

"Here."

White's features changed, became pinched, the skin bunched and wrinkled about his beaky nose. It was almost a fastidious expression, held to keep any stronger show of feeling in check. His features were in delicate, twitchy suspension. As Newlings took and handled the envelope White didn't seem to breathe. The air of sly triumph had been only that – an affectation, a silly mask of self-control.

Newlings undid the flap and looked inside. There was no paper, no writing, only a photograph. He hollowed the envelope and tipped the photograph onto his rosewood table.

It was a full colour still made up from a film slide.

Ah.

Newlings knew immediately that this photograph was meant to find its way onto his table, and that White himself might have been directed to this scene by a third party's subtle manoeuvrings.

"Horrible."

For the first time Newlings' voice was genuinely sympathetic. Until now the good doctor had always been, in the end, contemptible in his cuckoldry. Newlings had failed to see the blatant irony: that here was just another man, in a very similar situation to himself, who had had the very same hopes and fears and had tried to fulfil those hopes, vanquish those fears, with the help of this woman in the photograph – the very same woman, as it happened, about whom Newlings still entertained dreams of companionship and contentment in his own slavish way. But now, at last, he felt some measure of sympathy with the good doctor, and his imagination dragged in clues and scraps from other scenes and conversations, and he gathered together some vague idea of what poor old Whitey must actually have been through to get to this moment, this revelation, this point of no return. He remembered, even from the early days, when they were newlyweds, Dr. White's moroseness in the staff room, and the carping comments of colleagues when he left the room, the lewd jokes over shoulders, from curled, moustachioed lips, about his young wife, and his comings and goings to Woodlands in the middle of the day. And then of course in recent months, these visits to Newlings' apartment, these desperate and apologetic calls upon his time, when Whitey had searched for some friend to listen to his fears and give him honest counsel, only to meet more lies and bland assurances from Newlings himself, who continued to betray him week in and week out, and continued to pry into White's personal life, picking away like a merciless dentist, even as he dispensed his comfort and worldly wisdom and whisky mac.

"Horrible," Newlings said again softly, staring down at the photograph.

Dick Baker, caught at the moment of withdrawal, after anal intercourse with Clara.

Poor Dr. White had covered his face and begun to cry.

Chapter Twenty-two

The Spartan

There wasn't much room for Ossaf's bulk, nor the smell of his bulk, in Colin Scott's silo, and the visit didn't last long. Each had his own heavy-duty black rubber torch. As they crawled along the earthen floor on their knees, Scott directed his guest's attention to the various categories of inflammables, starting with the paper and cardboard materials. Orange baling twine, stolen from Rankin, secured the bundles in reef knots and half hitches. All knots were clipped short, no untidy ends. The bundles were arranged in rows according to size and weight, with the lighter materials (exercise paper, paper bags, old envelopes) the most readily accessible. Then cardboard of various degrees of thickness. Next carrier bags of wood shavings from Baker's Craft Shacks, a heap of dry sticks tied in armfuls, complete books (textbooks, dictionaries and hardback classics from the classrooms) bundled according to size, some chopped kindling, and finally, at the far end, the chemical stockpile of glue cans, tubes and aerosols.

Combustible vapours emanated so powerfully from this end that Ossaf's body odour was unnoticeable. Above all, there was the potent smell of petrol itself. In a pit covered with a plywood lid, which Scott now raised by a finger-hole, there nestled two gallon cans stolen from Rankin's tool shed. These were Scott's most treasured possessions. Two-stroke lawnmower fuel.

Scott shone his torch onto the shiny tops of the cans. They sat flush in their neat earthen pit. The tops were wiped so clean they looked polished. Scott unscrewed the caps. The stink of fuel intensified. Ossaf reached out and took a handle. He lifted.

"Both full," Scott whispered. "Two gallons."

Ossaf nodded and let the can slide back next to its twin, spilling some fuel. He shone his torch on the miscellaneous ranks of aerosols and glue tubes. Some of the tubes were full. Brand new. He recognized a particular kind from the Art Loft. Hallett was forever searching around for missing stock in drawers and cupboards. Here it all was. Expertly and lovingly cared for. There were even some old paintbrushes. They would be used, Ossaf surmised, to daub and smear the various incendiaries before igniting them. Ossaf stole a sideways glance at the puny Scott: the pale, triangular face and adult spectacles, the top-heavy head craning over his precious hoard. He was like a gnome with his treasure.

But understandable though that comparison was, it was misleading. No such associations belonged here, nothing fantastical or magical. Scott was concerned with things only as they were: the sticky, the volatile, the flammable. As if to prove the point, one incongruous bit of firewood lay tied into a bundle of twigs and sticks. It was a slender piece of black dowel, a wand - Rowell's baton, stolen from beneath the church lectern by his most treacherous chorister.

To Ossaf it seemed impossible to conceive of Scott parting with the contents of his silo. It was something he would want to add to forever. Here was a small boy's mania for collecting, the very spawn of boredom, taken to extremes, that was all. But again Ossaf was mistaken. Scott had assembled this material for a purpose and he intended to use it, and the time for executing his purpose was now. That was why Ossaf had been invited here. Scott had watched Ossaf and had waited for this moment, for the sea change, and had timed his invitation to perfection. Ossaf's mind was quick and treacherous, but not as quick and treacherous as the mind of the bespectacled eleven-year-old at his side, whose sensibilities had been tempered by years of ostracism and sadistic beatings, by continuous verbal persecution, and, worst of all, by never-ending taunts with half dead cockroaches, oozing their innards from the ends of wire coat-hangers.

Scott now chose this moment to shock his guest, to exercise power. From his shorts' pocket he whipped out a Zippo cigarette lighter - an item stolen from the prefects' room, and much missed from there. Ossaf recognized it immediately. Under the beam of his torch, Scott flipped up its hood single-handed. He had his thumb on the flint wheel. He glanced at Ossaf's face. Ossaf clenched his jaws. Did he remember the 'stoning'? Scott's eyes asked. Ossaf's mandible muscles bulged through his hairy jowls. The eyes, deep in their fatty sockets, were panicky, were fearful. No one had seen this in Ossaf's face for many, many years. A flick from Scott's thumb and the two of them would be cooked alive. They would be melted like wax, no merciful asphyxiation. Ossaf's downy face would burn from his skull; his muscle and gum would be boiled from the jawbone. His body fat, his lard, his vital organs, would all be melted into the humus beneath them. All that would remain of either would be a charred skeleton. A small boy's, and Ossaf's, not yet quite full grown.

Scott tittered, closed the lighter and gave it back to Ossaf. Ossaf took it and put it away: a weighty symbol of trust and partnership. Scott replaced the caps on the fuel cans and then their plywood lid. Master of Ossaf's attention now, he shone his torch to the other side. The old tennis net curtain, that had provided the original surface to the outer wall of the silo, was still visible as a neat latticework in this wall. Behind it, pressing through in places, was a mat of grass cuttings and twigs and small branches. But it was not the clever pattern of the wall that Scott wished to draw attention to. Fastened to the netting two thirds of the way down was a dirty sheet. Or rather two sheets, overlapping. Scott gestured to Ossaf to take up the other end of the sheet while he took up his.

Under the sheet, tied to the old tennis netting with slipknots of baling twine, were two long poles, and at the end of each was the shining axe of a crude halberd. The halberds faced in opposite directions. They were the products of Scott's labours in Baker's Craft Shacks, where he'd pretended to be working on a life-size mock-up of the Coxcomb crest, under Baker's neglectful eye, for The Grand Fete. Ossaf felt the axe of the halberd closest to him. It was razor sharp all the way round, right into the nick of the axe. The surface of the metal was lovingly coated in some fine grease or Vaseline to prevent any rusting of the head and blade.

Ossaf understood at this moment what he had been

brought here to understand: that Scott, this scrappy little fellow with his adult glasses, was actually ready to commit murder, to chop people's heads off and burn people in their beds.

Scott dropped his end of the sheet. It was a signal. Ossaf began his backward crawl to the exit of the silo, to the open air and safety of the rubbish pit. From there he disappeared again, slunk back into the depths of the woods, while Scott returned to the relative comforts of the Quad and the tuck box shed.

Sensitive and perceptive, Scott had gone out of his way to observe Ossaf's mood over the last fortnight, since Rowell's volte-face on the question of The Grand Fete.

Rowell had come out fighting after the Jimmy Tarbuck humiliation, determined to exercise his absolute power. The chipboard projects on the playing fields had become nothing more than an unsightly reminder of his humiliation, a mess to be cleared up. They ruined the view from his apartments. He instructed Rankin to break up the structures and clear them away, and to do it quickly, to use his tractor and his chain saw. Jarring adolescent fantasy had been allowed to take solid form in these extrusions, to erupt on his beautiful rugby pitches. With barefaced power he swept it all away. He consulted no one. He took charge and he acted. He didn't even go down there and have a look at what he was destroying. He never went near the half made tunnels of Magic or Love or The Giant Ghost Train, never saw the paintings suspended inside. Nor the elaborate system of belts that came off Baker's car, to drive the electrical gear that would power, eventually, the bogie-wheel carriage on its hired rails. He told Rankin to knock it all down and take it away with his tractor and trailer, and to return the hired railway to Gt. Yarmouth. Rankin did as he was told. Once he had smashed up and cleared away the chipboard tunnels and dismantled the hired tracks, he roughly hitched the front of Baker's frog-eyed Sprite above the gang mower and towed the car back to his shed, with its front wheels suspended in mid-air, turned in, droopy and forlorn. Rowell never bothered to find out what the purpose of the pyramid of tuck boxes around the rugby posts had been. He deployed the duty gangs himself to take all the boxes back to the tuck box shed, and that was that.

Rowell was at his most omnipotent. Away with this nonsense, he said, and away it went. The last thing to go was the first item made, and the most substantial and difficult to disassemble. He allowed a hoard of juniors, the very slaves who had erected The Giant Maze under Ossaf's command, to go inside and to knock it all to pieces, to trample it flat. There was a frenzy, a riot of destruction in there - shouts, screams, squeals of triumph and revenge, all quite disproportionate to the job in hand. It was over in a few minutes. Rankin loaded the smashed sheets of chipboard onto his trailer, folded up the tarpaulins and took it all away.

At last the Vampire squatted alone once more on the games fields. With all the uprights of Ossaf's constructions gone the plane looked less lopsided. Order was restored. The madness put away. Insurgency capped.

In this way, hardly thinking of what he was doing, Rowell destroyed not only the constructions themselves, of course. In taking away this scene, this set, he destroyed its creator and its protagonist too. Rowell did not care. There was no need to worry about Ossaf any more. His days were numbered now.

Ossaf sensed the laughter everywhere, around every corner, behind every door, titters from the youngest and weakest, guffaws from the oldest and strongest. It is a commonplace that the tyrant can endure all manner of hardship and censure, to the point of martyrdom, but he cannot endure being laughed at. Ossaf bore out this commonplace to the letter. Everywhere he went he overheard the whispers, the sneers, the jeers, the fleers:

'We all must make sacrifices for The Grand Fete!'

It became a malicious whisper on the breeze, and it cut him to the quick. In the end no one needed to utter it. The old refrain he'd used to lash his slave gangs now lashed his mind continuously.

He was a laughing-stock. With the debacle and demise of The Grand Fete he himself had been sacrificed, finished off. And Rowell had further news for his Head Boy. Payments stopped after his eighteenth birthday, just a few weeks away. Then he would be released into the world, the big bad world.

"The big bad world!" Rowell repeated, with a patronizing nod, playing with his glasses on his purple blotter.

"Then you'll find out what life is really about!"

Ossaf said nothing.

He stepped back. He retreated, hands in blazer pockets.

He took to the woods.

Chapter Twenty-three

Escape!

"Everyone's been worried sick! Where have you been?"

To Jackson, caught alone in his classroom, the boy was a disturbing sight - and smell. The breeze from outside wafted in a rancid mix of sweat, foot odour and halitosis. Ossaf couldn't have washed for a week or more.

He was covered by his cape, the academic gown of the hapless Mr. Wills. Sightings of Ossaf over recent days had all mentioned this cape, saying that it looked, according to the trusty Parsons himself, as if it had been 'savaged by wolves'. It was true that poor Mr. Wills' gown was in tatters, but it had not been savaged by wolves or any other animal. It had been cut in a stylised, deliberate manner. Jackson could see that the cuts were not rents, they had been made cleanly with scissors or a knife. The gown had been reduced to a kind of crepe paper that billowed and fluttered on the incoming breeze. The effect was certainly dramatic. Jackson did his best to compose himself but he found Ossaf's dark reappearance at the door of his classroom, from which there was no other exit, unnerving.

It was a miserable mid-March Friday afternoon and Jackson was again in his overcoat, behind the unbreachable wall of beige exercise books, trying to get up to date with his work. But suddenly none of that mattered. All the unhappy drudgery of his life, which he was too apt to dwell on these days, being bogged down as he was with more and more classes by Rowell, left with less and less time to implement his reforms - all these matters and duties that weighed down so heavily on his spirit were at this moment sloughed off. His senses were on heightened alert.

Ossaf's blackness absorbed all the weak March twilight in the doorway. His hair was no longer fastened back with its lick of oil. It hung in greasy tails across his forehead. His face, shadowed by his hair, seemed darker than ever and his pitted eyes all but disappeared in the shadows of his baleful countenance.

"Ossaf! Speak up, boy!" Jackson called. He didn't know quite what tone to adopt to give the right impression, to keep things on their sane and proper footing and retain an air of authority.

He attempted a laugh. "But to what do I owe this pleasure, Ossaf?" he asked cheerily. "Do come in!"

Cheeriness worked no charm either with the stolid

figure in the doorway. Jackson frowned, removed his reading glasses, and looked concerned.

"Ossaf . . ." Jackson turned in his seat. "Are you all right?" He adjusted his chair noisily on the suspended floor, giving himself room to move, to defend himself, to dodge and duck and flee, if need be.

With this movement from Jackson, Ossaf took from inside his shredded cape a long handle. He pressed a button and a bright blade sprang out, lean and silvery. A hoodlum's flick-knife. Another quality purchase from *Gun & Game*. Ossaf held out his arm and slashed in two a part of the dangling sleeve of his gown.

He stepped towards Jackson, with his opened knife. Jackson tried not to shrink into his chair.

Ossaf spoke at last. But so slowly. With such reluctance.

"*Do you . . . go back . . . dismay'd?*" he asked. His voice was very quiet and calm, very theatrical, stretched on the rack of this, his ultimate performance. Underneath the strands and tangles on his forehead his eyebrows rose and he asked again, more freely - "*Do you go back . . . dismay'd?*"

Jackson smiled and adjusted his position, "Now, Ossaf. No need for histrionics . . ." He searched for Ossaf's eyes under their raised brows, in their shadowed countenance. Although Ossaf's eyes returned his stare, and returned it steadily, there was no connection. They did not meet his own eyes. Jackson found this the most disquieting thing of all. He tried to remain light, friendly, normal, in control: "Now look here, Ossaf, you are not Othello, you know! You are aggrieved, no doubt, and not without cause, quite rightly so, but in the end you are simply Ossaf, Ossaf. Not Othello." Jackson looked to the floor then up again. He cleared his throat, thrust out his jaw. "You know,

Ossaf, I have been meaning to say this to you for some time. You know, you really do have a lot more going for you, a hell of a lot more going for you, than Rowell or O'Donnell might let on at times, and - "

But Ossaf stamped his foot and brandished his long blade, and spat out his lines at Jackson, so that his poison spittle actually landed on Jackson's clothes, on his desk and on his beige wall of exercise books –

> *"With this little arm and this good sword,*
> *I have made my way through more impediments*
> *Than twenty times your stop!"*

"Oh for God's sake, Ossaf!" Jackson cried out aloud, hoping that someone outside would hear his cry.

Ossaf took his knife in both hands and pointed it directly at Jackson, outstretched, as if steeling himself to attack, but then, with a flick of the wrists, he pointed the blade inwards to his own chest.

> *"I took by the throat the circumcised dog,*
> *And smote him - thus!"*

Saying so, he plunged the knife deep into his chest.

But of course he was smiling and unharmed. He had slipped the catch and the blade had retracted.

"Just a joke, old boy!" Ossaf mimicked Jackson's public school tones.

A squeaky laugh escaped from Jackson. "Quite so, Ossaf, but - "

"Do you like Othello, old boy?"

Jackson hesitated. He had to humour him, humour him:

"Othello is marvellous, Ossaf, but you really

mustn't - "

"Are you afraid to die, old boy?"

Jackson laughed again. Come on! Say something! Humour him, humour him:

> *"That we shall die, we know; 'tis but the*
> > *time,*
>
> *And drawing days out - "*

"That men stand upon."

"Quite so."

Ossaf came still closer, and with him his odour, his stink. Quite unignorable, yet he was oblivious to it. Jackson recognized that Ossaf was entirely within his own world now. There was something like a swagger in his movement, as if he felt the weight of a cutlass on his chubby hips, as if he felt its hilt move in its sheath, on his virgin hips. But now, incongruously, his voice was effeminate, almost whining with contempt:

"My little girly Colin Scott, sir . . ."

Jackson frowned his supercilious frown, unpegged and taken down from his range of frowns.

Ossaf continued:

"My little girly bade me say . . ."

A dramatic pause.

"Yes?"

"Jackson is noble, wise, valiant and honest – So he must be spared."

"Spared what?"

"Death by fire. Roasting on a spit."

"Ossaf! Snap out of it! What about Scott? What have you done to that boy?"

"*The ides of March are come . . . So says my master.*"

"Ossaf. What have you done to him? What have you done to Scott? Where is he? If you have menaced or harmed that boy in any way I will personally - "

At that incipient threat out came the blade again. Ossaf slashed the air in front of Jackson's handsome face, closer and closer, only inches from his face, his Roman nose –

"I see that nose of yours, but not that dog I shall throw it to!"

Ossaf stabbed his knife through the open exercise book on the desk, sinking the blade through the book into the wood. He turned about in his billowing cape and swaggered, as if encumbered with the weighty cutlass, out of Jackson's classroom. He called over his shoulder at the door:

"The ides of March are come . . . Avaunt! Be gone! . . . So says my . . . Master!"

"Wait!"

"Go! Go now! You must be spared! Death by fire!"

By chance some do not suffer. Such a one was Anthony Hallett.

Earlier that Friday afternoon he had come to the woods alone, as they had arranged, but Clara had been waiting for him at a spot some distance ahead of their rendezvous. There was the scent of an expensive perfume instead of her usual patchouli oil. She wore tight black corduroys, a fashionable roll neck jumper, and on her head - a very striking and unusual dash of colour - a broad, purple hair band. She was also wearing, deliberately perhaps, the same light black raincoat she had worn when Hallett had met her that very first time with Parsons, back in the autumn.

Tonight Hallett was in his best clothes too. She had told him to wear his best for this evening. He wore his flared jeans and his fisherman's smock, the outfit he wore for Sunday afternoons alone in the Art Loft.

Clara took Hallett through the arm. It was a deliberate effort on her part to start the evening off on the right note. She wanted to save him any awkward approaches. She led him back through the trees in the direction he'd come from, then across, towards the Woodlands drive.

"I thought we'd go away, tonight," she said.

Dr. White's polished, beige, Fiat 850 was sitting in the drive under the trees, facing the direction of the Quad. The sight of the car excited Hallett, but, as was his way, he covered his excitement with an air of detachment, of wry humour.

"I'm game," he said, and smiled his long curled smile, but then reddened. "I haven't got much money, though."

"Tonight, for once, we don't worry about money," Clara said. She opened the driver's door.

The car was very cramped and inferior inside, with a metal dashboard and rubber floors. To Hallett it smelled of that blend of Old Spice talcum powder and anxious sweat that came from Dr. White himself, that exuded from his Harris Tweeds, that predominated in his labs even over the formaldehyde. But this did not matter. Hallett was in a car, and for someone used to cycling everywhere in all weathers, a ride in any car was an interesting treat. When Clara turned the ignition he was startled and amused to discover the engine was behind them. He looked back and laughed: "Funny little thing!" he said. "Like a toy!" He saw her suitcase on the back seat. "Where are we going?"

Clara noted her passenger's moneyed arrogance and presumption. What did Anthony Hallett know about what it took to buy a car, even this car, this Fiat, and put it on the road? But she let it pass. She wanted to enjoy her young lover's company tonight and that would involve all sorts of compromises. Theirs was a delicate relationship: she found herself on the one hand tempted to be herself, to treat him as an adult lover, even to be quite passionate with him, and on the other hand she knew she had to keep a distance. At times she could tell he was getting in too deep. He had written her notes, letters, of late. He had taken to using her name a good deal too, unwittingly practising the role she had half-heartedly ascribed him for tonight.

"So where are we going, Clara?"

She made her delicious reply: "To a hotel."

Rankin was already at the gates to let a taxi out. Was that the back of Jackson's dark head in the rear seat? Clara waved and smiled at Rankin and passed through. The thought that Jackson was sneaking off somewhere too for the weekend caused any remaining fears and attachments to fall away for Clara White. Now they were on the open road and the reality of the adventure was taking hold. No one had stopped them in the woods or at the gates, no one was wagging a finger at them from a passing vehicle. They were alone in the Fiat speeding away at 40 m.p.h. - then a wobbly 50 m.p.h. - away from Coxcomb Hall.

For her, forever.

In the passenger seat Hallett leant back and allowed his excitement to flow from his belly to his groin. 'To a Hotel.'

Detecting something in this movement Clara reached over and squeezed his knee, his thigh.

Hallett hesitated, then covered her hand, drew it

closer.

"Any particular one?"

Hallett was familiar with all the Gt.Yarmouth hotels from countless token exeat teas with his brother Christopher, and his cold, unloving mother.

Clara glanced across. Such a fresh-faced, blue-eyed youth, with his quick wit and his blond cowlick. She was right to enjoy him.

"The Old Ship. On the front."

"Oh, very good."

She rested both hands on the wheel again and concentrated on her driving, but Hallett continued to look at her, in profile. She told herself to be careful.

She had left Dr. White reading the paper in his club chair in his spotless living room, warming his feet by the fire she had kindled for his return in the afternoon. Over the weekend she would be tackling upstairs – spring-cleaning the bathroom, hanging out the sodden candlewick - and then, last but by no means least, she would be cleaning, and then *redecorating*, from top to bottom, the bedroom. She would even plug up the hole in the ceiling with some Polyfilla she had bought.

Dr. White had told her what she was to buy at the shops and what she was to cook tonight. He had decided that tonight he would like pork chops in cider . . . and on Saturday he would have steak and kidney pie with puff pastry, and for Sunday lunch he would have roast lamb and rosemary, with a bottle of Spanish red wine, if you please. He had drawn up the shopping list, and given her the right money for everything, to within a shilling or two. And when, with a shy smirk, he had handed the list to her she could see at the end of the groceries, in his invisible hand, some other Friday night treats, some sex acts for the good doctor, some domestic bliss, at last.

Oh, everyone knew who wore the trousers now.

Clara had booked a suite at the very top of the hotel, the most expensive in The Old Ship, commanding magnificent views over the North Sea, the esplanade and pier. The evening was drawing in and on the horizon were black and angry skies. Another storm was coming. Turner skies, Hallett thought. He stood alone at the window looking into the distance with his painterly eye, while behind him, in the bathroom, Clara prepared herself. She had asked him to choose from a selection of fancy underwear.

Creeping along in silence close to the shore were a few weekend sail-boats, and in the middle distance some fishing smacks. A white ferry sat motionless further out, held in a lone sun blot between Felixstowe and the Hook of Holland. Everything held its place, from this far up, framed in a double-glazed and silent stillness. On the esplanade a newspaper seller hurriedly packed up his stand as the wind gathered force. Young Hallett enjoyed that detail. From here the struggle of life was something to be looked at and enjoyed, like art.

Chapter Twenty-four

Crossbows and crossbars

From the ramparts Ossaf surveyed things by the light of a cloudy moon. Behind and below him a dozen or so very junior minions, the weediest and most easily intimidated of all, laboured in exhaustion. The tuck boxes had been brought out again, under cover of darkness. They were now arranged in a double wall spanning the width of the nearest rugby posts, forming a battlement that reached a foot or so short of the crossbar. In the second wall six flights of steps led to three ramparts.

Behind the double wall another line of boxes was being put in place on the ground. These were laid out separately and arranged so that they could all be opened in the same direction, with their lids facing backwards, leaving ready access to their contents from the battlements.

These boxes had come, and were still coming, by silent wheelbarrow, from the Dell. Some were heavy and required careful handling. All were filled with a precious cargo. The exact order of their arrangement was a question of great importance over which the intellectual Scott took personal command:

"It's a question of logistics," he kept saying. "The logistics, you see . . ."

A toxophilite's pride, a six foot ash bow, a replica of a longbow from the middle-ages, some £60 worth, had been lashed sideways to the crossbar of the rugby posts. The fixing was more cunning and involved than it appeared: the bow was attached to a separate piece of wood held at either end by clamps around the crossbar. This arrangement allowed it to rotate, so that it could be used in the manner of a huge crossbow, sighted at any elevation, but pointing in only one direction.

Standing aside from the bow, Ossaf looked to the Victorian apartments, some seventy yards or so up a gentle incline. In the cloudy moonlight not much could be seen of the low trees, the laurel bushes, the horseshoe of rose beds that lay in the intervening distance. It would not be easy. It might not work at all. But as if to lend encouragement the moon emerged from cloud for a moment and showed the Victorian roof in ghostly silhouette. It was so clear Ossaf could see the ridges of the gables and the first runs of dewy pantiles. It did look very much within range. Scott had said it was well within range. He said the bow could reach five times that distance. Scott had calculated everything with the help of a trigonometry textbook: the angle, the distance, the parabolic trajectory - the only element unaccounted for was the wind. Tonight there was a strong following wind. Another storm coming, perhaps.

Scott was taking time off from the arrangement of

munitions to direct work on the final platform of boxes he needed behind the middle rampart. From this lower structure, which had to be very stable and secure, those who loaded and fired the bow and who adjusted its elevation would be guided by lookouts along the wall.

Ossaf turned from his view of the Victorian wing and spoke down to Scott. He demanded to see the plans once more and Scott went back to fetch them.

Scott's knees under his shorts looked so pale and weak, his frame was so slight in the moonlight, and yet all about him now, at last, was the insupportable weight of his long held obsession. He returned with the plans, now creased and grubby, attached to a clipboard. The drawings had been done to a large scale with a Rötring pen, leaving plenty of white space, so that they would be easy to follow in bad light by poor eyes. Nothing had escaped Scott's foresight.

While Ossaf puzzled over the drawings with his fading torch, Scott took the opportunity to check some details with his temperamental conspirator.

"Did you speak to Jackson?"

Ossaf nodded.

"He will not be in there?"

"He will not be there."

"Thank you." A pause. Scott had learned to take these pauses between subjects when talking to Ossaf. There should be no sudden movement of any kind. "Did you get spare strings?"

"Three."

"And spare arrows?"

"Thirty."

"Thank you." Pause. "Does the bow need any treatment? Does it need to be loosened up or stretched, oiled, anything like that?"

"The bow is made of ash," Ossaf said, turning a page of the plans over and fastening it under the clip. "It is unbreakable. Before the bow breaks, your arm will break, the man said."

In the dark Scott smiled. That was the kind of talk he wanted to hear.

"Did you know that a long bow can penetrate an inch of solid oak at two hundred yards?"

Ossaf didn't answer, didn't look up from the plans.

"At the Battle of Crecy," Scott continued, "in 1346, English archers so devastated the French with their long bows that the enemy lost thirty thousand soldiers and twelve hundred knights, for just one hundred men."

Ossaf still did not look up.

"You should have paid more attention to Mr. Newlings, Ossaf. I always listened carefully to Mr. Newlings. And after tonight you will never be able to listen to him again."

Scott no longer needed his plans.

Driven by the following wind the first drops of rain began to hit home even while Scott was finishing his platform. He was doing the last work himself, heaving heavy tuck boxes into position by their sharp metal handles, while other juniors stood by shivering in the wind that had whipped up across the rugby fields. The rain intensified and helpers slipped from the ranks. Ossaf's grip, even on the very youngest, smallest, weakest, was not what it had been. He still stood on the lonely parapet, in the strengthening rain, staring up at the Victorian apartments. The wind made the rain sting. Already he was soaked to the skin.

A few moments later, when Ossaf descended,

drenched but magisterial, to the loading platform, Scott stood alone. The rain had flattened his thin clothes to his child's body, and he looked pitifully frail in the stormy darkness that had overwhelmed them. Ossaf's torch was nearly finished, but he could still see Scott clearly enough to note his expression. Scott's nose was wrinkled up to stop his glasses slipping, which made him look questioning, as if he were seeking a decision from Ossaf, but behind his rainy glasses his eyes were resolute.

"It is over," Ossaf said, in a voice that betrayed the defeatism that had now settled in his soul. "You are washed out. You are a washout."

He stepped down from the platform and walked off into the rainy darkness, abandoning Scott and his plans and his logistical details, just like all the rest.

"Your binoculars!" Scott called after him, into the rain.

No reply.

Scott thought: It is better like this. Better by myself, and for myself, alone.

He knew exactly which boxes to take, but he could take them only one at a time. Already very tired, he heaved the first into the wheelbarrow and began the slow ascent towards the Victorian wing. He was pricked on by ideas and images from one of Mr. Jackson's classes - an early Conrad tale, the story of Gaspar Ruiz, the revolutionary whose zeal knew no bounds, who finished his campaign with a cannon strapped to his back, crawling up a mountain towards the enemy. So it was for Scott, heaving his barrow across the thick and sodden grass towards the path that led back up to the Quad.

Water rushed down the path against him, and he could not see where to direct the wheel in order to avoid the worst incline and the deepest ruts. He told himself that when he reached the gravel it would be easier. And so it was, but the gravel squelched and slipped beneath his boots and he lost traction, and the broad wheel of the barrow created an invisible bow wave that soon became impassable. Scott stopped and twisted the barrow, thinking that he'd hit some large stone or root. He had to get down on his knees and scratch away at the front of the wheel to discover the problem. He cleared a little distance, a yard or so in front, so that he had an easier start and a chance to pick up momentum. As the gravel thinned toward the top of the slope the barrow became lighter and easier to manoeuvre.

Twenty feet or so from the porch he stopped. He stood and listened to the wind and rain and his own fierce breathing. Then he heaved the box out of the barrow and carried it to the shelter of the porch. The rain penetrated at the front of the porch, but not far. He unclipped his father's flashlight and shone it briefly at the door. The door itself, and a semi-circle of stone before the door, were perfectly dry. He switched off his flashlight and clipped it to his belt again, then headed back towards the barrow and the battlements. The second box was not so heavy. He deliberately gave himself this relief, understanding that he might be taxing his strength more than he knew, before tackling the third and last, the heaviest of the three.

The first two boxes he set at an angle facing inwards, then opened them so their lids offered further protection. He left a gap to funnel the draught, and wedged his torch in the gap, pointing up, its base resting on the porch flagstone. Inside one box - the second and lighter one - was thick card and kindling and some wasted glue tubes. Inside the other was bone dry tinder in various lengths and sizes, with some full and half full aerosols.

He began to make his fire. He took his time,

distributing paper and card evenly, building a cone of sticks against the door, setting the aerosols strategically in the thicker kindling. By the time the boxes were empty he had created, from their contents, a wigwam of firewood some three feet high against the door, with the precious aerosols buried tight against the door itself. From the third box he took out the two gallons of two-stroke mix. He emptied half a gallon over the pyre, taking his time, making sure the card and wood had a chance to absorb the fuel, then emptied the rest into the empty boxes at his feet. The second gallon he poured all around the crack between the door and the rotten sill, pouring slowly so it had time to leak through and seep into the carpet the other side. He emptied the second can in this way. Intuition told him to keep some fuel in reserve, but he was too tired to think the question through and invested everything in this one conflagration.

Inside the lid of the petrol box was taped a book of Swan Vestas safety matches. His fingers were wet, dripping with fuel and rainwater. He had to step close to the pyre to keep himself out of the rain and rub his hands dry under his arms and between his legs. The first match lit with one strike on the book and even as he let it fall the flames and heat rushed up at him, singeing his eyebrows above his glasses. He whipped his torch away, lost balance and stumbled backwards out of the porch. He tossed the matches into the blaze and sprinted back down to his battlements.

By the time he had mounted the ramparts and found Ossaf's binoculars the front door itself was ablaze and the paint was burning and bubbling all around the architrave. The telephone wires into the Victorian wing were fastened to a wooden block above the porch. With luck the roof would come down and drag with it the block and wires before anyone awoke, but in case that didn't happen Scott had already taken precautions.

At around midnight Ossaf had secured the main gate with bicycle chains and padlocks. It would not cause much delay to a fireman's bolt-cutters, but it would create distraction and confusion and waste precious time. He had a second plan for dealing with the fire brigade, which again had depended on Ossaf's assistance, but which he would now have to execute on his own. He came down from the battlements and untied from the base of the rugby post one of his precious halberds and carried it back up to the top of the parapet. Standing on the furthermost box in his wall, Scott's task, which should have been Ossaf's, was to lob the halberd over the drooping telephone wire. For a short distance the wires ran parallel to the games fields. It was not something he had practised before. This part of his plan had been too remote to warrant close attention. He lobbed the halberd as high and as far as he could but it fell at least ten feet short of the wire. Ossaf might have had the strength to throw it that far but it was in truth a hopeless task now.

The halberd sank, pike first, into the longer perimeter grass. Scott left it there. He glanced back at the blaze. He took up the binoculars again and slipped the strap round his neck. The roof of the lead-lined porch was beginning to sag. The flames were already through the panels of the door – and beyond. The fuel inside had given a head start. But on the third floor, Rowell's floor, a light had come on. Scott let the binoculars drop to his chest and took up his torch. He skipped from box to box, binoculars dangling, back to his loading platform and the *Gun &* *Game* long bow. A quiver of arrows protruded from one of the boxes on the platform. Rowell's lighted casements made excellent targets – tall, oblong yellow targets -

exactly as he'd seen them in his mind's eye for so many years. But the first arrow went high and clattered against a wall somewhere, way off the mark. A gust took the second and it fell wide without a sound, landing God knows where.

Failure. Having come this far, he thought, reaching for a third arrow – failure, miscalculation, discovery. He was a washout. He couldn't risk tampering with the elevation of the bow, not at this stage, and anyway it was a two person job. Perhaps it was a question of power alone – he'd been using too much of the bow's power. For his next shot he drew the bow back only two thirds of the previous distance. A second after release, to his astonishment and delight, he heard glass shatter. He jumped up and down on the platform, stamped and shrieked uncontrollably with the thrill of this success, nearly losing his glasses in his excitement. The arrow must be stuck fast somewhere within the soft red linings of Rowell's apartment. Rowell's light snapped out and the targets disappeared. There were voices. Or rather one voice. Rowell was shouting, trying to penetrate the drunken slumbers of O'Donnell and Newlings below, and to rouse the supremely capable Tim Jackson. But, Scott knew, Jackson would not be there, and these wasted seconds looking for him would cost Rowell dearly.

If Rowell had set aside all thought of his neighbours' lives and his own ruin and disgrace and had contacted the fire brigade immediately, he might have had a chance - but Scott knew he would not do that. And while he thumped at the doors below, the roof of the porch came down and with it the block for the telephone wires, tumbling into the blazing hole at the front of the building.

"Fire! Fire!" called Rowell, in his fruity tones. "Fire! Fire!"

Egg Taylor

From where Scott stood the Victorian wing took on a ghoulish look. The windows of Rowell's living room, behind which Rowell - and O'Donnell too, very often - had spent so many afternoons gazing down at boys playing rugby, or juniors traipsing in, exhausted, defenceless, after cross-country, those two windows, in their sagging casements, had always given the building the look of a grim and overbearing human face. The face of O'Donnell or Rowell himself, in fact. But now the porch beneath those sagging eyes, the nose of the face, had gone. It had sunk inwards, releasing a tongue of flame below that licked around its own ghastly nasal cavity. There were frantic cries, shouts, screams even, from the apartments on the first and second floors. The screams did not belong to the face. The face ingested their noise, folded it in its flames and smothered it. Rowell's voice had fallen silent some time ago.

Had he been consumed, destroyed, or had he escaped through some back entrance Scott did not know about?

In order to make the fire spread Scott had to create a draught through the rest of the building. He climbed down from the parapet and took up his halberd from where it was stuck deep in the long grass. Carrying the muddied halberd at his side, and with Ossaf's binoculars banging on his feeble chest, he strode through the storm up to the Victorian wing. The blaze was now so powerful it illuminated the shiny gravel all around him and the driven rain shone in its light. Scott could be seen clearly. He even had a vague shadow. But the thought of a counter attack of some description did not even cross his mind. He felt invulnerable, he was both the inventor and the destroyer - he was, as Ossaf had put it to him, after visiting his silo, he was: *'the choice and master spirit of his age'*.

He approached the ground floor windows at the front of the wing and used his halberd to stave in the glass, knocking in all the lower panes to create the maximum draught at the base of the building. And while he went about this work he heard the fire speak back to him in pleasurable moans as it swept across the inner corridor, through doors innocently left ajar the previous evening, into the reception rooms of the building. He worked his way round, into the darkness at the far side, heading towards Rowell's gardens and garages, those private, sacred places where he'd laboured for so many weekends of his incarceration. After the brightness at the front of the building his eyes could not see much round here, and the cold and dark and wet were discouraging, but he soldiered on, feeling blindly for the window frames then knocking in the glass with the pike of his faithful halberd.

Fearlessly he went all the way to the adjoining garden wall. When he started back he was rewarded to discover that the flames had already penetrated the length of the corridor and now illuminated the interior of some of the rooms whose windows he'd just smashed, including Jackson's rooms. Jackson's wardrobe doors hung wide and his wardrobe was empty. The bed was neatly made. Nothing on the bedside table.

At the front of the building things had changed beyond recognition. All the lower windows were ablaze and the second story windows - Newlings' apartments - now contained an angry fireball that tossed and buffeted this way and that, obscuring everything. Scott stood back. The windows would shatter in the heat at any moment, it seemed, or the rotten casements would whip into flame and fall out one by one in huge, dramatic sections. That didn't happen, though, and Scott lost patience. He couldn't dawdle here in the rain. There was still too much to do.

Round the near side of the building he had to steel himself against the heat to get close enough to the windows, then use the full length of his halberd and bring the pike down on the glass from above. The work was harder, but no less pleasurable for that. He had finished the last of the ground floor windows and was about to make his way to the Quad buildings when he heard the sirens.

Without panic, at a leisurely gait, Scott left the scene and headed back to his battlements, his halberd by his side, Ossaf's binoculars bumping gently on his chest.

He cut down his longbow with the halberd's axe and retreated to the woods with his weapons, there to watch the spectacle of the fire engines, in all their red and shining glory.

Chapter Twenty-five

Paid in Full

It had fallen to O'Donnell to take charge of transport for The Grand Fete – the only responsibility he undertook - and he had ordered and paid for a sightseeing bus from *Gt. Yarmouth Pleasure Tours Ltd.* Ossaf came across the receipt in O'Donnell's filing cabinet. He noted the crooked stamp, *Paid in Full*, but could find no accompanying docket cancelling the order.

Over the last couple of days he'd been raking through various files and documents in O'Donnell's filing cabinet. There had been some interesting reading here. He'd also helped himself to O'Donnell's cellar of inferior scotch, laid down in serried half-bottle ranks in the bottom drawer. He enjoyed the vagueness the scotch brought to his days, despite the accompanying headaches. The receipt still in his hand, he swivelled back to O'Donnell's enormous metal desk - some quartermaster's cast-off - and consulted the calendar. It had not been flipped since the fire in March, the ides of March.

With that reference to the calendar he met, yet again, a familiar difficulty. He could not fix the date. How long had it been, exactly, since the fire?

He looked around.

His drunken mind drifted to life as it had been here, right here, in O'Donnell's office, prior to that date. He looked about this place.

The walls were drab and naked except for a few military prints. Men on horseback, very upright, staring across vacant, melancholy moors. Men alone against the dark and muddy elements, but in smart uniforms. In the corner behind the desk stood the wicker elephant's foot with the selection of canes, all present and correct. O'Donnell had made the juniors bend tight over his metal desk, reach across it and grip the other side, after they had pulled down their shorts. They'd always had to do that. Part of the ritual, that wriggling out of the shorts, to be naked and unprotected from him, then the reaching across to grip the opposite edge of the solid metal desk. Afterwards, the boy dismissed, O'Donnell slumped back with his scotch and his Gold Leaf in his warm fug.

Ossaf too had been caned in here as a little boy. But only once. His body had not pleased O'Donnell for some reason.

Now all of that, all that life, that way of life, all that activity and intensity of feeling, was gone forever from this office, from O'Donnell's cell, and day by day the stink of scotch and tobacco was getting staler and fainter on the chilly air, was becoming indistinguishable from the pervasive scent of burnt paint, wood and brick.

O'Donnell had been among the dead. His charred

corpse was discovered black and stiff and upright, much reduced, in its bed. He had been consumed by flames even as he tried to raise himself to the alarm. A fireball had leapt on his flammable screams as he sat up. For one mortal moment he had become one of the fire-breathing dragons of the Coxcomb crest.

Ossaf left the office chair and came round to plug in the bar heater in the corner of the room. In his drunkenness he had forgotten, yet again, that there was no electric power. No power in any of the buildings. He could not get used to living without electricity. There was none at Woodlands either, where he now spent his dark evenings and chilly nights. Before dusk each day he had to light a fire in Dr. White's living room for warmth and light, and keep it going until he fell asleep in his whisky stupor. He slept in his clothes in Dr. White's club chair, slumped before the dwindling fire.

But what was the date? What was the time?

It was morning, or midday perhaps. He emerged from O'Donnell's office, the receipt for the bus still clutched in his hand, and squinted up at the ceiling of grey sky.

Crows cawed. Sparrows flitted in the beech trees. Pigeons cooed and swooped. And behind the birds, all around them, all around their songs and movements, there was silence.

No telling what the time was.

Baker's wingless and unbonneted frog-eyed Sprite stood where Ossaf had left it in the Quad. It didn't run well on the two-stroke lawnmower mix and Ossaf only nursed it around the grounds, never drove it hard. There was no thrill in speed. It did not suit his mood. He used Baker's car as a convenience, to get him to and from Woodlands, round the Quad, down to the fields, round to Rowell's vegetable plots. Those plots now lay the other side of a vast, black, charred gap, where the Victorian wing had stood. It was actually possible - he had done it once, picking the route carefully - to drive over the place where the building had been. A demolition team had knocked down and cleared away the remaining structure. It had been too hazardous to leave standing.

Ossaf held the invoice up in the grey daylight.
Gt.Yarmouth Pleasure Tours Ltd. Paid in full.
This bus. This sightseeing bus.
Was it late, had it been, or would it never come?

He had his choice of bicycles. In their rush to get their sons away, many parents had abandoned - or guardians, uncles, friends, had abandoned - their boys' most prized possessions. There were bikes with mechanical speedometers, odometers, with chrome water carriers. There were fancy bells and horns. Ossaf went among the bikes trying the horns, each horn more mournful than the last. Their sounds seemed to draw in the burnt and morbid silence of the place tight around him. Like the noises he made in the tuck box shed as he went among the remaining boxes with a crowbar breaking open locks, looking for treats and secrets that had belonged to the lives now departed. The sounds of snapping locks and splintering wood were too loud and drawn out in the empty tuck box shed, were a giveaway to anyone passing.

No one was ever passing.

None better than Hallett's bike. The Dawes ten-speed. Swift and lean and handsome, like its owner. Remembering its owner Ossaf felt something. He shuddered, as if cold. These spasms, shocks, shudders of feeling, ran through him maybe three or four times a day.

They were not necessarily connected with Hallett, or anyone in particular, but they were always deeply painful. The cuticle of his drunkenness was scraped back to the quick of his sensibility. To what end he did not know, or care.

He refocused on the business in hand. He knelt and removed Hallett's locks with a set of bolt-cutters he'd taken from Rankin's workshop. Concentrating, scowling, worsening his headache, he walked around the bike, inspecting it, pinching the tyres. They were still firm.

In his uniform and his black cape still - all billowy shreds - Ossaf rode the bike one handed, while in his free hand he carried the bolt-cutters that he'd need again at the main gate.

Chapter Twenty-six

The Grand Tour

He could not help but note the looks from motorists and their passengers on his ride into town. The turning heads of wives in passenger seats, and then their children staring through rear windows. Ossaf's visits to Gt.Yarmouth had been few and far between. Someone else, some terrified fag or slave, had fetched and carried for him. Like the staff he felt out of his depth in town, but for Ossaf the currents were more cold and frightening: the young provincial English people, with their changing fashions and mores, made him feel such an alien, such a black alien, amid his own generation.

    This day, whatever it was, some time in late May, he was fairly sure, he felt more aware of his appearance in the eyes of others than ever before. Gt. Yarmouth was on holiday. He'd come at the Whitsun weekend and the weather was brightening up. The streets were crowded with young people but there were families too: young children with parents, escorting frail grandparents. Everyone was out to enjoy the sun and the festive spirit of the Bank holiday weekend. To Ossaf, in his defiled state and his weird garb, his black cape tattered and flowing, the whole town seemed like one enormous party from which he was absolutely and expressly forbidden. The noise of the party, though all around him, came from far off, as if through one of the seaside shells polished and set out on stalls, along with trinkets and beachwear and buckets and spades. Ossaf wheeled his bicycle through the crowd, realizing he was a nuisance, realizing too that he was so very unwholesome and unclean. The twelve-mile ride had dried him out and his mouth tasted sticky with O'Donnell's cheap scotch. His saliva had thickened to a savoury, unswallowable slime. He spat a gob of it in the gutter. People turned and stared and scowled. How long had he been like this? How many weeks had he lived like this at the Hall, idling his hours and days away, scratching around for food in the tuck boxes, the vegetable plots, the disgusting, derelict kitchens . . .

    Now that he was sobering up he became aware that his teeth had a filthy fur all over them. He had seen himself in the mirror every day in Woodlands, in the toilet upstairs, in Dr. and Clara White's bathroom, and he knew well how he looked. He had not cleaned his teeth for weeks. For months he had not bathed. There was only cold water. And besides, the bathtub was unusable. The Whites' yellow candlewick still lay soaking in the bathtub. Where it broke the surface, like a dead coral shelf, it was covered in an outcrop of mould that rippled in layers, in contours, in rising shelves, in lifted skirts of white and grey fungus, following the undulations of the sodden candlewick. Some prodigious spore had taken hold, thriving on the secreted proteins of Hallett, Newlings, Baker and Mrs. White. But not her husband.

Newlings. The late Jimmy Newlings. The life-giving proteins of the late Jimmy Newlings. Ossaf couldn't bring himself to touch the candlewick, let alone remove it. He couldn't go near it. It stank terribly.

He stank terribly. The stench of his own excretions, his sweat, piss, shit, and semen dribbles, all this stuck to him, stuck in his clothes, and only now, walking among his fellow citizens in their light, clean, summery clothes – the old people in short sleeves, their wrinkled, bony elbows jutting out everywhere - only now did he begin to feel the extent of his defilement. He would do something about his condition straightaway. He had money. Plenty of money. But where could he wash? Where could he clean his teeth? Should he go down to the sea and cleanse himself in the freezing waves?

He was in the high street, quite close, in fact, to the lane of antique shops which included *Gun & Game*, and on the corner of that lane was a men's outfitters. Ossaf propped Hallett's bike against the wall. He reached into his blazer pocket for his money and brought out a wad of notes that he'd tied with a rubber band from O'Donnell's desk.

Buying the new outfit was not a pleasant experience. He sensed the tittering of the staff and there was some hesitation before anyone came forward to serve him, but the wad of notes did the trick. He bought a brown worsted suit, a plain white shirt and paisley tie, and new underwear. He bought a pair of brown brogues and beige socks. His old uniform, including the shredded cape of Mr. Wills, he told the shop assistant to dispose of as he saw fit. The shop assistant did not object. The suit had been expensive, one of the most expensive they had. Ossaf wanted worsted, he said, because he knew the cloth well. He knew about worsted from Mr. Wills, who had told him that his own suit was worsted, and that he'd bought it because worsted was the local cloth. The yarn originated from the Norfolk village of Worsted in the Middle Ages, now Worstead, of course, only twenty miles away. All this Ossaf repeated to the salesman, bit by bit, as he tried on the various items he was buying, because the salesman, peasant that he was, had not known these elementary facts about the cloth he was selling from his very own shop window, hadn't even known that Worsted, now Worstead, was only twenty miles away.

Ossaf left the shop a different figure, but still bizarre because of his hair and unshaven face. He took directions from the gents' outfitters to a hairdresser's salon two minutes walk away.

By the time he left the hairdresser's he was unrecognisable. The figure who had entered the town on a bicycle this morning had disappeared. Ossaf's face was now clear of hair: both the dirty, oily twists that had fallen about his brows, and the down on his jowls that had been shaved off at last. All gone. He'd had a shampoo and his hair was now swept back, trimmed close at the sides, and held in place with a dry spray, a can of which he'd slipped into his jacket pocket when paying the enormous bill.

The effect of all this tailoring and grooming was to turn Ossaf, within a couple of hours, from a derelict alien into a rich, handsome and accomplished young man about town. But two things still marred the effect. His teeth remained furred up - they were nearly as brown as his skin - and his body remained unwashed beneath his new white underwear, his white shirt and expensive worsted suit. These details would now have to wait until he had finished his other business.

The modest offices of *Gt. Yarmouth Holiday Tours Ltd.,* the front room of a terraced house behind the bus station, were no match for Ossaf in his worsted suit, brogues and new haircut, not when he was able to produce the receipt for the double-decker sightseeing bus with the office's own crooked stamp, *Paid in Full.*

The assistant was a white haired fellow in his seventies, very tall and lanky, and with watery, uncertain eyes. The Hall had burned down, he said. There wasn't going to be any Grand Fete.

Ossaf knew all about that and appreciated that his request was a bizarre one, but he had his own reasons for requiring the bus nonetheless.

They wouldn't do it. They would offer a refund. Half the money.

But Ossaf didn't want any money back. In fact he countered that with the offer to pay the firm a bonus of 20% for fulfilling its obligation under these strange new terms - that there was no Grand Fete to ferry people to, that there would be only the one trip, and that there would be only the one passenger for both outward and return journey.

The proffered terms, though bizarre, were nonetheless extraordinarily favourable to *Gt. Yarmouth Holiday Tours Ltd.*

Ossaf was left waiting at the counter while the elderly assistant fumbled through a bead curtain into the back parlour.

The middle-aged entrepreneur and owner of *Gt. Yarmouth Holiday Tours Ltd.*, sitting alone behind an empty desk in the back parlour, was the son of the elderly assistant, and the driver of the company's one and only sight-seeing bus. The additional 20% proved an irresistible lure to the owner. He popped his greasy head through the fly curtain to double-check the details with Ossaf –

"That'll be cash, sir?"

"Of course."

He withdrew again to the parlour to discuss the matter with his father, behind the privacy of the fly curtain. The foreign gentleman obviously had his own reasons for the trip, he told his father. Perhaps he was considering buying the property, he speculated. Whatever he was up to, it was no business of theirs, and they could do no harm by putting themselves out for the young foreign gentleman. The bus was available. Available all day, in fact, despite the holiday weekend. He sent his father back to Ossaf with the terms: the trip would take place after lunch today, at 1.30 p.m., with the 20% surcharge payable in advance, of course.

"On your bus," Ossaf told the old man. "I'll pay it when I board the bus."

Before searching out somewhere to have lunch Ossaf bought a toothbrush and toothpaste from Boots and spent a full five minutes cleaning his teeth in a public toilet. With the last stains on his confidence removed he chose for his lunch the tearooms of a swanky hotel on the front - The Old Ship Hotel - where he enjoyed a plate of egg and cress sandwiches and two pots of tea. He found the food, which he'd never had before in his life, quite delicious, and fell in love with the tearooms of The Old Ship Hotel, overlooking the beach and pier.

When he returned to the bus station at 1.20 p.m. the sightseeing bus was already there.

The sun had gone and the sky had lowered when Ossaf sat down in his seat at the front of the upper deck of the open bus. It was a blustery twelve miles back to Coxcomb Hall but the worsted suit, with the lapels clasped tight about his throat, kept out the cold. He couldn't retreat to the lower deck anyway, because that might mean having to chat with the driver - the man from behind the fly curtain, in shiny cap and smart livery now.

At last the bus slowed at the gates of Coxcomb Hall, and the moment arrived when Ossaf could see the place from his new and lofty perspective. The gates were unlocked, as he'd left them, but the driver had to get out and draw them wide to make room for his bus, and while he did so Ossaf began his inspection.

The sharded walls. The walls that had circumscribed and confined his life for these last eleven years. From here he could see their shards. Their threat was a pretence. The rounded top of the wall itself was bare and harmless, spotted with soft yellow lichen. You could almost run around the walls.

The bus rolled between the gates and the driver got out again to close the gates behind them. He returned to his cabin and they trundled down the drive towards the Quad.

The trees were high along the edges of the drive, higher than the bus, and some lighter branches caught on the screen in front of Ossaf. He could see little. But when they arrived at the Quad and the driver slowed and stopped, uncertain where to go in the open space, Ossaf was able to take in a completely new vista.

From the front of the top deck all was diminished.

On his right the tuck box shed looked like an outsized, windowless garden shed, and its roof of asphalt matting was worn and holed. He noted the places where the water came through inside. It was a frail, dilapidated structure. And the beech trees. From up here they were magnificent in their spread and their reach, no longer the haunt of hungry boys squabbling during lock-out over a few sour nuts, or running from the maddened, short-legged Leery.

To the left was the block of classrooms in which the projection room was housed, where he had organized the private screening of the film of Newlings and Clara White. All that! All that life! Where had it gone? Ossaf stood up in the bus so that he could see across the roof of the building and along to the dirty skylight of the Art Loft, where Hallett had spent so much time at weekends, hidden away, slavishly copying ancient nudes. All Saturday and Sunday he could spend up there.

Ossaf looked down at the rubber floor of the bus. Another shudder of feeling. Only now did he remember that he had left the Dawes ten-speed outside the men's outfitters, propped against a wall, unlocked. He had forgotten it and it would be stolen. The shop assistant would steal it.

"Where do we go from here?"

It was the driver, the boss. He had left his cab and was staring up at Ossaf, his peaked and braided cap set back on his head. He sounded querulous and fed up.

"Take me to where the fire was."

Shaking his head the entrepreneur climbed back into his cabin.

The bus rumbled forward uncertainly across the gravel Quad, leaving the beech trees on the right and the Games Room and O'Donnell's office - where Ossaf had been sitting, drunk, earlier today - on his left. The bus

slowed, whining in low gear, and drew to a stop at the black gap where the Victorian wing had been, and the apartments of Rowell, Newlings, O'Donnell and Jackson.

With everything cleared away but a few stubby dividing walls, the original floor plan of the building was discernible between the blackened mounds. This building, in which Rowell had planned and schemed and masterminded The Grand Fete, and where he'd treated his favoured choir boys to cream cakes in his warm, red-lined apartments, and where he'd talked so grandly of his plans to bring the illustrious comedian Jimmy Tarbuck to the Hall, and where he'd listened to John Cussack and his *Black and White Minstrel* stars on his Ferguson stereogram, where he'd given his first aid instruction to so many juniors over the years, and rejected them coldly as they became pubescent, this building, this cosy nest of sentiment and gratification, this England, had now disappeared, and with it all the squeals and fears, the warblings, the orgasms, the ingenious human evasion, persuasion and enterprise, all over and done with. There remained only the wordless charred brick in even rectangles, vestiges of rooms drawn up by draughtsmen in the nineteenth century. The footsteps and voices and panicky whispers that in recent years had occupied the spaces the draughtsmen had described, were all gone forever.

The maudlin mood, the same paralyzing mood that had trapped Ossaf in the bogie-wheel carriage that gloomy afternoon back in February, was overtaking him again. He stamped on the floor. Twice. The driver released the brake and the bus rolled on.

And here was something special, before the descent to the games fields. Standing tall at the front of the top deck, in the middle, like a millionaire on his yacht, his hands clasped on the polished chrome railing, Ossaf was able to see over much of the woodland from here, and looking back, to his right, could detect the indentation of the Dell, and further on the clearing where Woodlands was. But neither of these things could mar the beauty of the canopy of the woods, which looked so fresh and pure, so unspoilt, as if the trees had resumed their supremacy over this corner of the world, and covered up all traces of human defilement.

The bus rolled slowly downhill, clutch in, worn engine idling, to the edge of the rugby fields, and stopped. Ossaf moved to the corner of the upper deck, above the driver's cab, and stamped on the floor again, and again, then three times, but the bus did not move. The driver left his cab once more and set back his cap. Ossaf leant down to speak to him.

"Over there!"

He pointed to the corner where the looming grey eminence of the Vampire stood. "To that aeroplane!"

"We'll get stuck in the grass! It's too long!"

Ossaf shouted down at the driver:

"To the aeroplane!"

Shaking his head and readjusting his cap, the driver climbed back into his cab. *His* cab, *his* old bus. His only bus. He released the brake and started across the field to the de Havilland Vampire.

Here was the chief change. This old grey monster had hidden its frailty while it stood higher than you, but from above it was nothing more than a gunmetal toy with faded roundels and shabby camouflage. Its lopsidedness was more fully exposed from above, and the grass had now grown so long beneath it that light brown seeds caressed the undersides of the wings, and the genitalia of its bomb carriage and undercarriage was modestly covered by a white skirt of cow parsley.

Rather than stop and turn about, the driver did a slow circle of the Vampire and then accelerated gently back across the rugby fields to the slope that had once drawn up to the Victorian wing, but which now led to nothing visible at all.

Ossaf had seen enough. He was ready, now, to leave Coxcomb Hall.

When they turned out of the gates onto the main road he moved to the shelter of the lower deck. He swung his way along the chrome bars to the rear of the bus and sat there alone, in the middle, arms outstretched across the back seat.

The Dawes ten-speed had gone, as he'd predicted. After several hours walking the town, the pier and the beach, Ossaf took a room at The Old Ship. He was lucky to get a room at all, at the Whitsun weekend, and only did so by hiring dear. He took the same suite at the top of the hotel that Clara White and Hallett had enjoyed on the night of the fire about ten weeks before.

Ossaf now knew the date. Everything was becoming fixed and substantial again.

The temporal world.

In his suite he sat by the window with a glass of beer. He still had not washed. He could smell his own stink rising clear and strong above the fresh scents of his new white shirt, his new worsted suit, and his hair spray, but he did nothing about it. He had not eaten since lunch downstairs. The beer, gentler friend of the whisky, gave a cold satisfaction high in his gut. The evening was drawing in and the holiday crowds were dispersing. A newspaper seller hurriedly packed up his stand on the esplanade. Ossaf stared out at the view of the darkening sea, and the frail lights of a trawler far out, bobbing under threatening skies, and he thought about the few banknotes he still had folded in his pocket, not enough to pay the bill, and about the stolen bicycle, and about his virginity.

Afterword

by

Christopher Hallett

Remembering E.G.Taylor

"Play it again, Egg!"

"Go Egg!"

Taylor clutched his scores to his chest and wrung them dry of false sentiment. It was true. He had just sent more tunes to Brian Epstein, manager of *The Beatles*.

"Yeah yeah yeah."

"Have you had a reply yet, Egg?"

Taylor could not look at that boy.

"Not yet," he admitted.

On 27th August 1967 Epstein's suicide hit the streets. All those dressing room scenes with John, Paul, George and Ringo, so brilliantly lit, were gone forever. Bleak headlines that day on Merseyside, and in every corner of this marvellous country of ours. The same morning a bulb in Egg's future must have popped out the Bakelite too: he'd been waiting eighteen months for Epstein's decision. Only he could have kept that plate spinning quite so long.

Looking back, it seems that for Egg Taylor earning a living, getting by, was not so much a struggle as a public brawl, or a brawl with the public, and how he died seems fated.

Aged 61, he was attacked as he left a pub –
The Belvedere, Caistor Sands - at closing time
on December 2nd 1969. He was felled by just
one punch, but a low punch from behind.

Given that he was wearing an overcoat
and that he was on the move, such a
blow shouldn't have done much harm, but it
came from an ex-boxer and a drunkard, the
publican himself. His punch broke a rib that
pierced Taylor's diaphragm. Taylor died in
hospital two hours later.

Why was he thus attacked?

Led on by some caustic remarks from
a drunk who fancied himself as the saloon
accompanist, the publican had accused Taylor
of tuning The Belvedere's shabby upright so
that it 'played like honky-tonk' - a remark that
for some reason incensed Taylor, threw him
into a frenzy. He insulted the publican and his
friend, and explained at length to anyone in
the pub who'd listen why their criticism was
as ignorant as it was absurd.

Come closing time he calmed down,
gave up the quarrel, and left unpaid, telling
the publican he could keep his £3 fee. But this
lordly dismissal was just another provocation
to the publican, who then assaulted him at the
door.

If his death was fated the Fates got it
all wrong for Egg Taylor that freezing
December night. He deserved better.

This book of his pays back some
dignity to a rotten life, and death.

Chris Hallett,

Caistor Sands, 2010.

www.ingramcontent.com/pod-product-compliance
Lightning Source LLC
Chambersburg PA
CBHW050016180626
46810CB00002B/440